Tell Me Why

Kay Bratt

Tell Me Why

A Hart's Ridge Novel

Books by Kay Bratt

Hart's Ridge Series
Hart's Ridge

Lucy in the Sky

In My Life

Borrowed Time

Instant Karma

Nobody Told Me

Hello Goodbye

Starting Over

Blackbird

Hello Little Girl

So This is Christmas

Every Little Thing

Now and Then

Tell Me Why

Ticket to Ride

By the Sea trilogy
True to Me

No Place too Far

Into the Blue

The Tales of the Scavenger's Daughters series

The Palest Ink

The Scavenger's Daughters

Tangled Vines

Bitter Winds

Red Skies

Life of Willow duology

Somewhere Beautiful

Where I Belong

Standalone Novels

Wish Me Home

Dancing with the Sun

Silent Tears: A Journey of Hope in a Chinese Orphanage

Chasing China: A Daughter's Quest for Truth

A Thread Unbroken

Train to Nowhere

The Bridge

Caroline, Adrift

The Wishing Tree series

The Wishing Tree

Wish You Were Here

Wishful Thinking

A Wish in the Wind

Dragonfly Cove Dog Park series

Pick of the Litter

Collar Me Crazy

<u>Children's Books</u>

Mei Li & The Wise Laoshi

Eyes Like Mine

Printed in the United States of America

First Printing, 2025

Red Thread Publishing Group

Hartwell, GA 30643

www.kaybratt.com

Cover Design by Elizabeth Mackey Graphic Design

RED THREAD
PUBLISHING GROUP

Chapter One

F ear is the moment before reality hits. Dread is knowing
something's coming and being powerless to stop it.
Both emotions made Taylor's fingers cramp as her grip
on the steering wheel tightened more and more. The words
Shane had just called with echoed relentlessly in her mind: a
burned-out car. Human remains. The vehicle registered to her
farm.

She drove through the winding curves inside the gates of the
farm, eager to get onto the highway. Her hands were steady on
the wheel, but her heart thudded with every second that passed,
the pit in her stomach growing heavier. She slowed as she
approached a break in the trees, and there—Anna's car was
parked in its usual spot outside her house.

Taylor exhaled. One sister safe.

But that left Jo. And Cate. And anyone else connected to
the farm.

Thankfully, Lucy and her babies were safe on the other side
of the world.

Suddenly she saw Cecil's familiar smile in her mind. His

1

kind but knowing eyes, and his huge hands that with one touch could bring her comfort like no other could give.

Had he changed his address to the cabin there? Or was his vehicle still registered to his house in town?

That was a terrifying thought, and she pushed it from her head. She couldn't let herself think too hard. Not yet. As she turned onto the main road and accelerated her speed, she prayed that everyone she loved was accounted for, that the registration Shane had found was a mistake. A number off. The wrong street name.

Time seemed to stretch on forever, each mile taking double its usual time to cover until she finally turned onto an old service route flanked by pine and scrub brush and saw the flashing red and blue ahead, stationed like warning flares in the growing mist.

Two patrol vehicles. One fire engine. A plain unmarked. And trills of smoke still trailing into the morning sky.

A familiar figure stepped away from the line of emergency tape and raised a gloved hand.

Deputy Penner. Solid. Gentle. One of the good ones. She had to remind herself to be professional and not fall into his arms for a supportive embrace the second she stepped out of the car.

She parked, hurried out to join him.

He met her at the tape, eyes soft with something close to sorrow. "Taylor. Where's Sam? You shouldn't have come alone."

"Thanks, Penner. He's with the kids," she said, her voice hoarse. "Shane here?"

He nodded and gestured toward the clearing. "He's by the car. Take your time. It's not going to be easy."

She nodded, then ducked beneath the tape and moved forward. The scent of burned rubber and scorched earth invaded her lungs, thick and acrid. Her boots crunched over charred gravel as she approached the wreckage.

The car was barely recognizable. A metal skeleton curled inward like a dying animal. Windows blown out. Paint peeled away in layers of black and rust. Whatever blaze had taken it had been thorough—merciless. Set to obliterate any possible evidence.

In the area that would've been the back seat a sheet was drawn. It hid whatever remained of the victim left to die in their coffin inferno.

Shane Weaver stood a few feet away, arms crossed, jaw tight. He turned as she approached, offering a nod.

Taylor didn't speak. She didn't ask. Her gaze locked on the remnants of what had once been the driver's side—now little more than a collapsed frame and twisted seat supports.

And there, just outside the door frame, half-buried in ash and soot, was something familiar.

A singed strap.

Bits of scorched leather.

And attached to the metal zipper—barely hanging on—was a charm. Heart-shaped. Gold once, though blackened now with soot and melted varnish.

Taylor froze. Her heart clenched.

Jo's satchel.

She hadn't seen it in a long time—distressed leather with braided straps and that tiny heart charm Jo had always said reminded her of a mama's locket. They'd found the bag while thrifting one weekend in Asheville.

Taylor took a step back, her hand pressed to her chest. Her breath faltered.

God, please, no.

Not Jo.

Not after everything she'd already been through.

3

And what about Levi?

Then her mind reached, clawed back through memory. And she saw it—clear as day.

Jo had given that bag away. Months ago.

To Quig.

Her sister had been sorting through some of her thrifted treasures, making a pile to donate to the women's shelter, when Taylor and Quig came to visit her at her cabin. Quig admired it for its worn, rustic look, and Jo had handed it over with a teasing grin. "Take it. You need this more than I do," she'd said. "You've got court dates and case files and nowhere to put 'em. Might even be able to clean you up one of my old laptops to use."

Quig had laughed, grateful. Clutched it like a treasure.

Now Taylor's knees nearly buckled.

Shane stepped closer, voice low. "We found what's left of a phone, but it's not functioning. We won't know for sure until forensics ... but the plate's a match. Belongs to your friend, Quig. Found it in the system."

Taylor swallowed hard, but her mouth was dry. Her thoughts splintered in every direction.

Quig?

The one who'd been sober for nearly a year and had fought tooth and nail to get her life back—to stay straight to get her kids back? The one she swore she believed in when no one else did, until the rest of the family had come around, realizing that, under the tattoos and bravado, Quig was a sweet girl with promise?

Taylor's heart raced. Her mind scrambled. She tried to find some other explanation, but all she could see was that damn bag. Quig took it everywhere with her.

And all she could think was—

Did she relapse?

Had the pressure finally been too much? Had Quig gone back to the thing that had once nearly killed her?

Taylor felt sick. How had she missed the signs? Was it her fault for being away so much? Not watching over Quig like she should've?

She blinked hard, fighting the sting in her eyes.

No. No, something wasn't right.

Not Quig. Not like this.

"She'd been doing better," she whispered.

Shane looked at her sideways. "You sure?"

Taylor didn't answer.

Because deep down, she wasn't. Addicts could be sneakier than anyone could imagine. They could hide their secrets beneath a ton of bullshit that even a backhoe couldn't budge.

No, Taylor wasn't sure. Not yet.

But she was about to find out.

And if someone had dragged Quig back into that darkness— or worse, if someone had put her there to shut her up—they were going to wish they'd never lit that match.

Chapter Two

Taylor sat in silence beside Shane as his car rolled through the winding back roads toward the sheriff's department. She stared out the window, eyes unfocused, haunted by the image she'd left behind. Eyeing Penner in the rearview mirror, driving her truck back to the station, she inwardly blessed the kind-hearted man. And Shane, for insisting she come with him.

It had taken everything in her to walk away from the scene.

Even as the forensics crew from Jasper arrived, unpacking equipment with methodical efficiency, part of her couldn't move. She'd stood at the edge of the burned-out car, her boots rooted in ash and gravel, staring into the wreckage like Quig might reach out—like she might whisper something Taylor had missed.

It felt wrong to leave her like that. Alone. Silent. Erased.

As though Quig had been trying to speak to her. Begging her not to walk away.

Don't let them forget me. Don't let them lie about who I was.

And Taylor had promised—without words, but with every aching beat of her heart—that she wouldn't.

Not this time.

Now, back in familiar territory with the tires crunching across the parking lot outside the department, that promise sat heavy in her chest.

"You okay?" Shane asked quietly as he put the car in park.

"No," she answered, just as quietly.

He didn't press.

They walked inside together, passing deputies who offered polite nods or awkward glances. Taylor felt out of place, like a ghost in a home that had already moved on without her.

In Shane's office, she shook off the awkwardness of being so close to him again, then took the chair across from his desk and accepted the file he handed her. The header read *Victim: Margaret Quinn Gallagher*, and just seeing Quig's full name in print sent a wave of sadness through her chest.

The door opened behind her.

"Taylor," came the comforting voice she'd known since the moment he'd pulled up to her walking from high school, his first gesture that led to many more to mentor her out of the pitiful life she may have had without his guidance.

Sheriff Dawkins.

She stood automatically, feeling a wave of relief. Sheriff always made things better. "Morning, Sheriff."

He gave her a nod as he stepped inside. "Heard you were here. Damn shame about your friend. I'm sorry, truly."

Taylor nodded but said nothing as she sat down again.

"She had a rough go, didn't she?" he went on, stepping around her chair to glance at the file. "Girls like her ... well, they attract trouble. Maybe she was trying to do right, but you can't run from the kind of crowd you've always known."

Taylor's spine straightened. "She was working hard to turn her life around."

He gave her a sympathetic smile. "Sure. But sometimes,

Taylor, it's not about hard work. It's about wiring. Some people are just ... wired to self-destruct."

She swallowed down her rising anger. This was Sheriff. The man who had stood in as a father-figure and changed her life long ago. Still, she had to defend Quig.

"She was sober."

His smile thinned, and he cocked his head just slightly. "When's the last time you gave her a drug test?"

"She didn't need one. She'd been clean. Focused. Saving for her attorney—"

He held up a hand. "I know you cared for her, Taylor. But you must be careful about who you let into your life. Into your family circle. Didn't you meet her in jail?"

Taylor stiffened. "Yes, I did. She was terrified and alone, and needed someone."

"Well," Dawkins said, adjusting his belt, "maybe next time you'll choose better. People like Quig ... they have a way of pulling others down with them."

He just didn't know Quig, Taylor reminded herself. Didn't see how hard she was trying. He didn't mean to be cruel.

Shane shifted in his chair, tension creeping into his posture. Dawkins took the hint.

"I'm glad to see you," he said, his voice softening. "But Weaver can handle this. It's open and shut, most likely. No need for you to get pulled back into the muck."

He tipped his head at Taylor. "My condolences."

And then he was gone.

The door closed behind him, and Taylor felt the air in the room shift. He'd been kind. Civil. But beneath the surface of his words was something that didn't sit right.

A dismissal. A judgment.

He was still angry at her for leaving the department.

Taylor looked up at Shane, pain flickering in her eyes before she shuttered it down. "I need to be a part of this, Shane. I can't just walk away. Quig was family."

He leaned forward, elbows on his desk. "Officially, you know I can't put you on this. You gave up the badge. Dawkins made that clear."

"What about unofficially?"

He paused. "If you can keep it low-profile, check in with me first, and don't go rogue—I'll work with you. But you do things by the book, Taylor. No solo visits. No kicking down doors."

Relief filled her chest. "Thank you."

He nodded. "No problem. You knew her better than anyone. You'll see things I won't."

Taylor looked down at the case notes. "She was doing everything right. Parenting classes. Working herself ragged to earn enough for a lawyer. Never complained, not once. Every animal at the farm adored her. Every kid. Every person she helped ..."

She trailed off, her voice cracking. "She finally felt like she belonged. Like she mattered. And now this."

Shane's voice was quiet. "Do you think she used again?"

Taylor's lips parted, but she couldn't answer. She didn't want to believe it.

"If she did," she finally said, "I want to find who gave it to her. And I want to burn their whole damn operation to the ground."

Shane gave a faint nod. "Alright. Here's what I'm doing today. I've got fire investigators coming back out with accelerant dogs. I've requested surveillance from every camera on the main highway, and I'll cross-check plate data. I want to know who was on that road in the hours before the fire."

He pulled out a small notepad. "You—start at the farm. Talk to anyone who saw her yesterday. Check her bunk, her routine. And I'll give you the address of the last employer she listed—it may not be where she was really working, but it's a start."

9

"What about family notification? I've met her mother. I know her kids. I think I should do it."

He nodded, relief evident that he wouldn't have to give the news.

"Let them know we won't know official cause of death until after the autopsy."

Taylor stood again, this time steadier.

"We'll figure this out," he said. "Whoever did this didn't expect anyone to look too closely for the death of a past drug addict. They just don't know you."

Taylor met his eyes.

"They're about to."

Chapter Three

Delivering bad news to someone's door didn't just make you a messenger. It also made you a witness to someone's heartbreak. It was never just about the words. Taylor took it more seriously than some, as, to her, it was also about carrying someone gently through the moment their world shifted. She turned onto the narrow gravel drive and eased her truck to a stop beside the modest one-story home. The yard was scruffy but cared for—grass trimmed in uneven patches, a trampoline sagging slightly in the back, and a plastic kiddie pool overturned near a row of wildflowers that someone had once tried to tame into a garden. A collection of bikes and scooters leaned against the porch railing. A basketball sat deflated by the steps.

She stared at the house for a moment, hands clenched on the steering wheel, willing herself to move.

This street wasn't new to her. She'd been here before—a few times. Before Cecil had helped Quig get her beat-up sedan, Taylor had driven her to the house for weekly visits with her kids. Sometimes they'd sit in the driveway and talk, not quite ready to face what waited inside.

Quig had always been nervous before seeing her kids. Always hopeful. Always trying. She wanted to be able to erase all the trauma she'd put them through. The missed birthdays. The crazy phone calls.

All of it.

They'd reminded her often it would take time, but one day they would trust her again. Now Quig's kids would never have that resolution.

It was heartbreaking.

She stepped out into the heat and made her way to the porch. Before she could knock, the screen door creaked open.

"Taylor?" the woman asked, squinting into the sun. Her thinning gray hair was pulled back in a tight clip, and she wore a faded T-shirt that read "I Don't Do Mornings." Her eyes, sharp and lined at the corners, held wariness.

"What's she done now?"

Taylor offered a small, tight smile. "Can we talk for a minute, Beverly?"

Beverly Gallagher's face tightened. She hesitated—then nodded and held the door open. "Come on in. But, forewarning, it's chaos in here."

Taylor stepped into the house and was immediately hit with a swirl of smells—laundry detergent, reheated mac and cheese, the faint bite of lemon cleaner. The small living room was alive with activity. Quig's three kids were scattered across the carpet, backpacks open, school supplies dumped into colorful piles. Pens, Sharpies, notebooks, and binders surrounded them like a rainbow minefield.

"It's the last week of summer," Beverly explained with a tired laugh. "Trying to get them organized. Fire department came through yesterday and donated all this. God bless them. I was still waiting on one more paycheck before I could even think about fulfilling class lists."

Taylor nodded slowly, taking it all in.

"And I'll give Quinn credit," Beverly added, lowering herself onto the couch with a groan. "She helped get their clothes. Picked up pieces here and there all summer. Some new and some from thrift stores. Said she wasn't gonna let them start school lookin' like nobody wanted 'em. Did a good job."

"She sure did," Taylor said softly, taking in the stockpile.

"Momma got me real Buckle jeans," Addie, the youngest girl, piped up, holding up a glittery pair of skinny jeans like they were the crown jewels.

Josh, the older boy, all knees and attitude, scoffed. "Yeah, well, they're used."

The girl rolled her eyes. "So? Used looks better than your new fake Levi's."

"Do not."

"Do too."

"Stop fussing," Beverly barked, not unkindly. "And Josh, quit acting like someone handed you a life sentence just 'cause you gotta go back to school. This year I need you to step up and help your sister with her homework. I can't do it anymore, not with all the crazy stuff they teach now. Whatever happened to simple math?"

Taylor smiled faintly, watching them, heart aching. Josh was fifteen but looked like he was in college. Already sporting a light mustache. This was what Quig had fought so hard for. This chaos. This love. A chance to be their mother again.

"Can I come back to the farm soon," Addie asked. "Bronwyn and I are going to make a fort, and the boys can't come in it."

"We wouldn't even want to, weirdo," her brother retorted.

Taylor cleared her throat. "Beverly, can we talk somewhere private?"

Beverly gave her a suspicious glance, but nodded. "Sure. Come on."

She led Taylor down the hall into a cramped bedroom that clearly pulled double duty. The far corner was partitioned by a floral curtain, behind which sat a narrow twin bed dressed in bright purple bedding with panda bears on the comforter. A small bookshelf held chapter books and a nightlight shaped like a mushroom. On the nightstand sat a framed photo in a glittery panda frame—Quig and her daughter grinning cheek-to-cheek, heads tilted together like best friends. They both had striking blue eyes. Blonde hair.

They could pass for sisters, to be honest.

Taylor swallowed hard.

"Addison wanted her own space," Beverly said, gesturing to the little corner. "Josh and Josiah share the other room, so Addie bunks in here. I'm sure rooming with your grandma isn't on anyone's bucket list, so the least I can do is try to make it a little special."

"It is," Taylor whispered. "It's sweet."

"I try," Beverly said, rubbing the back of her neck. "But I'm tired, Taylor. I'm too damn old to be doing this again. Josh needs a physical for football. Addie's got an eye appointment next week, and Josiah needs a deposit for a band instrument, or they won't let him in. And Quinn—she's supposed to help me with all this. Said she'd help with appointments. With rides. With the money. I pray to God you aren't here to tell me she can't work for y'all anymore."

Taylor opened her mouth, then closed it again. Beverly went on.

"I keep thinking maybe I can retire in a couple years when Quinn gets her shit together. Maybe finally tend to my flower beds. Get my house back and sit on the porch drinking sweet tea without wondering if somebody's gonna punch a hole in the drywall while I'm taking a breather. Yet, I'm still here. Still getting eye rolls and slammed doors and hearing 'you don't get it' from kids who don't know how hard this is from my side." She sighed deeply, sagging into the edge of the bed. "And I love them. God, I love them. But I just wanted to be their grandma. Not their ... plan B. I never wanted to raise more kids."

Taylor sat beside her, heart aching. "I'm sorry," she said quietly.

Beverly looked up, suddenly still. "Why are you here, Taylor ... what's going on? You've never come here alone."

Taylor reached for her hand. "There's been an incident."

The woman's lips parted. "What kind of incident?"

Taylor tried to steady her voice, but it broke anyway. "I'm so sorry but Quig's car was found this morning. It's been burned. And ... there were human remains inside. We believe they are hers."

Beverly didn't react at first. Just stared, blinking. Then her mouth opened slightly, and her hand jerked away from Taylor's as if burned.

"No." Her voice was flat. "No, I just saw her two days ago. She texted me just last night, too. She's fine."

"I know, but Beverly—"

She held her hand up, her face hardening. "Stop it. Don't say anything else. Quinn said she was coming back tonight. Said she had a shift and then she'd bring over some money. She'll be here. She told the kids she would."

Taylor felt tears press at the back of her throat. "I'm so sorry. Believe me, I didn't want to give you this terrible news."

Beverly stood abruptly, stumbling back toward the dresser, then turning to look at the photo of Quig with her daughter. "No. No, you don't understand. She was—she was finally doing things right. Working. Spending quality time with them. She and I were starting to get along pretty good. She was clean, I know it."

"Yes, I think she was, too," Taylor whispered. "She was trying so hard to make things up to the kids. To you. She wanted to repair all the heartbreak she's caused."

"Yeah, and I really believed her this time." Beverly's voice cracked and tears began to roll down her face. "I knew not to trust her, but I did. And once again she lied, didn't she? Damn it, that girl fools me every damn time! Just when I think she's finally kicked that life, she screws up again. I told her this would happen. That one day doing that junk would be her last day. That she'd be choosing drugs over her children. But did she listen? Did she think about them before being so selfish?"

"Hold on a minute. We don't know yet if drugs were involved," Taylor said, standing. "It's an ongoing investigation."

She reached for her again, but Beverly held up a shaking hand, blocking her from coming closer. "I don't want to hear it. That child has caused me grief her whole life. I gave her every-thing, and this is how she repays me? I can't—" she gasped, sinking to the bed again, as though her legs could no longer hold her. She put her hand to her heart. "I can't tell those babies that she's gone. Not right now."

"You don't have to. Not yet," Taylor said gently. "We'll help you. Whatever you need, call me and I'll be here. I'll be back tomorrow to ask you some questions." As she passed the dresser, she laid down three Benjamins. Hopefully enough for at least shoes and the instrument deposit.

Then she slipped out of the door.

Outside the room, the kids laughed, arguing over who got the blue binder. The last week of summer break. Bags packed with hope.

And just down the hall, their world had shattered.

Chapter Four

Tula Carrington, once known as Tula Rose Skaggs before she'd ditched her hillbilly name and chosen one more fitting for a future career under the big lights, turned off the highway and onto the winding two-lane road that led into Hart's Ridge, the late afternoon sun slanting across the cracked windshield of her rented sedan. A "Welcome to Hart's Ridge" sign flashed past her, its edges rusted and its painted letters fading like everything else around here.

God, she hated this place.

The trees thickened as she drove deeper into the town she'd left behind years ago. Her knuckles tightened on the steering wheel. She could almost feel the invisible cord of her past reeling her in—every mile a reminder of how hard she'd tried to break free.

Hollywood had felt like a salvation at first. Tula had always been the girl who stood out—the homecoming queen with the megawatt smile, the one who could command attention just by walking into a room. When she left Hart's Ridge to chase her dream, no one was surprised. She'd done alright for a while—a recurring role on a sitcom that lasted six seasons, a few commercials, a small part in a made-for-TV thriller. But the work had dried up just as fast as the curse of aging had leaped upon her, and the grind of audition after audition had chipped away at her until the dream felt like a punishment. Still, it had been better than coming home.

Until now.

She pulled into the gravel lot beside the county jail and cut the engine. Deputy Penner met her inside the lobby, a young, polite kind of man who called her ma'am and had likely heard stories about her from older folks in town.

"You're here for Waylon Skaggs?"

She nodded, her jaw tight. She wished she were anywhere but there. "I was told he's eligible for release."

Penner pointed toward the payment window. "You can take care of the bond there. He'll be out in fifteen."

She paid and then waited in the car, not wanting to run into anyone who might recognize her. It would be bad enough to run into an old friend, looking like a tired road rat, but to have to explain why she was sitting in the parking lot of the county sheriff's department would be the icing on the cake.

Eyes glued to the door, she impatiently thumped on the steering wheel of the rental car.

Fifteen minutes later, Waylon shuffled out, his hair a mess and his clothes wrinkled like he'd slept in them.

"Tula Rose," he said, like he couldn't quite believe she was real.

"Get in the car," she said flatly.

They didn't speak until she'd pulled out onto the road.

"I can't believe you came all the way back," Waylon muttered, rubbing the back of his neck.

"Well, I cannot believe that you got yourself arrested, Waylon. Again. You're lucky they called me and not one of our delightful brothers." She didn't mention it was a bit of good timing and had given her a reason to leave town for a bit, let things settle while she licked her wounds somewhere else.

He sighed. "It was nothing. Just a misunderstanding. You could've phoned in the bond."

"You were driving without a license. I felt like someone needed to come kick some sense into you."

"I've done it before. Nobody ever makes a big deal. Just a ticket. Usually just a warning."

She slammed her palm against the steering wheel. "Do you hear yourself, Waylon? You're going to end up just like the rest of them. Laws are in place for a reason. You can't even legally drive. And you thought it'd be smart to take a delivery job?"

Waylon looked out the window, avoiding her glare.

"Whose vehicle were you driving?" Tula asked, lowering her voice. She was going to give herself a stroke if she didn't calm down.

"Uncle Jimmy's old Ford truck," he replied. "Gotta pay to get it out of impound, if you'd like to help with that, too. Being how it was my third offense driving with no license, they took it in."

"What happened to the money I sent you for welding school?" she pressed.

He shrugged. "Didn't get around to going. Truck needed a paint job and an overhaul. Tires, too. It's blue now, by the way."

She exhaled sharply through her nose. She couldn't care less about the truck. What she cared about was saving her little brother from his own DNA. "So where are you working now?"

"A place called Shuffle Lounge."

"Doing what?"

"Just odds and ends. Whatever they need."

"Shuffle Lounge?" She raised an eyebrow. "What kind of place is that?"

Waylon shrugged again. "Bar. Restaurant. Kind of ... clubish. I clean up. Just whatever they need."

Vague. Too vague.

"And the delivery job?"

"Sometimes they ask me to drop stuff off. Supplies, food, whatever. Not often."

Something gnawed at her. An instinct. Or plain ol' distrust. His vagueness was bordering on stupidity. "You ever ask what's in the boxes you're delivering?"

He didn't answer.

Tula stared ahead at the road, her pulse ticking up. Hart's Ridge used to be a place where you couldn't sneeze without a cop writing it down. Now they had lounges hiring unlicensed drivers to do who-knows-what?

"What's happened to this town?" she muttered.

Waylon didn't respond.

Ten minutes later, they turned onto the familiar dirt road leading to their childhood home. The Skaggs place still looked like it was losing a slow, messy war with nature. The big house was flaking paint and sagging rooflines. A mobile home sat askew in the yard, the underpinning ripped out and strewn around, and a rusted-out camper leaned like a broken limb in the back.

Both most likely inhabited by her brothers, who couldn't get too far from their mama's nipple without running back for guidance. God knows they'd never make it on their own. But Waylon, she'd thought he might have a chance. He wasn't like them. He liked to read. Was smart in school. Cared about animals. And people.

She'd vowed that, like her, he'd live a different life than the average Skaggs. Now here he was, acting just like the rest of them.

Her frustration made her head throb.

Tula eased in closer to the house, and dogs barked and scattered. A litter of puppies rolled around in a dirt patch near a pile of old tires, the mother watching them tiredly, her teats sagging and ragged. Her jaw clenched. She was a volunteer for a dog rescue back in L.A. This kind of irresponsible chaos turned her stomach.

"I'm not going in," she said, shifting the car into park. "We'll talk tomorrow."

Before Waylon could answer, the front door banged open.

Their mother stepped onto the sagging porch, arms crossed, a cigarette dangling from her mouth. Her hair was bleached and frizzed from the summer heat.

"Well, well," she drawled, "look what the wind blew in. If it ain't Miss Hollywood herself."

Tula didn't answer. Just seeing the sarcasm pour out of her mother unearthed years of memories. The kind that should stay buried.

She reversed out of the driveway without another word.

Chapter Five

The ticking wall clock in the shabby motel room was louder than the hum of the old window unit. Tula lay flat on her back, zipped into the lightweight sleep sack she carried everywhere. No way was she touching the motel's floral bedspread—God only knew what was living in it. Bedbugs, fleas—or worse.

She could afford better than the local no-tell-motel, but everyone else was full because of some annual fishing competition at the lake. She stared at the water-stained ceiling, willing her mind to shut down. But Hart's Ridge had a way of stirring up everything she'd spent years burying. Sleep wasn't coming.

A knock rattled the door. Sharp. Urgent.

Her eyes flew to the glowing digits on the bedside clock. 2:07 a.m.

"Who is it?" she called, voice sharp from lack of rest.

"It's me," Waylon's voice came, low and uneasy. "Open up."

Another voice chimed in, raspy with cigarettes. "Tula Rose, it's Lorene. You gotta come."

Her stomach sank. It couldn't be good news at this hour.

She padded to the door and cracked it open, chain still latched. Waylon stood there, sweat dampening his hairline, shoulders hunched. Beside him, Lorene wore the same Skaggs features Tula saw in the mirror, only hardened—stringy hair, a washed-out T-shirt, eyes sharp with judgment.

"What happened?" Tula asked, already bracing herself.

"It's Mama," Lorene said. "Ambulance came and got her. They took her to County. Waylon says she was coughing up blood."

Tula's grip tightened on the chain. A small, ugly part of her whispered *not my problem.* "And where are the two brothers?" she asked, tone clipped.

Silence stretched. Waylon shifted. Lorene's eyes darted sideways at him, then back to Tula.

Tula let out a bitter laugh. "Drunk? Or strung out?"

Neither of them answered, which was all the answer she needed.

She sighed, pressing her forehead against the doorframe. "I told myself I wasn't going to get sucked back in. I came here for you, Waylon. Not for all this."

Lorene snorted. "Same old Tula Rose. Thinks she's too good for us now."

"Don't start with me," Tula warned, voice cracking around the edges. She took a long breath through her nose. "And stop calling me Tula Rose. It's just Tula now. Look, I'm sorry Mama's sick. But I can't—"

"Yes, you can," Waylon interrupted softly. His eyes found hers through the gap in the door, wide and pleading. "Please. I don't know what to do. You always fix it. Even when we were kids. You know I can't handle this on my own."

The words cut deeper than she wanted them to. She hated the responsibility, but she couldn't deny it. She had always been the one to patch holes, to shield him from the chaos of being a Skaggs.

"Damn it," she muttered.

She unlatched the chain and opened the door wider. "Fine. I'll go. But hear me when I say this, Waylon—this doesn't mean I'm back in the family circus. I'm here for only you. That's it. I'm still leaving in a few days."

Waylon nodded, relief washing over his face.

"Give me five minutes to get dressed," Tula said, waving them to the door.

Lorene rolled her eyes but stepped outside. "Hospital's twenty minutes. Hurry up."

Tula was dressed in less than three minutes. She locked the door behind her and walked with them into the parking lot. The night air smelled like damp pine and asphalt. Each step toward Lorene's beat-up sedan felt heavier than the last.

"We'll drive my rental," she said, and they changed direction.

She didn't want to see her mother laid up in a hospital bed. Didn't want to face the memories clawing at her.

But, once again, responsibility had her by the throat.

And as she climbed into the driver's seat and unlocked the other doors, she knew this was only the beginning of being pulled back into the life she'd sworn she'd never return to.

———

By the time the first weak threads of morning light crept through the hospital blinds, Tula felt like she'd aged ten years in a single night. Her neck ached, her back throbbed, and her legs were stiff from being folded into the miserable vinyl chair that had been her bed.

She shifted, stretching her arms overhead, then pressed her

palms against her eyes. She had sworn she wouldn't stay the night. That had been the plan when she'd walked into the ER behind Waylon and Lorene—get Mama checked in, let the nurses handle her, and get the hell out. But when it came time to leave, something had rooted her to the chair. Habit. Guilt. That old, rotten sense of duty she couldn't shake.

Now, in the pale gray dawn, her reward was a body that felt as though she'd been trampled and a mind restless with memories she didn't want. Arguments and accusations from years gone by. Hurt and disappointment she thought she'd long ago processed and let go of but was now circling around her again.

On the bed, her mama stirred. Her hand fumbled for the oxygen mask, tugging it down to speak. Her voice was ragged but laced with her usual sharp humor. "Well, I'm still thinking about last night with three of my babies together in a public place, gathered for little ol' me. People are gonna think I'm finally somebody important."

No, that ship had sailed long ago. Now the community would never expect anything different from Mama Skaggs. Her reputation was long and unforgettable, for many reasons. Many in the neighborhood thought of her as the mother of the Skaggs' kids, thus her "Mama Skaggs" moniker, but her given name was Dixie,

Tula leaned forward quickly, adjusting the mask back over her mother's mouth. "Save your breath, Mama. Literally."

Dixie's eyes glinted with mischief, even in her frailty. "Always the bossy one," she whispered through the plastic.

Before Tula could respond, the door opened and a nurse entered, chart tucked under her arm. She was tall, with blonde hair pulled neatly back, her expression brisk but not unkind. The badge clipped to her scrubs read, "*Anna Gray, R.N.*"

Tula froze and sweat broke out on her upper lip.

Anna paused, too, her eyes narrowing slightly as she studied Tula's face. "Do I know you?"

Tula straightened in the chair, spine stiff. She looked away. Pretending not to be the woman who was once the girl who beat out Anna for homecoming queen. "I don't think so."

Anna flipped open the chart, scanning the name. Her lips pressed together, then curved faintly. "Skaggs." Her gaze slid back to Tula. "You're Tula Rose, aren't you?"

The double first name felt like a spotlight, one Tula had tried to leave behind.

"It's just Tula now." She braced herself for the smirk, the jab. Back in high school, she and Anna had circled each other like rival cats—both pretty, both ambitious in their own ways. Tula had the crown, Anna had the attention of the high school quarterback, and neither had been generous with the other.

But the smirk never came.

Instead, Anna's expression softened. "Haven't seen you in years. How are you holding up? You need anything? Coffee? You can get some breakfast downstairs in the cafeteria, too."

Tula blinked, caught off guard. "I'm ... fine. Just in town for a short visit." She didn't mention Waylon's troubles.

Anna busied herself adjusting the oxygen line, her movements efficient but gentle. "Noted. Your mama's stable for now. Doctor will be in later with the full picture, but we'll keep her comfortable until then."

Her tone carried no judgment, no lingering resentment. Just kindness. It disarmed Tula more than cruelty ever could.

"Thanks," Tula muttered, unsure how else to respond.

Anna gave her a small smile, then left, leaving the room quieter than before.

Dixie shifted again, tugging at her blanket. "I remember that girl's sister, Taylor. She used to chase after everyone's approval like it was gold stars. Thought she was better'n everyone. Guess you two had that much in common, but she became a county sheriff and stayed around to support her family."

Tula ignored the dig. She'd expected that from her mother, and from others to still be seen as the shallow beauty queen, the one who'd left town chasing fame. Instead, Anna's acceptance was jarring. And it unsettled her more than her mama's barbs.

The door opened once more, and the doctor stepped in. A short man with thinning hair and eyes that had seen too much. He glanced at the chart, then at Tula. "You must be the daughter who stayed overnight."

Tula stiffened. "Stayed" implied more than she liked.

He pulled up the rolling stool and sat. "Your mother's lungs are in very bad shape. Severe COPD, emphysema, and she's battling pneumonia on top of it. I've seen her in here plenty of times over the years to know that this is the result of years of smoking, poor diet, and skipped medications. It isn't reversible, but we can manage it with the right care."

Dixie waved her hand dismissively, the oxygen mask fogging with each weak laugh. "Don't listen to him. Doctors always want to scare you into acting right. Ain't nothing wrong with me that a cigarette and a cup of coffee won't fix."

The doctor's expression didn't shift. He looked back to Tula. "She can go home, but she'll need oxygen around the clock. Possibly a hospital bed to keep her comfortable. And someone to monitor her for the first few weeks."

Tula shook her head, panic rising in her chest. "No. That's not possible. I don't live here. I was only passing through, so my siblings will have to handle it."

Dixie laughed harshly. "Fat chance. More likely they'll sneak in and turn the oxygen off and smother me."

"If no one arranges the care and agrees to follow through with it," the doctor said evenly, ignoring the sarcasm, "she'll be back here. And each time she returns, her chances of leaving decrease."

The words sank like stones in Tula's gut. She wanted to say no, to make it clear she had a life waiting elsewhere. She wanted to tell them all that she wasn't the responsible one, no matter what history suggested. That her mother hated her and had made her life a living hell.

But she could still see Waylon's pleading face from the night before. *You always did. I can't handle this on my own.*

She could see her mother's cracked fingernails curled into the blanket, her shallow breaths rattling through her chest as she watched the emotions flutter across Tula's face. There was a slight smirk on her face, under the mask. She knew she had Tula. Knew that someone up a few generations had passed something down to her daughter that made it nearly impossible for her to walk away from responsibility. Made her different than the others in her family who mostly lived for themselves in their own little worlds.

She was right. Her two older brothers were the most likely to screw something up, and Lorene—well, her little sister was filled with hate, bitterness, and, scariest of all, cunning like a fox. Her usual MO was to annihilate those around her with manipulation until they caved and gave her whatever she wanted.

She couldn't leave this all on Waylon.

"Fine," Tula muttered, her jaw tight. "I'll stay long enough to get the house set up. Oxygen, bed, whatever she needs. But then I'm gone."

The doctor nodded, scribbled on the chart, and left her there with the silence.

Finally, her mother pulled down the mask. "I'm assuming you'll want your old room back," she coughed and coughed, then started again. "I'll tell Curtis to clean it out. He was using it to piddle with building a taxidermy business, which failed, mind you, but I think there might still be a few critters around laying up there."

Tula leaned back in the chair, every muscle screaming from exhaustion, every nerve buzzing with resentment. She wanted out, but, once again, Hart's Ridge had its claws in her. And she hated that a part of her already knew she wasn't leaving as quickly as she had claimed.

Chapter Six

S orrow doesn't shout. It settles in quietly, folding itself into the spaces where love used to live—and waits to be felt. The church pew creaked beneath Taylor's weight as she shifted to glance down the row. Sam sat on one side of her, and her dad on the other. She was proud of her dad for coming, even if he hadn't known Quig all that well. He'd come to show Taylor his support, she decided, and that showed a lot of improvement on his usual selfish ways.

The sanctuary was barely half full. The scratchy mauve carpet looked like it hadn't been replaced since the eighties, and the dusty floral arrangements flanking the casket did little to brighten the room.

There was no music. No slideshow. No printed programs. With Quig's remains still with the medical examiner, there was just a pine box to represent her death at the front of the room—simple, unvarnished—and a small gathering of people who didn't know what to say.

Quig deserved better.

The second meeting with her mother was still on her mind. Beverly had passed the anger stage and could not stop crying when Taylor visited her again. It was hard getting any information from her, but at least now there was the beginning of a list of contacts. A few friends. Her exes, or at least the ones who'd fathered her children. An address of where she'd been going to meetings to work to stay sober.

Taylor scanned the faces in attendance. Other than Lucy, everyone was there from the farm, and even Sutton and Corbin had heard about the tragedy and come to support. Cecil had worn his best black suit and looked polished and well-to-do among all the white faces, most of them dressed in everyday clothes. He wouldn't care that he was the odd man out—nothing could keep him from paying his respects. He always did the right thing, down to even shining his shoes to show that Quig meant something to him and deserved his respect.

Mabel was there and currently had possession of Lennon, bouncing her on one knee as she whispered a nursery song in her ear. She hadn't known Quig well, either, but she had a heart for every young woman in town who had a history of trauma.

Of course, she'd come.

Della Ray and Faire sat on the same pew with Mabel, fanning themselves as they looked around and waited on their turn to hold Lennon.

There were a couple women from the church who'd known Beverly back in the day, and another one or two who looked like they'd wandered in from obligation rather than fondness. No framed photo graced the altar. No eulogy planned, either. Just a small speech from the pastor.

It wasn't that people didn't care. It was that they didn't know what to do.

Because when a woman dies young—burned and broken, rumors circling like vultures—people tend to sit in silence rather than say the wrong thing.

Taylor stared straight ahead, her hands clasped tightly in

her lap. She hadn't slept more than a few hours in days. The full forensics report still wasn't back, but word had gotten out that investigators found a used syringe near the wreckage. As far as the world was concerned, Quig had overdosed and died exactly the way people expected her to.

But Taylor wasn't convinced.

She kept asking herself—had Quig really fooled them all that well? Had she really managed to stay clean for months only to spiral in secret? To relapse and die alone on some back road with no one there to stop her? If so, how did the fire start?

It didn't sit right.

Not with the way Quig had fought for her kids. The parenting classes. The budgeting. The meals she packed and the soccer practices she tried to make. The way she'd glowed when she told Taylor she'd finally gotten a car that cranked on the first try.

None of that sounded like a woman ready to give up on her sober journey.

The sound of the door behind her made Taylor turn, and she saw the sheriff come in, remove his hat, and take the closest seat. Shane filed in next, sat next to him.

They weren't here out of care. Most likely only to do surveillance to see who showed up and if anyone acted suspiciously.

Taylor was already on it. So far nothing stood out.

The quiet service wrapped up in under twenty minutes. The preacher said his words and gave an invitation for sinners to approach the altar and give their lives to God.

No one moved.

Beverly sat pale and rigid, face unreadable, with Addison pressed into her side like a burr. The boys flanked them, both staring down at their worn sneakers, unmoving.

As the guests began filing out, Taylor lingered in the back, still seated, eyes sweeping the room. A few heads nodded at her in that polite, sad way people did when they didn't know what else to offer.

Sheriff Dawkins came by and dipped his hat, conveying his condolences to Taylor.

"She'd have appreciated all of you showing up, I'm sure," he said, gesturing to the whole pew of Taylor's family. She smiled weakly and he moved on.

"Good riddance," her dad said under his breath.

"Daddy, why don't you like him?" Taylor asked, frustrated at him for acting like a child. She already knew the answer, and it had to do with Dawkins treating her like a daughter for so many years. But her dad should be grateful that someone had stepped in and gave her direction, not envious that it wasn't him.

He scoffed. "I know you like to think of yourself as knowing everything to do with Hart's Ridge, but there's a lot about this town you don't know."

With that, he got up and walked out.

Taylor shook it off and continued watching the rest of the people gather their things and leave. There wouldn't be a graveside ceremony. Beverly hadn't wanted to prolong having to deal with everyone any longer than she had to. She was a private sort of woman, and wanted to get back to grieving alone.

A familiar face weaving in and out of the line of those leaving caught Taylor's attention.

Lyric Mitchell.

The last time Taylor had seen Lyric, they'd both worn county orange, squeezed into a concrete room with three others, one of them being Quig. Lyric with electric blue streaks in her hair and a talent for sketching anything with a simple pencil and paper.

Now, she looked ... whole. Long curls pinned back in a

messy twist, eyes puffy from crying, but her posture steady. She wore a modest navy dress and flats, and carried herself with the quiet strength of someone who'd earned every good thing that had come her way.

She spotted Taylor and crossed the aisle quickly.

"Georgia—I mean, Taylor," she whispered, voice breaking as she pulled her into a hug. "Oh my God. I'm so sorry."

Taylor embraced her, surprised at the sudden sting in her eyes. "It's good to see you, Lyric."

"I can't believe she's gone," Lyric said, stepping back, brushing tears from her cheeks. "I—I haven't talked to her in so long. Not since right after I got out on probation."

"I wasn't even sure you two stayed in touch."

"We didn't, really. Just ... friend of a friend stuff. I heard she was doing better. That she'd been brought into your family's farm, and had a job, and was trying to get her kids back."

Taylor nodded. "She was. She was doing so good. That's what makes this ..." She trailed off, shaking her head. "Did you hear anything? I mean, anything at all that seemed off?"

Lyric looked thoughtful. "No. Just the usual secondhand updates. But now that you mention it ..." She hesitated, then leaned in slightly. "I did hear something once—months back. Might've been nothing."

Taylor leaned in, pulse quickening. "What?"

"There was this girl I used to run into at meetings—said she knew Quig was working for you, but she made an underhanded comment that farm work wasn't all she was doing to put up money to get her own place."

"Are you saying it was something illegal?" Taylor asked.

Lyric shrugged. "I have no idea. I remember thinking that I hoped it wasn't to do with drugs—or Quig would backslide and lose all the ground she was making up with her kids."

"What was her name?"

"Lana something or other is all I know. She used to hang around that seafood place in the marina on the east side of Monroe. They'd let her work for tips when someone called out. Sometimes she ran food from the kitchen, too, if she wasn't too high to remember table numbers. I haven't seen her in a while there, though."

Taylor nodded slowly. "This is helpful, Lyric. If you think of anything else—anything at all—will you let me know? I want to find out all I can about what Quig was doing."

"Of course. And ... Taylor?" Lyric's voice softened. "Thanks for believing in her. Not many people did."

Taylor blushed. "Wasn't a big deal. She earned it."

As Lyric walked away, Taylor pulled out her phone and opened a new note.

Lana. Eastside Marina fish camp.

She stared at the screen a long moment. Quig had been up to something, that much was clear. Just what, Taylor didn't know, but she wasn't going to stop until she found out.

Chapter Seven

The table was scratched and mismatched, but it held them together better than any sermon could. Ellis and Cate's log cabin glowed with soft amber light, its wide beams catching the shimmer of oil lanterns strung from hooks. The kitchen smelled like roasted chicken, cornbread, and apple cobbler cooling on the counter. Laughter and clinking dishes spilled through the open great room, where the Gray family gathered to do what they did best—show up for each other when words weren't enough.

After the week they'd had, Taylor needed this. Her hands had trembled all day remembering the fire, the wreckage, the smell of burned metal that clung to her nose, no matter how far from the scene she was. She'd told herself she wouldn't think about it tonight.

Tonight was about family.

Diesel sprawled by the hearth, his big head on his paws, snoring softly. Cate's retriever, Brandy, had parked herself under the table, waiting for a dropped roll. Out on the porch, the faint sound of crickets hummed, their steady rhythm merging with the occasional clatter of silverware.

Taylor filled her glass with tea and took a deep breath. "I swear, Cate, you outdo yourself every time. You could open a restaurant."

Cate chuckled, wiping her hands on a towel. "And what—feed this crowd twice a day and strangers, too? No, thank you. Besides, family doesn't care if I burn the rolls."

"Burned rolls?" Sam lifted one, turning it over like evidence. "You mean these fine specimens?"

Bronwyn giggled. "Uncle Sam, you already ate two!"

Diesel's tail thumped. He knew the tone of a happy room.

"Mom's trying to outdo me, I think," Anna said, laughing.

Everyone knew Anna was the real Martha Stewart of the family.

Levi, sitting next to Jo, reached for another helping of mashed potatoes. "These are amazing," he mumbled between bites.

Jo smiled faintly but said little, her fork idle. Taylor noted it, the distance in her sister's eyes, how she laughed on cue but didn't join in. It was the same look Jo wore when she was trying to pretend life was fine when it wasn't.

Anna's cheeks flushed when her phone went off, signaling a text. She read it, then looked up. "Jack texted—said to tell everyone hi. He's covering night shift again, so he's sorry to miss this."

"Good man," Cecil said from the head of the table, voice warm and gravelly. "You tell him we appreciate him takin' care of folks when they're hurting. That's sacred work."

Anna smiled, eyes soft. "I will."

She never looked that way when talking about Pete, her ex-husband.

Conversation meandered easily—from the new calves at the farm, to Alice's latest science project, to how Teague had learned to whistle so loud it spooked the chickens. Sam leaned back, teasing Anna about hospital food while Bronwyn and Levi debated which dog was smarter—Diesel or Brandy.

"Diesel's part detective," Bronwyn insisted. "He can find anything."

Taylor smirked. "Except his way back to the house half the time."

"That's just strategy," Sam said. "He wants to make sure you come find him."

"Maybe he gets that from you," Taylor said, earning a round of laughter.

Brandy barked once, almost in protest, then went right back to scavenging.

Just as Cate was setting dessert on the table, Taylor's phone buzzed. The screen lit up with Lucy's name. She smiled and hit answer. "Well, look who it is!"

Lucy's face filled the screen—sun-kissed and radiant even through the video call, her dark curls piled into a messy bun. Behind her stretched the bright kitchen of her home in Uruguay, walls tiled in ocean blues and greens. "Hey, y'all," Lucy said, voice echoing with warmth. "Am I interrupting dinner?"

"Perfect timing," Taylor said. "We're just about to fight over apple cobbler."

"Then I'll make it quick before the battle starts. I just needed to see my family."

"Hi, Aunt Lucy!" Bronwyn shouted, leaning so close her forehead nearly hit the phone.

"Hi, sweetheart! Wow, you've grown at least a foot taller. Stop that—it makes me feel old."

Bronwyn grinned. "I can't help it. It just happens."

A little boy's voice piped up in the background of the tiled kitchen. "Mama, tell them about the lizard!"

Lucy turned the camera to a wiry five-year-old with wide eyes and dimples. "Johnny's been on safari duty," she said.

Johnny puffed his chest proudly. "I caught a lizard in the flowerpot. But Mama said I had to let it go because it hissed at Bea."

From somewhere off-screen came a baby's coo. Lucy shifted the camera, showing Bea strapped to her chest in a floral sling, blinking sleepily. "She's getting so big," Taylor said softly. "And those cheeks!"

"She's perfect," Lucy said, pressing a kiss to the baby's head. "Sleep's a myth, but I can't complain when she's looking at me with her daddy's eyes at two in the morning."

Cecil leaned toward the screen. "You're glowing, girl. Family life suits you. Always did."

Lucy's eyes softened. "Thanks, Cecil. It means a lot. I heard about Quig. Jo told me everything." Her tone grew quiet. "I didn't know her well, but it's awful. I hope they find whoever did it."

Taylor nodded, throat tightening. "We will."

Lucy hesitated. "Are you sure you're taking care of you, Tay? You look tired."

Taylor forced a smile. "Just long days. You know how it goes."

"Mm-hmm," Lucy said knowingly. "Promise me you're not doing that thing where you take everyone's problems and stack them on your shoulders like bricks."

Before Taylor could respond, Sam leaned close and grinned into the camera. "Don't worry, Lucy. I'm the brick inspector. I make her put 'em down sometimes."

"Good," Lucy laughed. "You keep her in line, Sam."

"Trying," he said. "But she's stubborn as a mule."

Cecil chuckled. "Comes from her mama's side. Can't fix it. Just admire it."

Lucy turned the camera, revealing Jorge passing behind her, paint-smeared hands and a sheepish smile. "Say hi to the family, love."

"Hola, familia," Jorge said warmly. "Jo, I owe you one for that tip about the art supply grant. It went through."

Jo's smile crept up. "That's great news. Heard you've got a new series?"

He nodded. "Not quite yet, but I'm working on it. Light of the South. Sun, sea, stories of home."

Lucy added, "And it's brilliant, but I might be biased. I've started helping a few local artists get their work into New York galleries. It feels good to be back in the mix."

"That's our Lucy," Anna said. "Can't sit still."

"I learned from the best," Lucy teased. "How's Jack, by the way? He still putting in double shifts?"

Anna's cheeks pinked. "He's ... busy."

Sam waggled his eyebrows. "Busy's good."

"Sam!" Taylor elbowed him, but laughter bubbled around the table.

Levi came around and waved at Lucy, over Taylor's shoulder. "You're growing like a weed, boy. Looks like he could be in college, Jo. Jeez, you blink and they're half grown."

"I know," Jo murmured, glancing toward her son. He was laughing now with Bronwyn, both sneaking Diesel and Brandy bits of chicken under the table.

Taylor felt a pang. They'd all been through so much, yet somehow they kept finding ways to laugh. Maybe that was their truest inheritance. She wondered if Lucy was staying on her medication like she was supposed to, but she wouldn't ask. Not when everyone was listening. She seemed good, though. Her smile appeared genuine, and her eyes were clear.

Lucy's voice broke the quiet. "Well, I better let y'all eat

before that cobbler turns cold. Jorge's burning dinner as we speak."

Johnny waved so hard the screen blurred. "Bye, Aunt Taylor! Bye Diesel! Woof woof!"

"Woof back!" Taylor said, grinning. "We love you, buddy. You too, Lucy."

"Love you more," Lucy said, then added softly, "I miss you all. Take care of each other."

When the screen went dark, the laughter and chatter resumed, but Taylor's chest stayed full with the ache of missing her sister—the good kind of ache. The kind that reminded her that love and family stretched across oceans and still held. And the ache that made her feel thankful that they'd not lost Lucy—or, better yet, she hadn't lost herself.

They finished dessert, lingering long after plates were cleared, talking about small things—the baby goats born last week, the price of hay, the neighbor's runaway rooster. An incident of dog fighting discovered just outside the county. Cate planned to take a few of the most battered pups, and was finding rescues for the rest. Those dogs would never have to see violence again if she had anything to do with it.

For a while, the world outside that cabin didn't exist.

Lennon finally got bored, and cried from her place on the living room floor. Taylor slipped outside with her for a minute or two of quiet. The sky stretched wide and soft, streaked with lavender clouds fading to blue-black. Fireflies blinked over the farm like tiny stars trying to return to the heavens.

The front porch creaked under her boots as she settled into one of Cate's rockers. Lennon stirred, then sighed, her small body warm and heavy. Taylor began to rock, humming a low tune she couldn't quite place—something her mother used to sing.

Diesel padded out behind her and curled up by the steps,

letting out a low groan. From somewhere near the barn, an owl called.

She didn't hear Sam until he eased the screen door shut behind him. He held two mugs—one steaming, one iced. He handed her the warm one and sat in the rocker beside hers.

"Thought you could use some tea," he said. "Decaf, so you can still sleep."

"Thanks," she said quietly. "Did everyone else head out?" She'd heard the back door slamming a few times.

"Yeah. Well, at least Anna's crew did. She said Teague has a project due tomorrow. Ellis and Cate are washing dishes, Jo's helping them dry. Alice and Levi are playing on their iPads. Cecil's pretending to fix the bathroom leaky faucet so he doesn't have to go home yet."

Taylor smiled faintly. "Bless him." Oh, how she loved that man. Sometimes she worried about him, about how his family wouldn't yet completely accept him back into the fold. But at least his son was speaking to him again. And the grandson, when he could find time to answer his grandfather's texts, between basketball and girls.

Cecil took the boy fishing off their dock sometimes. He seemed nice.

For a few minutes, they rocked in silence. Lennon's breathing evened out against her chest, her tiny hand curled around Taylor's finger.

"She looks peaceful," Sam said softly.

"She is. Wish I could bottle this feeling. Nights like this—it's the only time the world slows down."

He sipped his drink. "You should let it slow down more often."

She turned toward him. "You sound like Lucy."

"Smart woman," he said. Then his tone shifted. "Tay ... you know I'm proud of you, right?"

"That sounds like the start of a lecture."

"Not a lecture. Just—something we've talked about before. I think you might need a reminder." He looked out over the yard, where the barn lights threw long shadows. A goat bleated out into the dark. "You've got a heart that won't quit. But sometimes you don't know when to rest it."

"I'm fine," she said automatically.

"You're always fine," he said gently. "That's the problem. Between the farm, the investigations, and everybody else's emergencies—you leave nothing for you. And little for us."

Her jaw tightened. "You think I don't know that? I'm trying to balance it all, Sam."

"Honestly, I think you try not to think about it too much." His voice stayed soft, not accusatory. "But I see you running on fumes, and I get scared. For you. For the girls. I just don't want them growing up thinking they're second to every crisis that rolls through this town. I also don't think you are one hundred percent back to your full health. You keep pushing yourself, and you're sure to relapse."

Taylor stared out into the dark, the sting of his words tempered by their truth. Lennon shifted in her arms, murmuring in sleep. "Quig was family," she whispered. "If I don't fight for her, who will?"

"I know," he said. "You are so damn loyal. And I love that about you. She loved you, too. But loving someone doesn't mean burning yourself down for them."

She swallowed hard. "You sound like you've been rehearsing that."

He chuckled. "Maybe. Or maybe I've just watched this pattern long enough to recognize it, and I want to get ahead of it this time."

Taylor looked down at Lennon, tracing her tiny cheek with a thumb. "I just want to do right by people."

"And you do," he said. "Every day. That's what makes you who you are. I'm just asking you to save a little piece of that goodness for us. And for yourself."

She nodded slowly, eyes stinging. "You really think I'm doing too much?"

"I think you're trying to save the whole world when your own's right here in your arms," he said, touching Lennon's foot gently. "I just don't want you to forget which part matters most."

Taylor blinked back tears she didn't expect. "You always know how to hit where it hurts."

He smiled and rose from his chair, leaning down to press a kiss to her forehead. "I only aim for the heart, my love. That's where all the good stuff lives."

She let out a soft laugh, brushing at her eyes. "You and Lucy both. Ganging up on me from different continents."

"Someone has to keep you balanced." He started toward the door, then looked back. "You coming in soon?"

"In a bit. Gonna sit here with her awhile longer. Enjoy the warm snuggles."

He nodded. "Don't stay out too long. It's getting cool."

When he disappeared inside, Taylor rocked quietly, watching Diesel lift his head to sniff at the wind. Somewhere down by the creek frogs croaked, the night settling deeper around them.

She looked down at Lennon's sleeping face, the soft rise and fall of her chest. The porch light flickered over the yard, glinting off the silver of the fence posts and the rippling grass beyond. She heard Atlas whinny from his spot, a message to her that he was out there, watching for coyotes or any other unwanted guests.

It felt so peaceful.

This—family, harmony, the hum of home—was what Quig had fought to get for herself one day.

She thought about the girls.

Alice and Lennon. They needed to see her strong and competent. But also resting and enjoying life, or what would she be teaching them for their futures?

She pressed a kiss to Lennon's forehead and whispered, "I'll do better, baby girl. I promise." Then she rocked until the stars came out in full, and, for a rare moment, the world finally felt still.

Chapter Eight

The Hart's Ridge Fire Department sat squat between
the hardware store and the town's only dry cleaner, its
brick façade weathered from decades of harsh
summers and neglected paint jobs. A pair of faded garage doors
framed the front, one slightly rust-stained from a leaky gutter
above. The sign overhead, chipped but still legible,
read HART'S RIDGE VOLUNTEER FIRE STATION #1.

Inside, it smelled like rubber, motor oil, and burnt coffee.

Where the county tax revenue was going was a mystery
Taylor didn't want any part of, but she sure knew it wasn't going
to supporting the local fire department.

Or not much, anyway.

She hadn't set foot in the place in three years. She'd been
able to avoid the chief, Alex, since the night outside The Den a
few years back, when he'd wanted to take a swing at her. Diesel,
along with her pistol, had put a stop to that. The memory still
sat with her though, when his temper had blown up like a
dropped match in dry pine straw.

He'd always considered himself a prime piece of man, but,
in reality, he was a chronic womanizer with an ego the size of

Texas and a reputation that would make his father roll over in his grave. Not that Alex cared.

She followed Shane through the front, her boots silent on the scarred linoleum. He gave a short nod to a young firefighter who leaned against the bay door eating crackers from a vending machine bag. The guy looked too fresh-faced to have seen anything yet.

Taylor hadn't told Shane about the lead she held. Lana. Quig's side hustle. She didn't want to give him the opportunity to tell her he'd handle it. She wanted at Lana first. Shane had a way of intimidating people sometimes and, if Lana knew something, Taylor didn't want it to get lost. She'd tell Shane afterward.

Forgiveness before permission, in this case.

They found Alex in the back office, leaning over a stack of printed reports. He looked up when they entered, eyes meeting Shane's first—and only. Pretending Taylor was all but invisible.

Classic for him.

"Chief Jamison," Shane said.

"Detective Weaver," Alex replied, then motioned toward the chairs across from his desk. "Come on in. Shut the door, will you?"

Taylor shut it behind her, and sat without being invited.

Alex still hadn't looked at her.

He appeared ... smaller. Older. The hair that used to flop so carelessly perfect over his tanned forehead was now cropped close, with a streak of silver running along the pale temple. His tan had faded, and the easy swagger he used to wear like a second skin had thinned. Maybe age, maybe guilt. More likely, karma.

She wondered if the cheating had stopped when the attention did. Alex had quite a collection of past wives, divorces, and discarded mistresses. Everyone in town knew it.

He slid a file toward Shane. "Preliminary findings from the scene. We brought in the county fire investigator out of Jasper to confirm."

Shane flipped the folder open. Taylor glanced down and read upside-down.

Accelerant confirmed. Gasoline. Ignition pattern consistent with deliberate pour-and-light.

"So," Shane said, "arson."

"Definitely." Alex nodded, tapping a diagram with several burn pattern notations. "Whoever did it poured gas across the interior, mostly concentrated on the front driver's side and down into the footwells. Burn traveled fast and hot. Left minimal evidence behind. No accidental origin—no faulty wires, no engine fire, nothing like that."

Taylor kept her expression still. "Was a gas can found?"

Alex still didn't look at her. "No can. But there was residue on the gravel. Enough to know it was poured. Likely lit through the window with a match or lighter tossed in. Wind caught it quick and fanned the flames."

"So, the question is," Shane said, "did Quig pour the gas herself and crawl in as some kind of ... final act?"

Alex gave a long exhale. "Could be. Shame eats people alive. And relapse is a beast. Sometimes they'd rather disappear than face the fallout."

"Or someone set her up," Taylor said evenly. "Put her in there afterward."

That got Alex to look at her.

Briefly.

He raised an eyebrow, but didn't argue.

"We can't rule anything out," Shane added quickly. "We're heading to Jasper now. Autopsy results should be back."

Alex nodded, turning back to his paperwork. "Well. You'll have your answers soon enough then."

Shane stood, and Taylor followed. She didn't bother saying goodbye. Neither did Alex. Words would never make them friends again.

Out in the truck, Shane gave her a sidelong glance as he started the engine. "That was ... tense."

Taylor snorted. "You *think?*"

"He seemed nervous around you."

"He's lucky I don't tear his head off. One day I might, too, but that will have to wait. I want him on professional terms right now in case I need him again."

"I won't get in your way," Shane said, grinning.

"Sure, you won't. You know not to cross me when I'm mad."

He smiled. He liked that the banter between them was finding its way back.

They pulled out of town and turned onto the highway headed west, the road rolling in gentle dips past pine trees, farmland, and fields gone golden with late-summer heat. Cows lazed in clusters under shade trees. A billboard flashed by advertising tractor repair and peach cobbler.

"Jasper is about an hour from here," Shane said, turning on the air. "Hungry?"

"Starving."

They pulled through the Cook Out drive-thru just outside the next town over. Taylor ordered a cheeseburger and a sweet tea. Shane got a tray with a corn dog, a hush puppy, and fries. They ate in the truck, windows down, the smell of grilled meat and fried batter filling the cab before pulling out on the road again.

By the time they reached the Jasper medical examiner's building, the afternoon sun hung low in the sky. Taylor felt drained, but it was about to get even worse.

Crossing the parking lot felt like walking through quicksand, a sense of foreboding slowing her limbs. Inside, the fluorescent lights buzzed softly. A woman in a white coat greeted them at the front and ushered them down a quiet hallway lined with lockers and exam rooms. The walls were cold. So was the truth Taylor already felt coming.

Dr. Kerry Mendez met them in her office, gray hair tucked in a neat braid, glasses low on her nose. She gestured for them to sit.

"I'll be direct," she said. "We've only partially completed the autopsy on Margaret Gallagher."

Taylor nodded tightly. Quig would've hated the use of her full name.

"There's not much to go by, considering the shape of her remains," Mendez said. "But I have a hunch she was already dead before the fire started."

Silence.

Shane sat back slowly. "You're sure?"

"No. Not yet. But I can't find any impact trauma consistent with a crash. There were, however ..."

She paused, flipping a page in the file.

"... some deep nicks around the wrist bones. Could be defensive wounds. Could be restraint."

Taylor's skin chilled. "So someone killed her."

Dr. Mendez shrugged slightly. "I can't say that. We still have some investigation to go."

Taylor stood slowly, her heart thudding hard now, her grief shifting into something sharper. Something that coincidentally seared inside her.

Resolve.

Someone had taken Quig's life—and then tried to burn away the evidence.

But fire can't erase everything.

Chapter Nine

er mother's property looked even worse on the second visit. Tula parked on the dirt driveway and just sat behind the wheel for a moment, staring at the sagging porch and peeling paint. From here, she could see the leaning camper where Earl stayed, the rusted roof patched with duct tape and a tarp, and the raggedy mobile home that listed to one side like it had given up.

He obviously didn't have a lick of self-respect.

Curtis' trailer wasn't much better, but at least it had a real roof. Tula didn't have an issue with mobile homes, despite the bad reputation they got. She'd lived in one herself when she'd first moved out. It was only for a short time, but she'd rented one in a park where people took pride in their homes, no matter how humble or old.

They cleaned up their yards, kept the trash up, animals put away safely. Did what they could to have a family environment where their kids could play, proving that you didn't need a lot of money to live decently.

When she finally stepped out of the car, the chorus began.

Dogs barked and scrambled. A pair of hounds bounded toward her before veering off toward a pile of tires. Cats darted under the porch. A bird screeched from somewhere inside the trailer, the sound grating like nails on metal.

On her mama's porch, she braced herself and pushed open the front door.

The smell hit first. Cigarette smoke, fried food, and something she didn't want to identify. The house looked more like a junkyard than a home—stacks of newspapers, laundry piles spilling across the floor, fast-food wrappers, soda cans, an old recliner patched with duct tape. In the corner, three guinea pigs squeaked in a cage overflowing with wood shavings and other matter that shouldn't be so freely lying around.

How in the hell could people live this way?

Tula breathed through her nose as she came further inside, afraid to touch anything. It was all so familiar to her, and the memories flooded back, none of them good. Shame. Embarrassment. Never letting anyone come to their home.

But Curtis and Earl hadn't cared. They'd had friends over. Girls, even. Therefore, rumors had always floated about town about the dump the Skaggs lived in. The county had come round more than once, threatening to condemn the property.

Lorene shuffled through the kitchen, already lighting a cigarette.

"Damn it, Lorene. You can't smoke in here anymore. No one can. Did you hear how Mama was breathing? Coughing out a lung?"

Her sister rolled her eyes to the ceiling and walked out, sashaying provocatively in her skimpy shorts and tank top, her bare feet slapping against the dirty floor.

Tula went to the living room.

Waylon sat on the couch, picking absently at a hole in his

jeans as he stared at the TV. At least his room, Tula figured, was most likely the only space that ever resembled something clean. Her brother was like her and had a need for order and things to be where they should be.

"I tried to clean up," he said, gesturing toward the coffee table, the only cleared surface Tula had seen so far. "I didn't know where to put anything else, though. I'm sorry."

"Don't worry about it. Let me just take a look and see what I have to work with."

Her old bedroom was going to be a shocker, she was sure.

When she opened the door, she found piles of boxes, bags, and who-knew-what. Her once pale pink walls were grimy, and the bed sagged beneath a mountain of clothes. The room had once been a sanctuary for her, a place to get away from her brothers and pesky Lorene. Now it smelled like farm animals.

She shut the door again quickly, pressing her lips into a thin line. Not a chance in hell she was ready to tackle it.

Before she could say anything, the screen door banged open, and she went to investigate. Curtis swaggered in, his latest girlfriend on his heels, a dirty toddler perched on her hip. The child's face was smeared with something orange—Cheetos, maybe—and he clung to a can of Mountain Dew.

At least he was cute, unlike his sorry excuse for a father.

Curtis scratched at his unshaven jaw and gave Tula a once-over. "Well, look who thinks she's back from Hollywood to save the day."

"Don't start," Tula snapped. "At least someone was sober enough to show up at the hospital. Other than Waylon, I mean."

He smirked, hitching his thumb toward the back. "Yeah, heard Mama is sick. She gonna die?"

The girlfriend bounced the toddler, who let out a wail that pierced straight through Tula's temples.

Tula glared. "She's not dead yet."

"Good," Curtis said easily. "But if she does—dibs on the house. It's mine. Always figured it would be. Daddy would've wanted me to have it."

"Over my dead body," Tula shot back, heat rushing to her face. "You can't even keep your camper from falling apart. This house doesn't need another leech. Waylon is the only one who could keep it livable anyway, and only if he could keep the rest of you away. It's already like a bunch of vultures circling their dinner around here."

Curtis's eyes narrowed. "Funny stuff, coming from the one who ran off and never looked back. Seems like you could've been helping around here a little more and maybe it wouldn't look like this, Tula *Rose Skaggs*."

"I have sent so much money," she hissed, ignoring the barb about her name—none of them liked the fact that she'd changed it. "Money that was supposed to be *helping out*, not being poured down you and Earl's gullet. And this doesn't look like a money problem. This looks like a lazy problem."

"Oh, it's a money problem, alright," he said. "Something you have too much of and we don't have enough. Just the way you always planned it, little sister."

"Not my fault you never wanted to do anything with your life other than be a leech to everyone around you," she retorted. "Your lack of morals and ambition sounds like a you problem, not a me problem."

They stood nose to nose for a moment, and Tula thought he might just hit her, though she refused to show any fear. Finally, Waylon muttered something to diffuse it, and the girlfriend tugged Curtis toward the kitchen, muttering about the baby needing food.

Tula exhaled, pinching the bridge of her nose. He'd made her stoop to his level, arguing like a couple of banshees. She took some deep breaths, reminded herself she wasn't this person anymore. What she wanted to do was get in her car and just drive.

Keep going until Georgia was once again so far behind her that she didn't have to think about it or the terrible memories it dredged up just by being here. But how was her mother supposed to come home to this disaster?

Could she just walk away and leave her at the hospital? Let them sort it out?

The pressure felt like it would break her, right then and there, but she wouldn't let it. She took one more deep breath, then faced Waylon.

"Are there any trash bags around here?" she asked. No time like the present to get started. The faster she could get things livable, the faster she'd see this town in her rearview mirror.

———

Later that afternoon, back at the hospital, she stopped at the nurses' station and asked to speak with Anna. When Anna appeared, Tula leaned against the counter, her exhaustion plain. "Mama can't come back to that house. Not yet. I'm embarrassed to say it, but it's a filthy hoarder's nest. I need ... at least a few days to get it in order."

Anna studied her carefully, her professional façade crumbling into a look of pity. "I'm so sorry. Are you planning on staying there while you sort it?"

"God, no." Tula shook her head. "I wouldn't last one night in that place. I'd never be able to sleep. It's hopeless, I think."

Anna's lips quirked in a half-smile. "Not hopeless. Hard, maybe. But not hopeless. Listen—at our farm, we've got a cabin open. Simple, clean, and nothing fancy, but it's quiet. You could stay there while you work on getting your mom's house ready for her."

Tula blinked. "You're offering me a place to stay? I don't get it. You don't even like me. Or at least, you didn't before."

Anna chuckled softly. "High school was a long time ago, Tula. People change."

Tula wanted to decline, to brush off the kindness, but the thought of crawling back into that no-tell-motel, or worse, staying under her mama's roof with Lorene—made her skin crawl. Yet, it didn't feel right. "I don't take handouts," she said.

"It's not a handout," Anna said firmly. "It's practical. Clean. And temporary. If it makes you feel better, you can donate what you'd be paying that fleabag of a motel. Our rescue can use every penny we can get."

Silence stretched, Tula's pride wrestling with her exhaustion. Donation or not, it was still charity. But it sounded peaceful.

Finally, she gave a stiff nod. "Fine. A week. Just until I get things set for Mama."

"Good." Anna's smile widened just a little. "And while you're at it, if you need help with the house, I can point you to a service. They'll clean, sort, haul away junk. It'll cost you, but it'll get done a lot faster than you can do on your own."

Relief flooded through Tula so suddenly she almost sagged against the counter. That would let her get out of there sooner. "Yeah, that's a great idea. Give me their number."

As Anna wrote it down, Tula thought again how strange it was to find kindness here—least of all from Anna Gray. She sure didn't seem like the same Anna Gray from their high school days.

But then, she prayed she wasn't the same Tula.

Tula Carrington was a much nicer person to know than

Tula Rose Skaggs had been. She folded the slip of paper into her pocket and forced herself to meet Anna's eyes. "Thanks."

Anna only nodded. "Hey, chin up. You'll get through this."

Tula wasn't so sure. But for the first time since she'd driven into town, she didn't feel completely cornered and overwhelmed. She couldn't wait to get to the motel and get her stuff out, head to Anna's farm. A safe and clean place would make everything just a tad better.

Chapter Ten

Theheeee gravel road curved past a thick forest and then a field rimmed with golden-topped weeds before opening onto the Gray's farm. Tula slowed the rental car and just stared. The place looked like something out of a magazine—farm fencing stretched along the property line, a grand gate, opened in a welcoming embrace, pastures dotted with grazing horses, and tidy red barns that glowed against the fading light. She turned in slowly, taking it all in.

Further inside the gate, their boarding business building looked impressive, a logo of a pack of dogs next to the words, **Gray Escape Dog Boarding.**

The cabin Anna had directed her to sat back from the main house, tucked between trees, its porch light glowing warm and welcoming.

For a moment, Tula's throat tightened. This whole place epitomized what they'd made of themselves from nearly nothing. While she'd been chasing auditions and clawing for scraps of relevance in Los Angeles, the Gray sisters had overcome their past and carved out something real. Something solid.

Anna was waiting on the porch of the borrowed cabin, a

laundry basket balanced on her hip. She waved, her blonde hair catching the dusk.

"Got you some clean sheets," she said as Tula climbed out of the car. "A pair of pajamas, too—don't worry, they're new—and a few snacks. Nothing fancy, just fresh baked banana bread and trail mix. Some juice and milk for the fridge."

Tula blinked. "You didn't have to—"

"I wanted to," Anna interrupted gently. "Come on, I'll help you get settled."

Inside, the cabin appeared to have just been cleaned from top to bottom and smelled of pine and lemon oil. The furniture was simple but sturdy, a quilt folded across the bed, curtains pulled neat. The kitchen was neat, everything put away and countertops gleaming.

She set her bag on the dresser and ran a hand over the polished wood of a shoe cabinet just inside the door. Nothing fancy, just practical.

The home was nothing like the sagging disaster of her mother's house.

"I don't know what to say," Tula admitted.

Anna smiled, setting the sheets on the bed. "Say you'll come have dinner with us tonight. Nothing fancy, but the kids are excited to meet you. I told them you're a movie star."

"Not quite movies," Tula chuckled. "I wish that were true."

"Heck, anyone who has been on television is a movie star to them. Be ready for a lot of questions. Bronwyn already has a list."

Tula hesitated. She didn't like intruding, and she didn't like being pulled into other people's lives when she had no intention of staying there. But the thought of sitting alone, refreshing her email in the silence, thinking about what awaited her at her mother's house, made her stomach sink. "I guess I can manage that."

"Good." Anna's smile widened.

After a hot shower that washed away the stench of cigarette smoke and animals, Tula pulled on a clean set of leggings and a sweatshirt. She sat on the bed, checking her phone for emails— hoping, irrationally, for something from her agent. But there was nothing. Just spam, reminders, and silence.

Only gone a few days and already forgotten.

She tucked the phone away, squared her shoulders, and walked to Anna's house.

Dinner was surprisingly good. Anna's kids, Bronwyn and Teague, were quick to chatter, telling stories about school, friends, and a boy who had stolen the teacher's sandwich. When the subject turned to Tula, Bronwyn wanted to know if she'd met Justin Bieber.

Tula explained that was a whole different arena. Teague wanted to know how she remembered her lines, and she told them of some embarrassing moments on set. He asked if she was allowed to handle guns.

"Nope, I don't do that kind of TV," she said.

Their laughter was easy, and, for the first time in days, Tula felt herself relax.

Over roasted chicken and mashed potatoes, with to-die-for caramelized cooked carrots, Anna shared a little of her own story. "The divorce nearly wiped me out," she said matter-of-factly. "I was left with nothing but bills for a long time, until finally a bit of a settlement came through. I went back to school, earned my nursing degree. And now—well, I'm seeing someone. A doctor from the hospital." She smiled softly, almost shy.

Tula raised an eyebrow. "Impressive. You've really rebuilt yourself."

Anna shrugged, but her pride was clear. "Had to. No one else was going to do it for me."

Curious, Tula asked about the other sisters.

"Lucy's had a rough path," Anna said carefully, "but she's doing well now. Living overseas with her husband and two children. Figuring out a new culture. I think she's finally calmed the restless spirit inside of her that wreaked havoc most of her life."

She took out her phone and showed photos of Lucy, her husband, and the two kids. The new baby was beautiful, and Tula loved the name Bea. So simple yet lovely. And Johnny looked like a fun little boy, a mischievous twinkle showing in his eyes. Tula remembered Lucy being wild in school, and would've never guessed she'd settle down. Especially in another country!

"And your sister, Taylor? You two get along okay?"

Anna smiled. "Better than we used to. She's easier to deal with now, too. Less stressed since she resigned as a deputy sheriff. Now she and her husband, Sam, run their own private investigation agency. They've got a teenager named Alice, and now a new baby—Lennon. A girl. Taylor's pretty happy, I'd say."

"Yeah, I've heard how well she's done," Tula said, meaning it. She wasn't surprised. Taylor had always seemed to be the glue that held them all together. In school she'd stuck to mostly just her classes and keeping track of her sisters.

Tula didn't remember her ever being at any of the summer parties or events she'd gone to. Anna had, though. Lucy, too, when she was older. A lot of them used to hang out at a certain boat landing, passing around booze and a few other forbidden treats on the weekends. Stuff they weren't old enough to get on their own, but always had someone willing to provide.

Taylor was never there. Now Tula wondered if maybe she'd never been invited. Shame flooded through her at what a mean girl she used to be.

"I think your sister always did have a tenacious kind of spirit," Tula said.

Anna's brows lifted, a flicker of something unreadable

passing through her expression. Then she said, "Well, I was left penniless when my marriage crumbled, remember? I had to claw my way back. Every bit of respect I've got now, I earned."

The words carried weight, a subtle reminder not to overlook her own grit. Tula sensed a bit of sister rivalry. At least on Anna's part.

"You sure have," Tula said. "What about Jo? Is she doing okay?"

Anna grew more reserved. "Yes, she's here at the farm, too. You'll see her around, usually with her son, Levi. She's a single mom, too. Doesn't date. Oh, and, if you remember, our mother was dead. But miraculously, she came back to life a few years back and joined the family."

Tula's eyebrows raised to her hairline, all on their own.

Anna chuckled. "That's a story for another day. She and stepdad built a house on the next property over. To be honest, Mom is really the one who runs the place. She's the backbone of it all. It's been wonderful having her back with us."

"And your dad? Is he still living?" Tula recalled the girls had lived with him and that he was in and out of trouble. Possibly an alcoholic? And if she remembered correctly, the sisters were put into state care a few times while he got himself together. The kids at school had talked about it, spreading the word each time it happened.

Anna shrugged. "Yeah, he's around. He's a better version of himself than he was when we were kids, but he's still a work in progress."

"Aren't we all," Tula said, nodding.

She listened to Anna talk more about her family. Her kids. And her nieces and nephews. About her sisters and parents. An old man named Cecil they'd adopted as a stand-in grandfather. The animal rescue sounded like a fine outreach. Anna said the animal boarding business was already profitable after only a short time.

They were doing alright, it seemed, and it felt strange for Tula to return to her old town and find the Gray family completely different than what she'd left behind.

It was too bad her own family hadn't progressed that way. If anything, they were worse than they were back then, when Tula had done everything she could to hide the humiliation of being a Skaggs.

"Why is my cabin empty? Was it Lucy's? Were you waiting on a renter to come along?" she asked, suddenly curious.

"Yes, it was Lucy's place. But most recently, a friend of Taylor's lived there. Unfortunately, that's a bit of a recent tragedy. We don't plan on renting it out, though. There's always someone in our own circle who needs a place to stay now and then."

"Oh no. Did someone die in it?"

Anna shook her head. "No, not in the cabin."

She talked about "the girl," not mentioning Quig's name, being found burnt up in her vehicle. It sounded horrific, and Tula hoped the cabin didn't have any remnants of an unsettled soul.

After the meal, Anna poured them each a cup of steaming tea. Her gaze softened as she said, "I'm glad you're here, Tula. Even if we weren't technically friends years ago. Can we let the past go? Start fresh? I know I could use a friend, and I'm feeling that maybe you can, too."

Tula stared at her over the rim of her cup, wary. She hated needing anything from anyone, least of all from someone who used to be her rival. But there was something different about Anna now. Solid. Steady. Caring.

A friend would be nice while she was there, as long as they didn't dig too deep into her life back in Los Angeles. She didn't want anyone to know anything other than what was out there on the internet. Her secrets could stay just that.

Buried.

"I really don't plan to be here long," Tula said finally, her voice guarded but not dismissive.

Anna only smiled. "But you're here now, and that's good enough for me."

Chapter Eleven

Taylor pulled into the lot of Slick's Quick Lube, gravel crunching beneath her tires. The place sat off the highway like a metal shoebox, with a blinking neon OIL CHANGE sign that had seen better decades. She took a deep breath, grabbed her notepad, and stepped out.

Inside, the air was thick with grease and bad music. She found Jason Boyd, hunched over the hood of a pickup, wiping his hands on a filthy rag. He didn't look up.

"You Jason?" she asked.

"That's what the shirt says," he grunted, then gave her a once-over. "Who are you?"

Taylor gave a slight nod, reaching into her jacket. "Taylor Gray. Private Investigator." She held out her card. "Looking into Quig Gallagher."

At the mention of her name, his posture stiffened.

"What do you want from me?"

"She's dead," Taylor said bluntly and purposely, to watch his face for any flicker of guilt or surprise. She got irritation instead.

"Yeah, I heard. From my cousin. Or someone. That's some

twisted shit that she was found burned up." He tossed the rag onto a nearby cart. "You ain't thinking I had something to do with it?"

"I think I'm just doing my job," she said calmly. It pissed her off that, even knowing the mother of his kids had died, he hadn't even tried to reclaim them. "Where were you the night of the fifteenth?"

He snorted. "Fixing brakes till almost midnight. Ask Bill in the bay next to me. He was here the whole time. The next day was the same. We had a special that week and more customers than we could handle."

"Any problem if I look at your phone?" she asked.

He rolled his eyes but yanked it from his back pocket. "Knock yourself out."

She scrolled through texts. A chain of back-and-forths with a friend about a busted water heater. A timestamped receipt photo for brake pads. And more texts confirming the long work night. No gaps. No weird silences.

She suspected as much after doing his background check. He'd never been in trouble other than a parking citation or two. She handed the phone back. "Thanks."

"That mean I'm off the hook for child support now?"

Taylor blinked. "You think your kids died, too?"

"Well ... no, but—" he shrugged. "Figured maybe her not being around would make it stop."

She stared at him, deadpan. "Should've thought about that before you decided to bring them into the world. Full disclosure, your kids need a father."

He looked away. "I ain't got much to give, but I'll see what I can do"

Internally, Taylor thought *I'd bet you haven't given anything in months or even years*. Still, she just nodded once and turned to leave.

"Hey," he called after her. "She wasn't all bad, you know. Quig. Just ... lost her way."

Taylor didn't respond. She had one more on her list.

———

The drive to Jasper gave her time to reflect. Quig had been secretive, even with her closest people. But the father of her youngest daughter, Addie, had stayed on the radar. A landscaping company had come up on a background search, tied to Jacob Hensley, a boy barely out of his teens when Addie was born.

Taylor found him outside a ranch-style house, unloading mulch from a flatbed with another man—older, red-faced, and already irritated by her approach.

"Jacob Hensley?"

Jacob turned. His hair was wet with sweat, but his expression was open. "Yes, ma'am?"

She showed her card again. "Taylor Gray. I'm working a case involving Quig Gallagher."

His face fell. "Yeah, I heard about that. Really sad stuff. How's Addie doing?"

"Maybe you should check in on her yourself," Taylor said. "I'm going to need to ask you where you were the night she died."

Before he could answer, the older man—probably his father —stepped forward.

"You don't need to drag him into this. That girl had issues. Told him she was on the pill, then bam—pregnant. She tried to trap him. Ruined his college plans."

Taylor stayed professional. "No one's accusing him of anything. We're just covering all ground. We could do this at the sheriff's department if you wish? Make it more official?"

Jacob looked down, awkward. "I was with my girlfriend. We went to that drive-in movie over in Dahlonega. She's got the receipt from the ticket site. I can give you her number."

Taylor nodded. "Please do."

He pulled out his phone and read it off. The alibi sounded solid—and the nervousness she saw wasn't fear. It was guilt. And grief.

The older man wasn't finished, though. "You're not gonna try to push him into takin' the kid, are you? That baby ain't his problem."

Taylor's jaw tightened. "Actually, that baby is a little girl now and is the best part of a mother who was trying to do right. So maybe show a little respect."

What the hell was wrong with these young fathers trying to leave their responsibilities to someone else?

She turned to Jacob. "Thank you for your time. You need to go see your daughter."

He nodded, silent again.

As she walked back to her truck, she scribbled in her notepad: Two men. Two different reactions. But neither one felt like the killer.

Chapter Twelve

They gathered near the lake. The water lapped gently against the dock, its movement soft and hypnotic, the same way it had probably soothed Quig after a long day.

It felt right to remember her here now.

They were building a memorial, not for show, but for remembrance.

Taylor's heart felt so impossibly heavy. Diesel could sense it and hadn't left her side all morning, escorting her around as though her bodyguard. Sam stood on her other side, telling her about a recent PI case he'd taken on. Something about a man suspecting his wife of hiding assets before a divorce—nothing exciting, but steady work. "I caught her with a second storage unit and a bank account under her maiden name," he said, offering a shrug. "It'll get ugly."

She tried to smile for encouragement, but guilt prickled at the back of her neck. "Thanks for taking that one solo. I'm sorry I haven't been more help."

Sam brushed her shoulder gently. "Stop it. You're doing enough. More than enough. I can handle it."

She knew he could. Sam had surprised her with his investigation skills. While she worked more on instinct, he was hard-wired for logic. Hard proof. He was smart and did his share of their PI work as well as kept the books and helped his dad oversee the auto garage.

The two of them together were quite a team.

The breeze stirred the air, carrying the scent of fresh-cut grass and sun-warmed water. Down the slope, Cecil and Ellis hoisted a hand-built bench between them, maneuvering it toward the dock. Anna followed close behind, paintbrush in hand, a half-finished sign under her arm that read:

"Still Waters: In Loving Memory of Quig."

Taylor liked it better than their original idea, Quig's Garden. It fit. This had been her quiet place. "She used to sit here after dinner sometimes," she said quietly. "Let the breeze hit her face. Said it helped her breathe."

Sam nodded, already digging into the flowerbed beside the dock with a small spade. Taylor joined him, pressing a bright cluster of zinnias into the soil—Quig's favorite. Bright, messy, a little wild. Just like her.

Behind them, the kids ran barefoot through the grass, laughter rising into the still evening. Levi's fishing line jerked, and, with a whoop, he pulled a fat bass from the water, grinning ear to ear.

Jo jumped up from the picnic blanket and rushed over. "Yes, baby! That's what I'm talking about!" She threw her arms around her son, ruffling his hair as he laughed and flailed. He was going through the time of life when it wasn't cool to have your mother fuss over you.

Taylor watched, her arms wrapped around Lennon in the cloth carrier across her chest. The baby stirred slightly in her sleep, her face soft against Taylor's heart.

Her mind slipped to Addie. To Josh and Josiah.

They'd never feel their mother's arms again. Never hear her cheer from the sidelines or get scolded for something stupid but harmless. Never have the chance to make new memories. Not with her.

Whatever had happened to her was unfair. Senseless. Quig had loved those kids, and was making a better life for them.

Diesel nudged her leg, and, when she looked down, he was staring into her eyes, concerned at the avalanche of emotions he felt coming off her.

"Good boy," she whispered, rubbing his head.

His tail wagged slowly, but his expression remained vigilant. The other dogs ran around, enjoying the outdoor family get together, but Diesel didn't join them.

Once the bench was in place and the sign propped against a rock, the adults gathered on the dock. The sun was nearly gone now, and the kids had settled on a blanket with snacks, fireflies beginning to blink around them. The mosquitoes would soon drive them away—to their separate homes—to simmer in sadness alone.

Taylor sat with her sisters, while the other adults gathered at the picnic table. Jo sat cross-legged beside Anna, both quiet for a long while until Taylor finally asked the question gnawing at her.

"Did either of you notice anything strange about Quig lately?"

Jo glanced up, then looked away. "Strange how?"

"I mean ... was she acting off? Seem different?"

Jo hesitated. "I didn't think it was my place to say anything."

Taylor frowned. "Say what?"

"She was coming home really late. A lot. I mean, two—even three—in the morning sometimes."

Taylor's stomach dropped. "Jo ..."

"Don't be mad at me," Jo said defensively. "I didn't know she was on a curfew. She *is* an adult, Taylor."

Taylor turned to Anna, already knowing what was coming. Jo wasn't a surprise. She wasn't one to talk much anyway. Never gossiped. But Anna—why hadn't she spoken up?

Irritation flooded through her.

"I saw her leave late a few times," Anna admitted softly. "Not as often as Jo saw her, but enough to wonder. After ten or eleven, usually."

Taylor's voice came out sharper than she intended. "And neither of you thought to tell me?"

Jo crossed her arms. "What were we supposed to do? She was doing her job. Getting her work done. Helping with the animals. She seemed to keep her cabin clean. I figured she was dating someone or maybe needed some space."

"You both knew her background," Taylor snapped. "That she was vulnerable. That every move mattered for her getting those kids back. You should have said something. And now you give away her home, just like that, Anna? A little soon, don't you think?"

"Trust goes both ways, Taylor," Jo said, voice tight. "You trusted Quig. So did we. Maybe too much. And you know she would've been the first to offer up her place to Tula."

"She's just here for a week," Anna said. "I didn't give anything permanently. The place is just sitting there empty, after all."

"I know. I'm sorry. I just wish I'd known that Quig was acting strangely," Taylor muttered, knowing her anger was displaced. "If it was drugs, if she was struggling—maybe I could've helped. Maybe she'd still be here."

Cate's gentle voice cut through the tension, calm but firm. "All this what-iffing won't change the past. What matters now is finding out what happened."

Everyone turned toward their mother, who sat watching them, her hands resting in her lap. She was always the lighthouse.

"So what's next, Taylor?" Jo asked.

Taylor took a breath. She thought about the faceless girl named Lana. "Her exes have been cleared, but I'm going to keep digging. I'll interview anyone she talked to recently. Visit that NA meeting she goes to. See if anyone knows more about where she was going or what she was caught up in."

Anna nodded. "We'll help. However we can."

Jo sighed. "Just tell us what you need."

Taylor looked out over the water, the dock now holding pieces of Quig's spirit—flowers, wood, memories. But it wasn't enough. Not yet. Someone knew what had happened to take her down. And Taylor was going to find them.

Chapter Thirteen

S aturday morning dawned bright and cool over the
Gray's farm. A thin veil of mist floated above the
pasture, burning away as sunlight spilled across the
fields. In the little cabin, Tula woke to the sound of birdsong and
the faint scent of hay drifting through the cracked window.

For a fleeting second, she forgot where she was. The quilt
beneath her smelled faintly of lemon detergent, the sheets soft
and unfamiliar. She could almost believe she was back in Los
Angeles—an off day, no auditions, no chaos.

Then memory returned, heavy and suffocating: her mother
in the hospital, the wreck of the house waiting for her, the
cleanup crew on their way from Atlanta.

Her stomach tightened.

She rolled from bed, rubbed her temples, and forced herself
upright. The mirror on the dresser showed a pale, tired woman
with smudged eyes and hair that had given up. Her L.A. friends
would be horrified. Probably pitch in to send her to the spa.

Tula stared at her reflection for a long moment before
turning away.

She laid out the thick work pants and long-sleeved shirt

she'd picked up at Walmart—cheap, stiff fabric that smelled faintly of plastic—and pulled them on like armor. On the chair sat her rental car keys, a stack of receipts, and a box of rubber gloves. The large arsenal of cleaning supplies in her trunk looked like it could handle a war. She hoped it was enough.

"I should've gotten a tetanus shot," she muttered, running a hand through her hair. It had been years since she'd even thought about one. Maybe a decade. "Too late now."

No time for doctors or fear. She had a job to do.

By the time she pulled into her mama's yard, the place looked like a construction zone. A giant green dumpster blocked half the drive, its steel sides already streaked with rust and flies buzzing thick around the rim. A trio of workers in gray coveralls —two men and a woman—hauled trash from the porch like an assembly line. Plastic bags, broken furniture, blackened pans. The clang of metal hitting metal echoed through the air.

A pickup truck idled near the oak tree, its bed stacked with fresh lumber. Two men were unloading boards—a tall, older Black man with a salt-and-pepper beard and calm eyes, and a freckled teenager with bright red hair and the kind of energy that hadn't yet been dimmed by the world.

The older man caught her staring and gave a courteous nod. "Morning. I'm Cecil. This here's my right hand, Levi. Anna said you'd need a ramp built. We're here to oblige."

The boy grinned wide. "I'm his apprentice."

Tula blinked, caught off guard. She hadn't asked for a ramp, hadn't asked for any of this, and yet here they were—tools, trucks, purpose. She glanced toward the porch, remembering the nurse's warning that her mother would need wheelchair access. These people were already making that happen.

Before she could respond, a stout woman in stretch pants and a bright floral blouse marched across the yard with grocery bags looped over both arms and a casserole balanced precariously on top. She blew past Tula like a force of nature, muttering, "Fridge'll need scrubbing before I put this in."

Tula followed her inside—and nearly gagged.

The smell hit like a slap: sour milk, animal musk, old grease, and decay. The air felt sticky, heavy with years of neglect. She pressed a hand over her mouth as the woman yanked open the refrigerator door.

"I'm Mabel," the woman announced without looking up. "From The Den. Anna said you folks could use some meals to get through the week."

Within seconds, Mabel was tossing expired cartons and molding containers into a trash bag, muttering to herself about "science projects" and "bless her heart." The rhythmic sound of clinking jars and tearing plastic filled the kitchen. She scrubbed shelves with a vengeance, then lined up fresh milk, eggs, butter, and the casserole with military precision.

Tula stood there, dumbfounded. She couldn't remember the last time someone had done something for her without asking for something in return.

A familiar voice broke through the chaos. "You just gonna stand there, or you want to help?"

Tula turned. Anna stood in the doorway wearing faded overalls, a red bandana tied over her hair. She carried a clipboard and passed out bottles of water to the workers like she was running a command post. The organized calm in her eyes made Tula feel, for the first time in days, that maybe she wasn't alone in this nightmare.

"You can't know what this means to me," Tula said, lowering her voice. "But I didn't mean for you to take all this on. It's awful."

Anna shrugged easily. "Some of us have seen worse. And you're not alone here. We're all friends, even if you don't know us yet."

Tula swallowed the sudden lump in her throat. "Thank you."

Outside, new arrivals pulled up—a tall man with kind eyes unloading fencing from a pickup, and, beside him, a woman with quiet grace crouched to examine the ragged dogs milling nervously around the porch.

The woman's voice was soft but firm. "I'm Cate," she said, straightening. "Anna's mama. That's my husband, Ellis. We'll set up a station for these dogs—food, water, shelter. Some of them need a vet pronto. I'll take them. We'll separate the rest, males and females."

Tula blinked. "I—thank you. I hadn't even—"

Cate's smile was small but understanding. "You've had your hands full. We'll handle this." Her tone left no room for argument, and Tula was too relieved to give one.

By midmorning, the yard buzzed like a hive. The sun climbed higher, beating down on their backs as the cleaning crew carved pathways through the wreckage. Inside, the constant rustle of garbage bags filled the air. Every few minutes, a worker would hold up something half-broken or unrecognizable.

"Trash?" they'd call.

"Yes," Tula answered sharply, not even glancing up.

"No," Lorene snapped from her post near the doorway, arms crossed tight over her chest. "That's good stuff. Mama will want it."

And so it went, object by object—an endless tug-of-war between denial and reality.

The battles wore everyone down, but the work continued. Piles disappeared, floors emerged. For the first time in years, light reached corners that hadn't seen a broom since Tula was a teenager.

Waylon was nowhere to be found. His truck was gone; she

could only assume he was out driving without a license again. The thought made her stomach knot.

Curtis and Earl, on the other hand, had planted themselves in lawn chairs near the shed, cigarettes hanging from their lips, beers sweating in their hands. They watched the cleanup like it was a show.

When one of the workers tripped over a box, Curtis hollered, "Ten points!"

Earl cackled, nearly spilling his drink.

Tula clenched her jaw until her teeth hurt.

Things escalated when two of the dogs, wound tight from all the commotion, began snapping at each other. The scuffle broke out fast—growls, dust, fur flying. Before Tula could move, Ellis and Cecil were already there, calm but quick, separating the animals with quiet authority.

"Easy now, fellows," Cecil murmured. "Ain't nobody losin' fur today."

Cate knelt, checking for wounds, her hands gentle but efficient. "They'll be fine. Just scared of all this ruckus. They aren't used to so many strangers around them, are you, guys?"

Earl, watching from his chair, smirked and nudged a stray with his boot. "They don't like outsiders either."

Something inside Tula snapped. "Don't you two have jobs? Or you could pitch in, you know. It wouldn't hurt you to break a sweat."

Curtis blew smoke in her direction. "House'll be mine soon enough. Might as well let you do the dirty work."

"Good one, Curtis," Earl said, laughing like a donkey.

Tula's pulse jumped. "You're both unbelievable."

Lorene's voice cut through from the porch, defending her brothers. "Leave 'em alone. Nobody wants you here anyway, Tula Rose. Why don't you go back to your fancy city life—

hobnobbing with the one percent, pretending you're better than us?"

Tula's voice shook. It was laughable that they still thought she was living the high life. That she was rich. "Because Mama wouldn't last a week in this mess, that's why. Someone has to fix it. Don't see the three of you doing anything about it, do we?"

Almost on cue, a delivery truck rumbled up the drive, brakes hissing. Two men climbed out, unloading a hospital bed and oxygen tanks. The sight stole the air from her lungs. It was one thing to hear the doctor talk about her mother's dire prognosis — it was another to see it rolling up her childhood driveway.

Her hands trembled, but Anna was suddenly there beside her, clipboard in hand, her tone calm and professional as she directed the workers where to go. "Bedroom's through the hall on the left. We've already cleared it. Careful of the door frame."

Tula nodded, silently grateful for the structure, the steadiness. Without Anna, she might've fallen apart.

By late afternoon, the chaos had taken on a rhythm. Inside, the cleaners hauled the last of the trash to the dumpster, their coveralls streaked with sweat and grime. Pathways now stretched clear from the front door to her mama's bedroom, to the bathroom, to the kitchen. Sunlight streamed through the freshly cleaned windows, catching dust motes that looked like tiny ghosts fleeing the scene.

In the kitchen, Mabel and Anna worked side by side, humming along to an old country song playing from a phone speaker. Mabel's chili simmered on the stove, filling the air with the comforting scent of tomatoes and spice.

Tula leaned against the doorframe, watching them. For the first time all day, her throat loosened enough to swallow without effort.

"You alright?" Anna asked, glancing up.

"Better than I was this morning," Tula admitted. "I don't know how to thank you."

"Don't bother," Anna said. "Just pass it on someday."

Outside, the sound of hammering echoed. Levi and Ellis were fitting the last boards on the ramp, their laughter rising between strikes of the hammer. Cecil held the frame steady, offering quiet guidance.

"Little more on that corner," Cecil said. "You want the slope even, else Ms. Skaggs is liable to roll backward before she even hits the porch."

"Yes, sir," Levi said, tongue caught between his teeth in concentration.

Tula smiled, a genuine one this time. "He's good at that. For a kid."

"Hard worker," Cecil said proudly. "This is Jo's boy. Got more sense than most grown men I know."

Cate walked by leading two of the calmer dogs on makeshift leashes. "We found the worst of the fleas," she said. "These two are clear now. The others are separated out. Once your mama's feeling stronger, we'll figure out which of the lot can be rehomed. I've got low-cost spay and neuter vouchers ready."

Tula nodded, relief softening her shoulders. "Thank you, Cate. Really."

Earl, still in his chair, snorted from across the way. "Ain't nobody cutting on my dogs."

Curtis joined in with a bark of laughter. "Yeah, how'd you like your balls cut off?"

Cate didn't even blink. "We won't remove anything without your mother's permission," she said mildly, then went right back to work. The kind of calm that made grown men look foolish.

By dusk, the transformation was astonishing. The yard smelled of cut grass instead of rotting trash and the dirty diapers that had been flung out on the trailer's porch. The house, though still scarred, breathed easier. The dumpster was full, proof as to what could happen when good people refused to give up.

Jo arrived quietly as the sun sank, her car pulling in without fanfare. She'd stayed at the farm to man the boarding facility all day, and looked tired, but had still come.

Tula watched her move through the house like she'd always belonged there, scrubbing, sorting, and carrying boxes without needing instruction. When Mabel asked her to stir the chili, she just nodded and did it.

Tula watched her work, noticing the quiet connection she shared with Cate—a few looks, a shared smile, something unspoken. She didn't know their history, but it carried warmth.

As night settled in, the last load of trash thudded into the dumpster. The dogs, newly fed and watered, curled up in the straw beds Ellis had made. The air hummed with the soft sounds of crickets and low conversation.

The Gray family had pulled off a small miracle.

Tula stood on the porch, her body aching, her clothes damp with sweat, but her heart lighter than it had been in years.

Inside, Mabel ladled chili into bowls while laughter drifted out through the open windows. The savory smell wrapped around Tula like a blanket. Her brothers—who'd done nothing all day—finally slunk inside to fill their bowls, drawn by the scent of real food.

She leaned against a porch post, too tired to move, and watched the stars begin to blink through the gathering dark.

She still didn't understand these people—their easily given kindness, their refusal to judge, the way they simply showed up and worked without question. Hours ago, they'd been almost strangers. Now, they'd given her something she hadn't felt since she was a girl.

Hope.

And that humbled her more than she could ever admit.

Chapter Fourteen

It was funny how guilt could sneak up on you—like showing up where you used to belong and realizing you'd been gone long enough that nobody noticed.

Taylor sat in her truck outside the church, the old white steeple rising over the oaks, paint peeling near the bell tower like skin after a sunburn. The parking lot was mostly empty except for a few older sedans and a motorcycle with saddlebags that had seen better days.

She remembered coming here as a kid for Bible school, sitting on hard wooden pews while sunlight streamed through colored glass, turning the floor into a patchwork of blue and red light. Those were fun summer weeks, when the neighbors stepped in to try to direct them toward God's grace, making sure they were included in the annual fun by picking them up, transporting them to the church.

Their father had always looked forward to that week, when someone else was totally responsible for his kids, giving him even more free time than he usually took.

Back then, faith had felt simple.

Now it felt more complicated.

It wasn't that she didn't believe in God anymore. She did—deeply. She just didn't believe that finding Him required fluorescent lights and coffee-stained carpets. Somewhere along the line, religion had turned into something people endured instead of embraced. It had become another to-do list: attend, donate, smile, repeat.

Where was the joy in it that she'd felt as a child?

Taylor still prayed, but her church was different now. Her sermons were carried on the wind over the lake, her communion the quiet that fell after dusk.

God didn't need her to dress up or pretend.

She sighed, shutting off the truck, then checked herself in the rearview mirror. Her reflection stared back—barefaced, tired. She'd scrubbed off all traces of makeup and pulled on jeans and a plain T-shirt. No badge, no weapon. Just a woman trying to disappear into a crowd.

Her stomach churned as she opened the door. She hadn't walked through this church's back entrance in over a decade, and her boots echoed down the stairwell like small betrayals.

The basement smelled faintly of burnt coffee and cleaning spray. A circle of folding chairs filled the center of the room, the cheap metal kind that creaked when you sat wrong. A coffee pot hissed in the corner beside a tray of Styrofoam cups, and someone had left a box of off-brand donuts half-open on the counter.

She spotted a woman unfolding another chair near the wall. Short gray hair, sensible shoes, a kind face that had seen both joy and grief. "Evening," the woman said. "You're welcome to join us."

"Thank you," Taylor said quietly, taking a chair near the back.

The fluorescent lights buzzed overhead, lending a washed-out glow to everything—the kind that made even the living look a little ghostly. A dozen or so people shuffled into their seats, murmuring soft hellos.

At seven sharp, the woman—Helene, as she introduced herself—folded her hands. "Let's begin," she said. "We'll start with the Serenity Prayer."

Voices rose and fell in uneven unison.

God grant me the serenity to accept the things I cannot change ...

Taylor mouthed the words but didn't speak them aloud.

One by one, people introduced themselves.

"Chad, addict. Five months sober."

"Jenny, alcoholic. Eight days."

"Raymond. Trying again."

Some voices were strong, others barely whispered. The words, "one day at a time," floated like a lifeline through the room.

Taylor stayed quiet. She wasn't here to speak. She was here to listen.

Helene's gaze drifted toward the empty chair beside her, and her voice trembled slightly. "I'm sure most of you have heard we lost one of our own last week," she said softly. "Quig. She died in a car fire."

The room went still. Taylor watched carefully.

"The girl who had the teardrop tattoo?" someone asked.

Helene nodded. "Yes, that was her. As you recall, she had that removed. She'd been doing so well on her healing journey. I don't know what happened—whether she relapsed or didn't, or if it was something else entirely. But she was one of us, and we'll miss her."

A hush fell.

"If anyone would like to share something about Quig," Helene said, "the floor's open."

A woman with a flannel shirt and rough hands raised hers.

"I knew her as Margaret. She always sat by the window. Used to bring brownies on Fridays. Said she baked because it kept her from thinking too much. They were from a box and lopsided as sin, but good."

A faint ripple of laughter broke the tension.

Another woman, younger, added, "She was funny. The quiet kind of funny. Once, I was bawling my eyes out over my ex, and she handed me a tissue and said, 'Girl, don't waste good mascara on bad men.'"

That earned a few chuckles. Taylor smiled through the ache in her throat. That was Quig to a T—never loud, but cutting in a way that made you feel seen instead of scolded.

After a moment of remembrance, others began to share their struggles.

A man with hollow eyes and a worn denim jacket spoke next. "My daughter's graduating next month," he said. "Told me I can come if I pass a drug test first. Guess that's her way of saying she believes I can."

A middle-aged woman clasped her trembling hands. "I slipped last month. Eighteen months sober, and I still thought I could have 'just one.'" Her voice cracked. "Didn't even taste good. It just reminded me how quick I can lose everything."

"You came back," Helene said softly. "That's what matters."

A man with prison tattoos down both arms nodded. "Yeah. Door don't lock behind you here. You fall, you just get back up and walk through it again."

Laughter, murmured agreement.

Then a teenager with bitten nails spoke. "My mom said, if I don't come to these, I'm out. So here I am."

A few people clapped.

Then a woman around Quig's age smiled shyly. "I just got my license back. Means I can keep my job. I don't have to depend on anyone for rides anymore."

That earned a genuine round of applause.

For a while, the group was just that—people telling truth to each other without fear. Taylor found herself sinking into the rhythm, their stories weaving into one another.

One older man told a story about losing his brother to fentanyl and how guilt kept him coming back every week. "I figure if I stay alive long enough," he said, "it means his death wasn't wasted."

A younger woman shared about her teenaged son—how she'd promised him pancakes every Sunday if she stayed sober. "Fourteen Sundays in a row," she said proudly. "He keeps count better than I do."

Another man admitted that every night before bed he made a list of three things he'd done right that day. "Sometimes it's just 'didn't steal,'" he said, laughing quietly. "But, hey, it's progress."

Taylor listened to all of it, letting the words settle like rain. Each story was a small miracle—proof that even broken people still reached for light. And somewhere in all those voices, she heard Quig's echo.

When the meeting finally ended, people lingered for coffee refills and small talk. A woman hugged Helene, a few exchanged numbers. The air buzzed with quiet comfort.

Taylor waited until most had gone before approaching. "Helene?"

The woman turned, her face soft. "Yes, honey?"

"I was a friend of Quig's. She lived on our property."

Helene blinked. "Oh, you must be Taylor. She talked about you."

Taylor's breath caught. "She did?"

"Oh yes. Said you gave her a chance when nobody else would. Loved working at that farm. Said it felt like home." Helene smiled faintly. "She used to make us laugh with stories about the animals. Last week it was about a goat getting loose. Said y'all were chasing it across a field like a band of fools."

Taylor managed a weak laugh. "Raspy. He's always the troublemaker. We should've named him Houdini. Nothing can keep him in. Nothing makes him happier than to make us chase him."

Helene's smile faded into something wistful. "Well, she was proud of that job. Said it gave her a reason to get up in the morning. That there she was part of something bigger and was trusted to do her part. You don't know how rare that is for some of these folks. Trust is something they long for again."

"Quig never mentioned anything about ... being afraid? Or trouble?" Taylor asked carefully.

Helene frowned. "Not afraid, no. But she did stop coming as often. Said she got a second job. Night shift. Not exactly official."

Taylor felt her pulse pick up. "A second job?"

"Yes. She said it paid cash. I asked if it was safe, and she said, 'Safer than what I used to do.' I didn't push her. Should I have?"

Taylor shook her head. "No, you couldn't have known."

"Why do you ask, honey? Is something wrong?"

Taylor hesitated. "Just trying to understand what happened to her."

Helene's eyes searched hers. "You're not just a friend, are you?"

Taylor looked down. "Let's just say I'm someone who cares."

Helene nodded slowly, accepting that. "She was close with Rae, but she left before you came over. You could try again Wednesday. Same time."

"Could I get Rae's number?"

"Sorry, no. We keep anonymity here. You know how it works."

"I understand," Taylor said. "I'll be back Wednesday."

Helene hesitated, then added softly, "She was making amends with her kids. Talked about buying them each a birthday present next month. She was so proud of that. Said she'd finally saved enough to do something right."

Taylor's eyes burned. "Thank you, Helene."

"If I remember anything else, I'll call," Helene said.

Taylor handed her a folded note with her number. "Please do."

When Taylor stepped outside, the night air hit cool against her face. The church parking lot lay quiet except for the hum of a lone streetlight flickering at the corner. Crickets sang in the grass.

She paused at the truck door, staring up at the steeple silhouetted against the sky. The wind shifted, carrying the faint smell of rain.

Her phone buzzed.

Shane.

She answered on the first ring. "Hey."

"I've got something," he said. "Where are you?"

"NA meeting just let out. Southside church."

"I just talked to the medical examiner," Shane said, voice grave. "She died from asphyxiation. Hyoid bone fractured—strong sign of strangulation. No soot in her lungs, no carbon monoxide in her blood. Means she was dead before the fire."

Taylor closed her eyes, the world narrowing to the sound of her own pulse.

"This changes everything," she whispered.

"Yeah," Shane said. "We've now officially got a murder on our hands."

Taylor drove home with the windows cracked, letting the cool night air wash over her face. The road stretched empty ahead, her headlights cutting long tunnels through the mist.

She replayed the meeting in her mind—the smell of church coffee, the murmured prayers, Helene's tears when she'd mentioned Quig's name. Every story had carried pieces of pain that mirrored Quig's life, but none explained her death.

Quig had been doing so well.

Taylor gripped the steering wheel tighter. She thought of Helene's words—a second job, night work, not official. That detail gnawed at her. It fit too neatly with the other loose threads she'd been tugging: the anonymous tips, the cash payments, the whispers of back room deals at the Shuffle Lounge.

Raindrops began to speckle the windshield—soft at first, then steadier, drumming a rhythm that filled the cab. She flipped on the wipers and let their steady swipe accompany her thoughts.

Her mind wandered back to the faces at the meeting—each one had walked into that basement carrying invisible weights.

So had Quig.

They'd all thought she was turning a corner. She'd been showing up, smiling. Joking about goats and sobriety chips. She'd made everyone believe she had momentum, like she was clawing her way back from the brink.

And maybe she was.

But Taylor had learned the hard way—sometimes, when people seemed the strongest, they were holding on by a thread.

The rain thickened. By the time she turned down the gravel drive to the farmhouse, her chest ached with a mix of sorrow and rising fury.

Diesel's silhouette appeared in the porch light, tail wagging. Always vigilant. Always waiting.

She parked but didn't get out right away. The rain tapped gently on the roof of the truck, a soft percussion that gave her cover to finally let herself feel it. The grief. The helplessness. The guilt.

She dropped her head back against the seat and closed her eyes.

And suddenly—she was back there.

It had been a breezy, golden Easter Sunday on the farm. The big family hunt was one of her favorite traditions—plastic eggs filled with chocolate or loose change, tucked into fence posts, tucked into the flower beds, even floating in the watering trough.

Addie had darted across the yard, a pink basket flapping at her side, squealing with delight every time she spotted an egg. Bronwyn had taken her hand early on, leading her toward the "easy finds," and within minutes they were giggling like sisters.

Quig had stood back with Taylor near the barn, watching her daughter with misty eyes. She looked more alive that day than Taylor had seen her in a long time—her cheeks flushed from the sun, her curls wild in the breeze.

"My baby's got a real friend now," Quig had said, almost in a whisper. "That's all I ever wanted. To give her something real."

Her boys had skipped the egg hunt, claiming they were too grown, but Taylor had found them later sitting out by the lake with Levi and Teague. Fishing poles in hand, chewing on sour straws they'd snuck from the treat table. Quig had spotted them, too, and there was this ... stillness in her expression. That soft, quiet pride only a mother could understand.

She had glowed that day.

Not just because of her kids—but because she belonged. She wasn't the outsider anymore. She was one of them.

Part of the Gray family.

Taylor had taken a photo that afternoon—Addie and Bronwyn on the porch swing, barefoot and sticky-faced from Easter cupcakes. Quig had snuck into the background, grinning at the chaos.

Taylor opened her eyes, the image still seared behind her lids.

She whispered into the quiet cab, her voice raw, "We'll get you justice, Quig. I promise."

It cracked on the last word, but the promise held steady.

When she finally stepped out, the scent of wet earth wrapped around her like a shawl. Diesel trotted down the steps and nudged her hand, sensing something off. She scratched behind his ears, grateful for the constant.

Somewhere across the dark field, a whippoorwill called—a long, low whistle that echoed across the trees like a warning.

Taylor tilted her face to the sky, letting the rain fall freely now.

The storm had only just begun.

Chapter Fifteen

The next morning dawned with the farm already humming with signs of life—roosters crowing, goats bleating, and the distant sound of a tractor starting up as everyone began their chores. The dogs must've already been fed, because, if they were hungry, there'd be barking coming from the rescue barn.

Taylor stood on the porch, the last remnants in her tea mug warming her hands, Lennon snuggled tight against her chest in a wrap. They were both still in pajamas, taking a lazy introduction to the day.

She watched quietly as across the way Cecil was teaching Levi how to fill a new pothole in the driveway, shoveling gravel from the wheelbarrow and smoothing it out, then stamping it down, their quiet conversation lost beneath the calls of blue jays overhead. The rest of the morning chores were done, and he'd already released the kids to prepare for breakfast, then the school bus, but Levi didn't like to be idle or hang around waiting.

Like Cecil, Levi was always doing something outside. Busy, busy. She had no doubts that, out of all the children, Levi was growing up to be the most helpful around the farm. He jumped out of bed bright and early, eager to do chores with Cecil and Ellis. It was a shame that he'd never had a father figure before now, and the truth of his own paternity haunted Jo, and would one day do the same to him.

Life was a series of hard times, pressed between the good ones, competing against each other for space.

Behind her, the kitchen was a flurry of motion.

Cate stood at the stove, flipping pancakes while giving Jo instructions about a vet appointment for one of the horses. With her hair piled up on her head, and her face bare of makeup other than a touch of mascara and lip gloss, she reminded Taylor of an older Audrey Hepburn.

Ellis was taking her to Dahlonega for the weekend, and Cate was nervous about leaving the farm in everyone else's hands. She knew they could handle things without her when needed, it was just her connection to the animals that made her so careful with instructions.

Anna was off work from the hospital and would be handling the front desk for boarding. She'd oversee checking in and checking out the animals, and whatever she could do in between to help care for them and clean up. It was probably not the best weekend to take Cate away, seeing how Hart's Ridge was having a huge vintage car show and their bookings were full, but Ellis hadn't known that when he'd made the reservations for a cute Airbnb, and they all wanted Cate to take some time away when she could.

Anna helped Teague and Bronwyn gather signed papers and stuff them into their backpacks. She usually did her own mornings at her house, but Cate had wanted to do a family breakfast before she and Ellis took off, so today was it.

Even with all her favorite sounds of family and farm life around her, Taylor couldn't shake the heavy cloud of sadness that enveloped her. Quig was on her mind constantly, her ghost urging Taylor toward justice.

Sam came up and put his arms around her, including Lennon in his embrace. His warmth spread through Taylor, reminding her that he always showed up to bring her comfort. She could get through anything with him by her side. She was lucky, and she knew that.

"Talk to me," he whispered. "I can see that brain of yours working overtime, even if your face says something different. You know keeping all that inside of you is going to wreak havoc on your nervous system. Tonight, your whole body will be in pain from you internalizing everything. So spit it out."

Damn, he knew her so well. She laughed softly, pulling away. Lennon stirred and Taylor shushed her back to sleep as she went to the porch swing and sat down.

Sam joined her.

"I just can't imagine who would want Quig dead," she said, her voice low enough that no one other than Sam could hear her. "I need to start digging harder. Talk to more people. See who she was spending time with. Someone out there knows something."

"Want some help on this?"

"I wish you could, but Shane said I had to keep real quiet that I'm working with him. I think adding you to the mix would make him shut me out. You know how he is."

"Yeah, I know he hates me," Sam said.

Taylor could hear a tinge of jealousy in his tone, but he was too proud to come out with it. He was right, though. Shane didn't seem to want anything to do with Sam. Made Taylor feel like she was always walking a tight rope between the two men. At least Shane had learned from the last time and was respecting her boundaries.

Treating her like a colleague and nothing more.

"I don't know about that. Anyway, I have a lead from yesterday. Someone from the NA meeting said she thought that Quig had a second job—possibly off the books, working night shifts. If I can figure out what it was, I'm going to follow her tracks. Go where she went. Talk to anyone who might've seen her the night she died—or even the nights before."

Anna peeked out the screen door. "Are you talking about Quig again? Taylor, you're going to make yourself sick over this. Let the sheriff's department figure it out."

"Listen," Taylor said, irritation flooding through her. "I don't need you telling me what to do or how to process her death. This isn't one of your patients in the emergency department where you see them for half an hour, send them off, and never think of them again."

A flush crept up Anna's neck and filled her face.

She let the door slam as she flounced back into the house.

"Great," Taylor said, shaking her head "Now look what I've done. She probably went in there and told Mom that I just verbally attacked her. I can't even explain and tell them that we know Quig was murdered, or they'll wonder how I have inside news before it's released. So, I just look like an asshole now."

He squeezed her hand. "Anna will be fine. Well, maybe after a day or so."

His joke fell flat. He didn't realize how long Anna could hold a grudge when she wanted to. In her youth, Anna had been known to stop talking to one of her sisters for weeks on end.

Lennon broke the tense moment by opening her eyes and looking around, a slight smile creeping up as she saw her two favorite people in the world hovering over her.

Just then, Anna came back out with two mugs of steaming tea. "Peace offering," she said, glancing at Taylor. "Breakfast is ready, too."

Taylor accepted a cup, relieved that her sister was going to give her grace. "Thanks. Look, I'm sorry, Anna. We're all on edge. I just ... I don't want Quig to be dismissed as though she doesn't matter. Not like some junkie who made bad choices. She really was trying so hard."

"I know she was," Anna said. "Believe it or not, I miss her, too. She was always so eager to please around here. Couldn't help but like her. I hope they figure out what happened."

Taylor nodded. Yes, she also hoped "they" did. And she planned to be on the top line of that team. Quig would've done anything for the Gray family, so finding her killer would be the least that Taylor could do for her.

Chapter Sixteen

Taylor pulled into the gravel lot of the Eastside Marina Fish Camp, and the scent of deep-fried fish greeted her. She stepped from the truck, gravel crunching beneath her boots. A string of faded triangular flags fluttered above the covered deck where a handful of patrons were dipping hushpuppies into plastic ramekins of honey butter.

It was a modest place—just a screened-in dining porch and a small shack for the kitchen, patched together with weather-worn planks. The paint was peeling, the porch sagged slightly on one side, and a hand-painted sign that read FISH FRY FRIDAYS – CASH ONLY swung gently in the breeze.

She'd gone to another support meeting, and Rae still wasn't there.

Now Lana was her best hope for getting any behind the scenes information.

Taylor adjusted the strap of her purse, scanning the area. A couple of waitstaff bustled about in T-shirts and cutoffs, dropping off pitchers of sweet tea. A lanky teenage boy with sunburned cheeks handed out menus. She stepped up to the counter window where the cook—middle-aged, shirtless under a grease-stained apron—was taking an order from a woman with two little kids in tow.

When it was her turn, Taylor smiled politely. "Hey, I'm not here to order. I'm looking for someone who used to work here, off and on. Name's Lana. Ring a bell?"

The man squinted at her. "Lana ... blonde girl? Real skinny, always smells like bubblegum vape?"

Taylor nodded, though she had no idea. "That's her."

"Yeah, she used to run plates for us, when one of the regular girls flaked out. But she hasn't been around in a few weeks. Month maybe."

"Any idea where she hangs out now?"

He shrugged, flipping a burger on the grill behind him. "Not really. I think she was living down near the boat slips for a while. Might've had a friend with a camper, or a boyfriend with a boat. Can't remember. Sorry."

Taylor thanked him and wandered toward the marina. Behind the fish camp, a long wooden dock snaked out toward the water, lined on either side with boats ranging from pristine cabin cruisers to beat-up fishing vessels barely floating. At the far end, a handful of RVs and campers were parked along the dirt edge of the lot, some surrounded by makeshift furniture and tarps for shade.

She walked slowly, her eyes scanning the area for anything —or anyone—that looked like it might belong to a Lana.

At the third camper, a busted-up Jayco with a blue tarp pinned over the roof, a woman lounged on a folding camp chair with a magazine in her lap and a cigarette between her fingers. She looked up warily as Taylor approached.

"Hey there," Taylor said, keeping her tone casual. "I'm looking for someone named Lana. I heard she used to work at the fish camp and might be staying around here?"

The woman took a drag and exhaled slow. "Why?"

This was the kind of place where people protected each other, whether they were close or not. Taylor paused. "I'm not with the law. Just trying to figure out what happened to a friend of mine—Quig. Lana might've known her. Might've worked with her."

The woman's face softened just a bit. "Quig? The one who died in the fire?"

Taylor nodded.

"Damn shame," she muttered. "She was good people."

"So, you knew her?"

"Not really. Just seen her around a few times. Way back, actually. Lana knew her better. They'd talk sometimes, mostly late nights. I heard about what happened to her."

"Is Lana around?" Taylor asked.

The woman gestured with her chin. "She's over on dock five. Stays on an old sailboat—The Phantom—ugliest green thing you ever saw. She don't like visitors, but tell her Cindy sent you."

"Thanks," Taylor said, already turning.

She found the boat exactly where Cindy said it would be—fifth dock, middle slip. It wasn't just ugly; it looked haunted. Dull olive hull, mildew on the windows, and a faded decal of a palm tree peeling off the stern.

Taylor stepped onto the creaky dock and rapped her knuckles on the fiberglass.

After a moment, the door creaked open, and a young woman with tired eyes and a messy topknot peered out.

"Yeah?"

"Lana?"

Suspicion flickered across her face. "Who wants to know?"

"My name's Taylor Gray. I'm a friend of Quig Gallagher."

Lana's expression changed instantly. Her chin quivered, just slightly, and her fingers tightened on the edge of the door. Her bloodshot eyes suddenly went from apprehensive to sad.

"Can we talk for a minute?" Taylor asked gently.

After a pause, Lana stepped aside and waved her in.

The inside of the boat smelled faintly of mold and air freshener, with a hint of skunk weed. A worn blanket was crumpled in the corner, a cooler doubling as a table, and a few candles melted halfway down beside an open bag of chips and a messy jar of salsa.

"I'm not in trouble, am I?" Lana asked. "They dropped that warrant weeks ago. No evidence."

"I'm not a cop, and I don't know about any warrants. I just need to know what you knew about Quig. Anything you can give me. I'm trying to help her mom find closure. She's suffering, as you can imagine."

Lana sat, pulling her knees up to her chest. "Yeah. Like— damn. I'm so pissed off about it, too. Quig was trying so hard, you know? Like, actually trying. And she was getting close. Closer than anyone I'd ever seen get to pulling themselves out."

"Where did you know her from?"

The question was met with Lana visibly flinching. "From another kind of life, actually. Like way back when both of us were doing anything and everything we could to stay high. I'm too tired to chase it now."

That's not what it looked like, but Taylor kept that to herself.

"Okay. Understood. What else can you tell me about Quig's current life. Or—the one she had."

"Not much. After she got out of jail, she stopped hanging out with anyone from her past, as far as I know. I also know she was working two jobs. Said she had to stash away everything she could for a place of her own. She missed her babies so bad when they weren't with her."

"Do you know what the second job was?" Taylor asked.

Lana hesitated. "It wasn't anything ... official. Not at first. It started with her getting pulled in to clean up after some private parties. Like, little get-togethers out at this place between Jasper and Hart's Ridge—Shuffle Lounge, I think they call it. Behind the old liquor store out on Deer Point."

Taylor's brow furrowed, a thought occurring to her about it sounding familiar. "Shuffle Lounge?"

"Yeah. It's all 'members only' club or whatever. Basically just a bunch of guys playing poker, smoking cigars, and talking like they run the world."

"Did she say who got her the job?"

Lana shook her head. "She just said it was hard to get into but someone she trusted vouched for her. That it was easy money. But ... I saw her one morning after she pulled an overnight there. She looked scared. Wouldn't say why."

Taylor's gut clenched. "Did she keep going back?"

"Yeah. She said she had to. Said she was close to getting enough to get her into her own place. Three bedrooms and a real backyard. But from what I heard through the grapevine, she started acting weird after that. Kept saying she felt like someone was watching her."

Taylor's pulse quickened. "Watching her how?"

"Like ... not just at the Lounge. Like ... everywhere. Maybe she said following her. I don't know."

"Can you tell me who else may know more about this?"

"So yeah, that's like ... classified," Lana said, winking at her. "I sort of have people all over in a few counties. I used to travel back and forth a lot, and I still hear things through my own little network. But I swear, I don't know what happened to Quig. I wish I did. She didn't deserve to die like that. She really had her shit together."

Taylor stood, already reaching for her phone. They hadn't

yet released that Quig dying in the car fire wasn't an accident. Maybe Lana's network knew more. "Lana, if you remember anything else—any name, license plate, conversation—you call me, okay?"

She pulled a fifty-dollar bill from her pocket and handed it over.

Lana took it. She looked like a kid in a candy store as she nodded. "I sure will."

Hopefully that fifty would net some more leads. As Taylor stepped off the dock, she texted Shane:

> Have you ever heard of Shuffle Lounge?
> Behind the old liquor store on Deer Point?

Chapter Seventeen

Tula sat at the foot of the hospital bed, her arms crossed tight while the discharge nurse went over instructions for oxygen use and medication schedules. Her mama wasn't listening. She was clutching the bedrails with both hands, her lower lip thrust out like a sulky child.

"I don't see why I can't stay here," Dixie complained, her voice scratchy but strong enough for the whole ward to hear. "Got me a clean bed, three meals a day, and a television remote that don't go missin' every time I get up to the bathroom. Nurses check in regular, and I don't hear all that fussin' from my young'uns. You sendin' me home is just 'cause I'm on Medicare, ain't it? Cheaper to kick me out."

The nurse kept her professional smile, but her patience was wearing thin. "Mrs. Skaggs, your vitals are stable. You now have a recuperation plan in place. I promise you'll be better off recovering at home with your family."

Dixie cut her off with a snort. "Home health, my butt. Y'all just don't want me takin' up space. Going to put someone else in this here bed that has that fancy insurance."

Tula pinched the bridge of her nose, her pulse rising. If she opened her mouth, she'd scream. Instead, she pulled out her phone and texted the only person she could think of: Anna.

Can you come up? She won't budge.

A few minutes later, Anna appeared in the doorway, still in scrubs, her auburn hair tucked behind her ears and her eyes red with fatigue. She slid right into the room with the kind of calm confidence that Tula envied.

"Morning, Mrs. Skaggs," Anna said warmly. "I hear you're giving the staff a hard time about going home. Don't you know, that's a good thing!"

Dixie perked up, clearly pleased to have new attention. "I'm not ready to leave. Don't trust 'em to send me home and forget about me."

Anna pulled up a chair and leaned close. "What if I told you Medicare will provide a caseworker? They'll come see you once a week, check your vitals, make sure your oxygen is working, answer your questions. And if anything isn't right, you can always come back."

Dixie narrowed her eyes. "You swear that's true? Someone will come out to my place? Check on me?"

"It's true," Anna said firmly.

Silence hung heavy. Then Dixie jabbed a finger at Tula. "I'll only go if she promises to stay another week. One week. No less. She's trying to run out of here so fast you'd think her ass is on fire."

Tula's stomach dropped. She wanted to shout no. Wanted to tell her mother she had a life waiting in L.A., that she couldn't keep drowning in this family quicksand. But it was the only way to get her to go home. If she didn't discharge from the hospital, this nightmare would never end.

"Fine," she said, her voice tight. "One week."

Her mama smirked triumphantly.

Anna's hand brushed Tula's arm as if to steady her. "You can stay at the cabin as long as you need."

Medicare transport arrived soon after, two men with a wheelchair and a white van. Getting Dixie into it was its own ordeal—bumps over the elevator threshold, bumps down the ramp, bumps across the parking lot. She complained at each jolt.

"Judging on what they've done just getting me this far, I'm sure you'll hit every pothole on the way to my house that you can find," she accused the driver, scowling. "This oxygen is going to blow up right in my face."

Tula clenched her fists and kept her mouth shut. She stayed sane by picturing her apartment back in Los Angeles: the tidy white sofa with its turquoise throw pillows, the framed art prints she'd collected from street fairs, her kitchen counters gleaming and clear, her bedroom with its soft duvet and lavender candle.

Each room, neat and clean, safe from the drama of her family, was her mental life raft.

At the curb, Anna squeezed her shoulder. "Good luck. You've got this. Give me your car keys." Tossing them to the second attendant, Anna shut the van door, leaving Tula alone with her mother's muttered complaints.

———

The moment the van pulled into the Skaggs yard, followed by the second paramedic driving Tula's car, her mama sat straighter, her eyes narrowing. "What in God's name happened here?"

The dumpster was gone, the yard cleared, the corral with tarps and straw standing where a swarm of half-feral dogs had once roamed.

Tula was proud of the transformation.

"Where's my stuff?" Dixie demanded. "What's going on with my dogs? Why aren't they running out to meet me?"

Tula forced calm into her voice. "Most of it was trash, Mama. We had to clear paths. And the animals—some were sick. The Grays helped separate them, get them food and bedding. Medical care. Cate is going to find homes for some of them."

Dixie's face turned red beneath the oxygen tubing. "Them dogs don't need no corral. They like freedom. And you best not let anyone take what's mine!"

"We'll talk about this once we get you settled," Tula said. Hopefully her mother had no idea how many animals she had, and wouldn't be able to figure out which ones were gone. Her heart thudded as they wheeled her up the brand-new ramp. She prayed her mama wouldn't explode when she saw inside.

But the moment the front door swung open, Dixie froze. "Where's the rest of my things? My boxes? My table piled with magazines? Who gave you the right?"

Before Tula could answer, Curtis and Earl sauntered in, both reeking of smoke. Curtis smirked. "You gonna die, Mama? If you do, dibs on your room."

Tula spun on him. "Shut your mouth."

Their mother stuck out her hand. "Cigarette."

Curtis obligingly pulled a pack from his pocket and tapped one free.

Before her mama could take it, Tula snatched it away. "You can't smoke anymore," she snapped. "Not with oxygen tanks in the house. You want to blow yourself up?"

Waylon jumped in, trying to help. "She's right, Mama. You gotta stop smoking if you want to get—"

Dixie cut him off with a huff, tugging at her oxygen tubing. "I can't breathe with this contraption! Feels like a leash."

"Better than the alternative," Tula muttered.

Lorene drifted in, already whining. "Mama, you got any cash? I need twenty bucks."

"Stop taking her money," Tula barked, her voice sharp as glass. "She needs it for medication copays!"

"She was going to give me some money before she got took by the ambulance," Earl said, trying to shove Lorene aside.

The air thickened with shouting, dogs barking, Dixie coughing into her mask. Then she wheezed, "Somebody make me fried chicken for dinner. I'm starving."

"Doctor said no fried foods," Tula ground out. "You need a low-sodium—"

"I want fried chicken!" her mama bellowed.

It all collided at once—Curtis lighting another cigarette, Lorene demanding money, Earl laughing like a maniac, Dixie wheezing and cursing, Waylon trying to reason with her.

The chaos pressed in like a storm cloud.

Tula's chest burned. She couldn't breathe. Couldn't think.

"That's it!" she shouted. "I'm done for today. Y'all enjoy your little powwow. I'm out of here." She grabbed her bag and bolted for the door.

The outside air hit her lungs like salvation, even if it was tinged with the pungent smell of dirty animals. At least it wasn't the air from inside. From a place that suffocated her.

She gulped, breathing hard, tears blurring her vision, her hands trembling on the steering wheel as she climbed into the car. How could she share the same blood with these people? How could responsibility for all of them keep landing on her shoulders?

Grabbing the keys the paramedic had placed in the console, she drove back down the dirt road, shaking, angry, heartsick. Saddled with responsibility she didn't want and love she couldn't kill.

And for the first time in years, she had no idea how long she'd be stuck in Hart's Ridge.

She cranked the radio up and listened to an old song by Alan Jackson, letting the sweet Georgia air flood through the windows, lifting her hair and teasing her face. He crooned about loss and forgiveness, and she reached up and turned it off again, nearly pulling off the knob in her anger.

Guilt began to eat at her, reminding her that no one of any decency would run away and leave their parent during their time of need. That if she did so, she'd be just like Earl and Curtis. And Lorene.

Good for nothing.

A memory flooded back to her. Her father swinging his belt at her and her brothers, yelling at them that they were good for nothing, just like their nagging mother. Most of the time Tula had done nothing to deserve the discipline. Was only lumped in with the rest of them and paid the price, too, for their shenanigans.

Her brothers had never apologized for that either.

If she ever had children, she would never use a belt on them. Damned if she'd give them permanent scars on their souls.

Back at the cabin, she didn't bother turning on the lights. She dropped her bag just inside the door and collapsed onto the bed, still in her jeans and shoes. Her body trembled with left-over adrenaline, and the silence pressed heavy after the chaos of her mother's house.

Tears came hot and sudden. She pressed her fists against her eyes, furious at herself for breaking down. She wasn't supposed to care this much. She wasn't supposed to be the one holding the wreck together. And yet here she was, caught in the same net she'd fought all her life to escape.

A knock startled her. She swiped at her cheeks, sat up.

"Tula?" Anna's voice was soft through the door. "You awake?"

Tula debated ignoring her. But something in the gentleness pulled her up. She opened the door to find Anna, dressed in jeans with her hair down now, her expression careful.

"You look like you could use some air," Anna said. "Walk with me?"

Tula nodded, too drained to argue.

Outside, the farm was alive in a way that soothed her nerves. Kids chased each other across the yard, their laughter echoing under the star-pricked sky. A cluster of dogs bounded after them, tails wagging. From the barn, the low clucking of hens carried on the breeze.

Anna's Great Dane loped up, tall enough that Tula instinctively stepped back. "Good Lord," she muttered. "That thing's half a horse."

Anna laughed. "He's a sweetheart. Just don't leave food on the counter. He'll take it."

They walked along the fence line, gravel crunching underfoot. Tula filled Anna in on the rest of the day with her mama, the cigarette, the money fights, the fried chicken demand.

Her words came fast, brittle.

"Sounds like a circus," Anna said quietly.

"Circus would be kinder," Tula replied. "More like an insane asylum."

Near the barn, another figure approached. Taylor, her dark hair pulled back, her baby tucked against her chest in a wrap. Little Lennon stirred but didn't wake, her tiny hand peeking from the cloth.

"Hey," Taylor greeted. "Anna said you could use some company."

Tula managed a nod. "She wasn't wrong."

They all leaned on Apollo's fence, and, other than a low nickering, Lennon's soft breaths the only sound for a while. Then Anna asked, "So what's the plan? Can't Waylon pick up where you left off so you can get back to L.A.?"

Tula's throat tightened. "Waylon's ... better than the rest. At least he's working now. But I can't depend on him. Not yet."

"Where's he working?" Anna asked.

"Shuffle Lounge," Tula said flatly.

She didn't miss the way Taylor's head swiveled around, her eyes sharpened, interest sparking there.

Tula narrowed her gaze. "Why? What's that mean to you, Taylor?"

Taylor's expression smoothed. She couldn't give anything away just yet, but maybe Tula's brother could be of help. "Just heard things. That's all."

Before Tula could push, Sam appeared, striding across the yard with easy confidence. He slid Lennon into his arms without a word, kissed Taylor's temple, and murmured something that made her smile. Then he carried the baby back toward the farmhouse, rocking her gently as he went.

Tula watched them, her chest twisting. She'd never had that. Someone steady. Someone who carried part of the weight without being asked.

She'd had boyfriends. A few proposals, even. One engagement that went on too long. Somehow, they all seemed to slip away, moving out of her life so slowly she wouldn't recognize it until it was nearly final. Too late to repair.

Her mind slipped, unbidden, to what she'd left behind in California. Another mess waiting for her, one she couldn't yet face. One she didn't dare speak aloud.

She pushed the thought away, pressing her arms tighter across her chest.

111

Anna touched her elbow gently. "You're not alone here, Tula. Whatever you think, you're not. Or, you don't have to be."

Tula didn't answer. Because if she opened her mouth, she wasn't sure if she'd laugh, cry, or scream. Instead, she kept walking under the stars, surrounded by a family that wasn't hers but felt a hell of a lot steadier than the one she was born into.

Chapter Eighteen

T aylor sat at the worn kitchen table, Lennon tucked against her chest in a sling, her tiny little fists curled under her chin. Other than *Good Morning America* on the tube, the rest of the house had quieted. Alice was at school and Sam was out on a minor skip-trace job in Monroe. Diesel was taken care of, and Taylor had a few hours to herself before she had to relieve Cate at the boarding counter.

She clicked the television off so she could concentrate better.

For once, the silence didn't feel peaceful. It felt like a challenge.

She opened her laptop, typed Hart County Business Search into the bar, and began digging. The Shuffle Lounge didn't have a website or any social presence she could find. No Yelp reviews. No Facebook page. Just a blip on Google Maps with an address, a blurry street-view shot of a long, one-level brick building with bars over the windows and a warped vinyl sign.

She entered the address into the business license database.

Shuffle Lounge
    License issued: October 28
    Registered to: DFC Hospitality Group, LLC
    Principal Address: Gainesville, Georgia
    Registered Agent: C T Corporation System
    Business Type: Food & Beverage

Taylor leaned back, chewing her cheek. "DFC?" she murmured, jotting it down in her notebook. She ran the LLC through the state registry, but the trail went cold fast. A corporate service had filed it. No names. No real address. Just boilerplate paperwork.

Her gut tightened.

"A two-year-old shell company running a business out in the woods with zero police activity? That's not restaurant stuff. That sounds like something fishy."

She clicked through a few more tabs, searching public records for any code violations, complaints, or health inspections. Nothing. It was like the place operated under radar—no complaints, no attention, no digital footprint.

Until Quig.

Taylor stared at the screen, then back to the name in her notebook.

DFC. Three letters.

Three people? A silent partnership?

The thought came uninvited.

It could stand for anything. Even something totally above board and innocent and just kept under the radar for personal reasons that didn't matter. But, deep down, Taylor knew. Things like this didn't come out of nowhere.

Someone was purposely keeping it quiet.

And she intended to find out who.

The narrow country road leading to Shuffle Lounge curved through woods. Trees pressed close on both sides, creating a natural canopy net that felt more like it was closing in on Taylor.

Shane drove with one hand on the wheel, the other holding his phone, texting and scrolling occasionally, a habit that drove her crazy. One of these days his distracted driving was going to be the death of him.

Or them both.

Yet she was glad he was letting her help investigate this case, so she had to mind her manners. "I can't believe this place has been operating for two years, and I've never heard of it," she said.

"Same. I asked around at the department, too. No one's been out here for any calls, either," Shane said.

Taylor nodded. "Exactly. Not a peep about it. Not even a noise complaint. It's like it's invisible."

"Or someone is keeping it invisible."

They reached the end of the tree-lined road, and the building came into view—a squat, gray-block structure with no signage other than a neon OPEN sign glowing faint red in one corner of the window. The lot was gravel, poorly lit, with a few rusting floodlights mounted haphazardly on the roof. Still, more than a dozen cars were parked out front, headlights flicking on and off as some vehicles came and others went. An old blue Ford was backed up to the rear door.

Taylor tried to imagine Quig coming there, parking in the weed-filled lot.

Why was it a secret? What about the job made her not want to confide in Taylor?

Shane pulled off the road into a grassy patch behind a line of trees, giving them a clear but concealed view of the building. He cut the engine, and silence fell around them—except for the thumping bass that spilled out every time the door to the building opened.

"This doesn't scream restaurant," she muttered.

"I don't see anyone coming out with food. I'm going to run a few of those car plates."

Taylor raised a pair of binoculars and scanned the entrance. Two men stepped outside—one in jeans and a blazer, the other in camo and a trucker hat. They shared a cigarette, laughed about something, then disappeared around the side of the building.

"It's a strange mix of clientele," she said. "I've counted at least three luxury cars, but also two beaters with mismatched doors."

Shane looked up. "I've run five tags so far. All residents from Hart County, Franklin, and one from Elbert. No priors. No warrants. No connection between any of them."

"At least not that we've found yet," Taylor said. She lowered the binoculars and checked her notes again. "So, let's say that Quig started working here a few months ago. If something about her job went sideways—then someone here knows more than we do."

They sat for a while longer, watching. More cars arrived. Loud laughter drifted across the clearing, followed by the crack of pool balls and the hum of a bass-heavy playlist. A young man came out with two bags of trash and headed to the back of the building. He looked a lot like Tula. Could be Waylon.

Taylor made a mental note.

Shane stretched his arms across the dash. "You sure this is the best way to dig into it? Recon? A stakeout? We could just go in there and investigate. Talk to them and see what's up."

Taylor didn't look at him. "Like that will work. They'll smell cop and won't say a word. Anything we might've learned will be hushed up and covered and we'll be back to square one. Quig deserves more than a box checked. If this place has anything to do with her death, I'm not letting it go."

He nodded slowly. "I didn't say stop. Just ... be careful."

She offered him a rare smile. "You too, Shane."

The smile faded as her eyes settled back on the building. A new figure stepped out into the night—tall, broad-shouldered, sharply dressed, and clearly out of place among the others. He spoke briefly to someone by the door, shook hands, then slipped back inside.

Taylor lowered the binoculars again, pulse quickening.

"Run that Benz over there," she said, pointing. "The black one with the chrome rims. I think we've found someone worth noting."

Shane tilted the laptop toward him, his fingers flying across the keys as he ran the plate. It took a few seconds for the results to populate.

"Huh," he said, leaning closer. "That's interesting."

Taylor turned to him. "Talk to me."

"Registered to a Marcus Jenks. Lives in Gainesville. Not much on him—clean record, owns a small import/export business. But guess what his business address is?"

Taylor raised a brow.

"Same principal address listed for DFC Hospitality Group."

Bingo.

Taylor's heart thumped harder. "So he's tied to the LLC."

Shane nodded. "Looks like it."

She stared at the building again, her mind turning gears. "Import/export is one of those vague umbrella terms people love to use when they want to sound legitimate but don't want anyone digging too deep."

"Especially when it shares a corporate address with a shell LLC tied to a place like this."

They watched as a woman exited the club, wobbling slightly in stilettos, pulling her skirt down with one hand and clutching her phone with the other. She tapped around on her screen, then stumbled toward a car and leaned against the hood, waiting.

"This is one hundred percent not a food-and-beverage establishment," Taylor muttered.

"Now to figure out what really is going on," Shane said.

She felt a pang of guilt. If Quig had gotten involved with something here, something that got her killed, then Taylor had failed her. She should've asked more questions. Paid closer attention. Trusted her gut instead of assuming everything was fine because Quig had been smiling at dinners and keeping up with her responsibilities at the farm.

Taylor clicked her pen and jotted down:

Marcus Jenks. Gainesville. Shared business address. Import/export.

"Let's give it another hour," he said. "See who else comes and goes. Then tomorrow, I want to pay a visit to the county clerk's office. See what else I can dig up on Jenks and anyone else tied to DFC."

"I can do that," she offered.

Shane nodded, glancing at his watch. "Fine with me."

A beat passed. Shane sobered. "You think Quig found out something? About what's going on in there?"

Taylor's jaw clenched. "It's possible. Maybe they hired her to clean or serve drinks, but she saw something. Overheard something. Maybe she tried to walk away or said she'd go to the cops."

"Or maybe," Shane added darkly, "someone found out she used to be an addict and made a pass at her. She refused. Set them off and they figured no one would look twice if she ended up dead in a burned-out car."

Taylor's stomach twisted. "Well, they were wrong. There will be justice."

Movement at the front door again. Two men stepped out—one older, wearing a suit that didn't fit quite right, and the other a thick-necked guy with arms like tree trunks. They looked like muscle, not customers. Noticing the car lights in the lot flicker again, Taylor pulled out her phone and snapped a few discreet photos.

"I want facial recognition on these guys," she said. "I wish we had that at the department."

"I'll see who I can tap for a favor," Shane said.

"Let's pack it up, then" Taylor said, sitting straighter and twisting to look behind them. "We've seen enough for tonight."

As they drove off, the Shuffle Lounge shrank in the rearview mirror, its dull red glow pulsing faintly in the darkness like a warning beacon. Taylor kept her eyes forward, hands tight on her thighs.

They weren't just chasing ghosts anymore.

Now, they had names.

Chapter Nineteen

The marina was quiet in the early morning, the sun just starting to stretch over the water. A breeze came in off the lake, rustling the mast flags and sending tiny ripples across the otherwise still surface. Taylor walked slowly along the dock, careful to step around a curled-up rope, a tipped-over bucket, and a cat that blinked lazily at her before going back to sleep.

Taylor spotted Lana instantly, kneeling on the deck of her boat, hair in a messy bun, smudges of soil on her bare legs and under her fingernails. A half-dozen terra cotta pots were arranged in rows, each cradling a small tomato plant just beginning to stretch toward the sun.

Taylor cleared her throat lightly.

Lana looked up, shielding her eyes. "Oh. Hey." She didn't sound surprised. Just resigned. "Figured I'd see you again."

"Figured right," Taylor said, stepping closer and gesturing at the plants. "They're coming along nice."

Lana wiped her hands on her shorts and reached for another seedling. "Been meaning to get them in the dirt all week. Felt good to do something with my hands. If I get some more money freed up, I'm planting lettuce and cucumbers. Maybe I'll have the makings for my own salad soon."

Taylor knelt beside her without asking. Took the next pot and began loosening the root ball. They worked in silence for a few minutes, side by side, the air rich with soil and the metallic scent of lake water.

"Might as well spit it out," Lana said, not even looking up. "I'm sure this ain't no social call."

"You know I wouldn't be here if this wasn't important," Taylor said.

"I know nothing other than people like you are like a dog with a bone."

"I've been to the Shuffle Lounge."

Lana's hands froze mid-scoop.

Taylor continued. "Quiet little place for a food and beverage establishment. No social media. No website. No paper trail to speak of. But somehow there're still plenty of people coming and going. You ever work there?"

Lana pressed soil around the base of the plant. "Nope. Well, not officially anyway. And wasn't around there long before I took off."

"Why?"

She shrugged, avoiding eye contact. "Didn't like the vibe."

"What kind of vibe was that?"

"A vibe with too many secrets," Lana said. "Too many rooms you weren't supposed to ask about. Doors that only opened for certain people. Names not said aloud."

"So, what goes on in there? Don't tell me it's a great place for a hot dog."

"They have hot dogs," Lana said casually. "One of the things on the menu that is edible, to be honest."

Taylor knew it wasn't a hot dog joint. Lana was being obtuse. Time to press her more. She reached into the tray for

121

another seedling. "You said before that Quig might've been working there. That's what you heard."

Lana nodded once.

"I think it's time you told me what you really know, Lana."

"I don't really know anything for sure," Lana said, her tone suddenly clipped and brittle. She took the plant from Taylor's hand, her movement abrupt.

"But you suspect something," Taylor pressed, coming to a stand. "You cared about Quig. You said that yourself. If there's even a sliver of a chance that something happened to her because of that place, don't you think you should say something?"

Lana looked down at the tomato plant in her hand, her thumb rubbing absently over a curled leaf. "Look, that place has people connected to it. People you don't mess with. I need to keep my mouth shut so that I don't end up like her."

Taylor's breath caught. "What do you mean, like her?"

Lana set the pot aside, her eyes flicking out toward the lake. "Like ... well, I heard things. You know how it is. You overhear a joke. A whisper. A warning passed like it's nothing, but it sticks with you."

Taylor waited. Let her sit with her guilt.

"Fine," Lana said finally, voice low. "I've got one thing and one thing only, then you leave me alone. There was a man. He drove a black Benz. Wore suits, nice shoes. Too polished for that place."

Taylor's pulse jumped. "Marcus Jenks?"

Lana shook her head. "I don't know his name. They called him Boss. He didn't talk much, but, when he did, people listened."

Taylor leaned forward, eyebrows raised. "Was he the owner?"

"No one really knows. I heard the place is owned by

someone out of Gainesville. But rumor is the one really calling shots doesn't show his face."

Taylor opened the small notebook she kept in her jacket pocket. "Come on, Lana. Give me something else. Anything."

Lana didn't answer.

Just then a man came sauntering up the dock, glaring at the two of them. He kept walking, but he didn't look like he wanted to.

Taylor softened her voice. "Please, Lana. If there's more ... now's the time."

Lana whispered. "I'm scared. Don't you get it?"

"Yes. But Quig's already dead. And if she got caught up in something bad, we need to know what it was before someone else ends up just like her."

"Yeah, like me. I'm done here. I don't know any more names," her jaw clenched. "Get off my boat and don't come back."

She sounded like she meant it this time. Taylor stood slowly, brushing her hands on her jeans. "You have my number. If you remember anything else—"

Lana turned back to her plants. "I won't."

Taylor lingered a beat longer, then stepped off the boat and onto the dock. As she walked away, she glanced back once.

Lana hadn't moved.

But something in her posture said she was fighting a war inside.

And Taylor wasn't about to give up. She'd come back again if she had to.

Chapter Twenty

Tula pushed her mother's wheelchair through the narrow hall toward the Office of Aging Services of the administration building, smack dab in the middle of Hart's Ridge. Getting her out of the car and into the contraption had already drained Tula of whatever energy she'd woken with, and it looked like it was going to be a long day.

Dixie grumbled the entire way. "Don't see why I gotta come down here like I'm some kind of charity case."

"Because you need help," Tula muttered, jaw tight. "And I can't do it all myself."

The representative, a woman in her forties with glasses perched on the end of her nose, greeted them with brisk warmth. "Mrs. Skaggs? And this must be your daughter. Come in, sit down."

Dixie folded her arms, glaring at the paperwork stacked on the desk. "Don't see the use. Ain't no one ever gave me nothing. They'll just tell me no."

"Not at all," the rep said cheerfully. "I talked to your daughter on the phone, and I'm up to date on your situation. Now we'll see what you qualify for. Possibly statewide

Medicaid Managed Care, for one—it covers nonmedical services to help you stay at home. Personal care, meal prep, that sort of thing."

Dixie perked slightly at meal prep, then scowled again. "If you're talking about bathroom stuff, I think I can handle my own personal care. There're some things no woman wants anyone else doing for them."

"True. But some patients need a bit of help with showering. If you don't, that's fine. There's also the Home Care for the Elderly program," the rep continued, tapping her pen against a form. "It can provide financial assistance to help family caregivers—supplies, accessibility modifications, subsidies."

"You mean my kids could get paid for taking care of me?" Dixie looked suddenly interested.

Tula could see the wheels already turning in her mother's head.

"Well, it depends," the rep said. "We can certainly apply for that if you already know who your main caregiver will be."

Dixie turned and looked at her, a smug smile on her face.

Tula ignored it. "And home health? She'll need skilled nursing sometimes, won't she?"

"Possibly, depending on the level of care you need. We can connect you to certified agencies for nursing, therapy, and aides."

Dixie sniffed. "I don't know. It kinda sounds like too many people in my house."

Tula ignored her. "Food and nutrition assistance?"

"Yes," the rep said, flipping pages. "Meals on Wheels, SNAP, TEFAP—emergency food boxes."

"That'll be helpful," Tula said. She hesitated, then added, "I'm also worried about my siblings. They ... take advantage of her. Her money, her benefits. I don't want her to lose everything because of them."

Dixie's head snapped up. "Don't you go talkin' about your brothers and Lorene like that, Tula Rose. They help me more than you ever did."

Tula's neck flushed red as she stared her mother down "Help you? By draining your check every month? Yeah, that's some real good help, Mama."

"Earl has a good job, anyway. He don't need nothing from me."

That was the first that Tula had heard of her brother having a job. Before she could probe deeper, the rep interjected gently. "We do have Adult Protective Services. They investigate allegations of neglect or exploitation. If you ever feel your mother is in danger—"

"I'm not in danger!" Dixie barked. "My kids look out for me. What I want is for Tula to move back here and stop actin' like she's better than the rest of us."

Tula's face flushed hot and she shushed her mother before turning back to the rep. "I'm sorry. Please excuse us. I live in L.A. My jobs, my life—they're there."

Dixie snorted. "Jobs. You don't have jobs anymore. Not since that fool reality show. Whole town saw what a mess you made of yourself. You think you're still somebody?"

The rep's eyes widened. "Reality show? You were on television?"

Tula's stomach twisted. She forced a bland smile. "Small thing. Not worth talking about."

But the rep leaned forward, intrigued. "What kinds of shows? Acting? Competition?"

"Just ... projects. I was on a soap opera for quite a while. Then a sitcom years ago, a couple commercials. The reality show was a mistake." Tula kept her tone flat, hoping it would kill the curiosity.

Inside, though, her thoughts churned. Her mother was right

about one thing. She shouldn't have pivoted to reality TV. That one season had undone everything she'd built. And it had led to her having to leave L.A., though she hadn't told a soul here the full truth.

The representative said brightly, "You should be proud. TV credits are impressive."

Tula forced a polite smile. "Old news." She didn't elaborate. Couldn't. Not when the memory of that show, and her ineptitude, still curdled in her stomach like spoiled milk.

She pushed the thought away, forcing her attention back to the forms.

Dixie slumped deeper into her chair, muttering, "All I need is my oldest daughter home again. Not a bunch of useless papers."

Tula swallowed hard. She couldn't give her that. Wouldn't. But the way her mama said it—like love and ownership were the same thing—still lodged under her skin.

Mama Skaggs was a master at emotional manipulation.

The meeting at the administration building dragged on for more than an hour. By the end, Tula's head was full of acronyms —SMMC, HCE, SNAP—and her mother was full of complaints.

"They'll send strangers into my house, rifling through my things," Dixie muttered as Tula steered her back toward the car.

"They'll send help, not criminals," Tula corrected, her patience thin. "And you said you were glad to have someone come by and check on you."

"What I need is you to stop being a stubborn little brat." Dixie's voice had that wheedling edge Tula remembered from childhood. "Come on back home, Tula Rose. You know you don't belong out there with them crazy Californies."

"I do belong out there," Tula said firmly, pushing her

mother toward the exit. "You're going to have to accept that my life is in L.A., not here."

Dixie smirked. "Not after that reality show mess, it isn't. Washed yourself up on national TV. Everyone saw it. You'll not be getting any more roles, I'll bet."

Tula's jaw clenched. She didn't answer or follow her instinct to stuff a sock into her mother's mouth just to shut her up. Instead, Tula got her loaded into the car, buckled her oxygen tubing carefully, and slid behind the wheel.

The drive back to the Skaggs place was tense. Dixie dozed in the passenger seat, mouth slack, but the silence gave Tula no peace. Her thoughts churned—services, paperwork, her siblings circling their mama's check like vultures. And always, under it all, the whisper of her apartment in L.A. calling her back.

When she pulled into the gravel drive, the sight that greeted her made her stomach plummet even more. The truck that Waylon drove was gone again, and Lorene sat sprawled on the porch steps, phone glued to her ear, a cigarette dangling between her fingers. Smoke curled lazily around her as she laughed at something the caller said.

Across the yard, Curtis and Earl leaned against the hood of an old truck, beers in hand, watching a cluster of dogs. The animals had been let loose, darting and snapping at each other. Tula's stomach turned as she spotted two in the corner, tangled together. More puppies. More mouths to feed. More suffering.

Dixie let out a cackle sharp enough to cut glass. "Well, look at that. Nature taking its course. Can't stop what God intended."

Tula cringed, heat flushing her face. She parked and came around to help her mother out of the car. "Little help?" she called.

No one moved. Lorene kept laughing into her phone. Curtis

sipped his beer, smirking. Earl stubbed out his cigarette on the porch rail, his dead stare penetrating down to Tula's soul.

Her blood boiled. She'd had enough. "Earl!" she snapped. "Make yourself useful for once and help me get Mama's wheelchair out of the trunk."

He straightened slowly, his eyes narrowing. The dead stare dropped. What replaced it made Tula's pulse spike—something dark, dangerous, the kind of look that promised retribution later.

"You watch how you talk to me," he drawled. "You might think you pull the strings on Waylon, but here's a clue, you won't be doing it for long. And you'll never tell me what to do."

What was he talking about Waylon for? For a heartbeat, Tula thought he might refuse to help. Then, with exaggerated slowness, he pushed off the truck and stalked toward them.

Dixie grinned from her seat, oblivious or maybe amused. "Now, now," she said, her voice thick with glee. "Ain't nothin' like family pulling together."

Tula swallowed her fury, tightened her grip on the wheelchair handles, and braced herself. Because she knew—it was only getting worse from here.

Getting Dixie settled required Tula to pull from an energy source she didn't know she had. She then whipped up some soup and grilled cheese sandwiches, enough for them all to eat for dinner later, too.

Meanwhile, Dixie complained about the hospital bed being too firm, the oxygen tubing pinching her nose, the soup being too hot, then too cold. But eventually she ate the soup, tore through a grilled cheese sandwich, and settled back with a sigh that sounded suspiciously satisfied.

Tula tip-toed away. What else did she need to do?

She'd left a plate of leftovers in the kitchen—grilled cheeses stacked high, chips on the side. For the hyenas that surrounded her mother.

Waylon appeared in the doorway as she was wiping crumbs from the counter. He kept his eyes down, shoulders slumped. "Smells good."

"Your plate's in the microwave," Tula told him. She'd kept his separate.

He nodded, retrieved it, and without another word headed for his room.

Tula dried her hands and followed, pausing in the doorway. His space was like another world compared to the rest of the house. Bed neatly made, books stacked in careful rows, sketchpads spread across his desk. The faint smell of pencil shavings and soap lingered, clean and sharp.

"Looks good in here," she said softly, stepping inside.

He sat on the edge of his bed, fork halfway to his mouth. "It's just a room."

"No," she countered, picking up a sketchpad. "It's order. You're the only one in this house who seems to know what that looks like."

Waylon shrugged, cheeks flushing. "Keeps me sane."

She flipped through the pages, pausing at a drawing of the family's broken-down camper. It was rough but surprisingly detailed. A few dogs lay sprawled out in front, giving emotion. "This is good. Really good. You ever think about taking art classes? Doing more with it?"

"Classes cost money."

"Could've used the welding school funds for it." She sat beside him. "But instead, you're out driving without a license, probably making less than minimum wage. What's it going to take to get your driving privileges back?"

He shrugged again, a gesture that seemed practiced. "Court fees. More classes. Don't matter, anyway."

"It matters," she pressed. "You can't keep running from it.

What if you get pulled over again? You'll end up worse off than Curtis or Earl."

He didn't answer, stabbing at his sandwich instead.

She tried another angle. "So, you dating anyone?"

That earned her a faint smirk. "No."

"Good. Don't waste your time. Relationships are hard." She tapped his sketchpad. "Stick with things that lift you up, not drag you down."

He gave a noncommittal grunt.

"Then tell me about your job," she said, careful to keep her voice light. "Shuffle Lounge, right? What do you do there?"

"Clean up. Make deliveries. Whatever they need." His tone was vague, eyes sliding away.

She narrowed her gaze. "And how did you find it?"

The door creaked. Slowly.

Tula turned, her pulse hitching. Her eldest brother stood half in, half out, a cigarette tucked behind his ear, smirk curling his lips.

"I hooked him up," Curtis said, his voice thick with warning. "If you got more questions, sis, you can direct them my way."

Waylon froze, fork still in hand.

Curtis' gaze lingered on Tula, sharp as broken glass. "But I suggest you mind your own business. We don't need Hollywood snooping around."

Tula's instincts screamed. Something was off. Waylon's vagueness. Curtis protecting him. The whole setup reeked.

But she forced her face smooth, snapping the sketchpad shut. "Fine. Just trying to catch up with my little brother."

Curtis grinned like he'd won something and sauntered back down the hall.

Tula sat there, her stomach knotting. Nothing that had Curtis in the mix could be good. She didn't like it. Not one bit.

Chapter Twenty-One

When Tula pulled up at the farm cabin, the last thing she expected was company. But there, sprawled on her porch steps, were Anna, Taylor, and Jo—each with a grocery bag in hand.

Anna grinned. "Surprise. We decided you needed a girls' night."

Taylor lifted her bag. "Mocktails and cards. Chips and salsa, Oreos for dessert. No kids, no men, no expectations."

Jo shrugged sheepishly. "They talked me into it."

Inside, they made quick work of the cabin's little table, setting out fizzy sodas, fruit juice, a shaker, and mismatched glasses. Anna dug out a deck of cards from her bag while Taylor mixed cranberry and lime into sparkling water. Jo curled onto the couch, slipping into her socks like she was at home.

"Mocktails?" Tula teased, raising her glass.

"Best we can do with nursing shifts and babies to get home to," Anna said, clinking her glass against Tula's before moving around the small kitchen to set up the snacks.

Soon the cards were flying, laughter bubbling up easy. They teased each other mercilessly, Jo slyly winning nearly every round, Taylor tossing her cards down in mock disgust, Anna keeping tally.

For the first time in years, Tula felt ... relaxed. In L.A., her girlfriends had been cutthroat—every gathering a silent contest of who had the bigger role, the tighter dress, the shinier life. Here, no one was competing. They'd shown up in slouchy clothes, hair messy, faces bare. They weren't trying to be anything other than what they were.

And Tula loved it.

She found herself talking more freely than she expected. About her mama's dramatics, about the constant drain of Curtis, Earl, and Lorene. Then, hesitating, she told them about Waylon. About his job at Shuffle Lounge. About Curtis barging into his room.

"Curtis said he got Waylon the job," Tula said, voice low. "Told me if I had more questions, to ask him. And the way he said it—" she shivered. "It felt like a warning. Like I was supposed to back off. Something is off about it."

Taylor's eyes sharpened instantly. "Shuffle Lounge," she repeated. "I'd really like to know what goes on in there."

Anna leaned forward. "Why? You think Curtis would be able to pull Waylon into something shady?"

Tula shrugged. "Maybe. On the other hand, Waylon has always been different than the boys. Smarter. He keeps his room neat, he reads books. Got good grades in high school, even. He could've had a shot. I had him going to welding school. But now? He's shutting down. And I don't like what Curtis has got him doing, even though I can't exactly pinpoint why."

Taylor nodded. "I'll look into it," she said quietly.

Tula bristled. "No. I didn't say this to ask for help. I don't want to get Waylon into trouble. I just—I needed to tell someone."

Anna reached over, squeezed her hand. "Tula, you're not alone anymore. Let us at least be in your corner."

Something in Tula's chest loosened, just a little. She leaned back, letting the fizz of the mocktail tickle her tongue, the sound of the cards shuffling filling the room.

For once, she wasn't performing. Wasn't competing. She was just Tula Rose, sitting in a cabin in Hart's Ridge, playing cards with women who were starting to feel like friends.

And for the first time in a long time, that felt like enough.

The game slowed as the mocktails dwindled, laughter softening into easy conversation. Jo was curled sideways on the couch, her chin resting on the armrest, while Anna leaned back in her chair, bare feet tucked under her.

Taylor shuffled the cards idly, not dealing yet. "You know," she said, "I used to think I had to be the strongest person in the room. Deputy badge, gun on my hip, all of it. But the truth is, I left the sheriff's department because it nearly swallowed me whole. Nothing I ever did was going to be enough to gain the same respect that my male counterparts got."

Tula blinked. "I heard you were doing well since you left. A PI, right?"

Taylor gave a half-smile. "Yeah. We're doing okay. The money is a hit and a miss, but Sam makes the best partner. For a long time, I thought I had to carry it all. Protect everyone. It nearly broke me. Sam has saved me from myself more than once."

At that, Anna snorted softly. "At least you've got him to save you. After my divorce, I didn't have a partner. If it wasn't for you guys helping me with the kids, I couldn't have got my nursing degree. Y'all really stepped up. I remember working those night shifts, then sitting in the back of class half-asleep just to get through. And still, there are days I wonder if it's all going to fall apart again."

"You're stronger than you give yourself credit for," Jo murmured. "Anyway, your kids feel like our own. Family is supposed to be there as a safety net. We only did what was right. You are the resilient one who made it all worth it in the end."

Anna smiled faintly. "Maybe. But I don't want people thinking it was easy. It wasn't. Thankfully, now I have Jack." She explained that Jack was a doctor at the hospital, and they were now exclusive, but still taking things slow. It was hard for her to trust a man after everything her ex had put her through.

"Yes, you mentioned Jack to me," Tula said. "I'm glad to hear you're taking it slow."

Jo's gaze drifted down to her hands. "My story's different. Levi's dad. What he did. I haven't been near a stage since. Can't even think about theater anymore without feeling sick." Her voice was quiet, but steady. "Every day I remind myself I'm more than what happened. That Levi deserves better. That I do. But some days I don't feel like enough for him."

The silence that followed was gentle, not heavy.

Tula studied the three of them—honest, open, unguarded. The warmth of the moment tempted her to go one step further, to share something she'd buried so deep she barely admitted it to herself.

She cleared her throat. "There's ... something I haven't told anyone here."

Taylor's brows lifted. "About L.A.?"

Tula hesitated, then nodded. "Yeah. Everyone thinks I left because I got voted off a reality show and couldn't handle the humiliation. But that's not the full story."

The women went still, listening.

"One of the contestants—her name was Eden—she disappeared. Mid-season. The producers said she left for 'personal reasons,' but I believe that wasn't true. I heard her fighting with someone that night. There was a crash, shouting ... and then nothing. The next morning, she was gone." Tula swallowed. "When I asked questions, I was told to keep my mouth shut if I wanted to keep working. Then suddenly, my contract was canceled, my access card didn't work, and the producers announced my departure by saying I'd had a breakdown."

"Did you?" Jo asked.

"Not even close," Tula answered. "But to get the rest of my contract money, I had to keep my mouth shut."

"Sounds like everything I've heard about that scene is true," Jo said. "Hollywood is like a pit of vipers."

"That's more accurate than you'd realize," Tula said.

Taylor's voice softened, curious but careful. "You think this Eden girl was hurt?"

"I don't know about that, but I think something happened to her," Tula said quietly. "And whatever it is, the network covered it up. Her family's hired someone to investigate, so it's not my place anymore. I just ..." She rubbed her arms. "It still feels like she's haunting me. Like I should've done more."

"I'm sure she's fine," Taylor said. "Statistics show that adults running away from their lives is on the rise year after year. It used to be mostly teenage runaways, because, as we age, we learn how to regulate our emotions. But some people never gain that skill and, with it, life and all the anxiety and responsibilities that come with it can be too much to handle. Especially in high stress arenas."

Jo nodded. "Whatever happened to that girl isn't your fault. Don't let it steal any more of your peace."

"Y'all are right," Tula murmured, then realized she'd slipped back into her Georgia accent and slang. Unwillingly, too. Next thing she knew, she'd be shopping for boots and sucking on a toothpick.

Taylor leaned forward slightly, all PI instinct flickering in her expression. "Also, if the family still has someone looking into it, maybe one day the truth will come out. Until then, the best thing you can do is hold your head high. You didn't do anything wrong."

Tula forced a small smile. "I wish it felt that simple. The gossip online hasn't stopped. Every few months the story resurfaces—my face, that old footage. A few comments wondering if my so-called-breakdown is connected to Eden's dropping off the radar. It's like I can't escape it. Sometimes I think my career's just ... over."

"Then start new," Anna said softly. "Here. You've got a fresh slate and people who see the real you."

Something in Tula's eyes glistened as she nodded. "Maybe I can believe that someday. When Eden comes out from under her rock, if she'd do an interview with me maybe we could get my reputation cleaned up."

"That's a good idea," Anna said.

The moment lingered, tender and quiet, before Taylor gave the cards a playful flick. "Okay, enough heavy talk. New rule—whoever wins this hand must name our next girls' night spot."

"Easy," Jo said, grinning. "Somewhere with better snacks."

Laughter rose again, easing the weight in the air.

Anna raised her glass. "To surviving, however we got here."

They clinked their mismatched glasses together, mocktails fizzing as if to toast their messy, imperfect victories.

Tula felt something loosen in her chest, something she hadn't even realized was clenched. For the first time since setting foot back in Hart's Ridge, she didn't feel like an outsider.

The night stretched on, their laughter mellowing to soft voices, then yawns. Around midnight, Anna gathered the empty glasses, Taylor shuffled the cards back into their box, and Jo slipped on her shoes.

"Thanks for letting us invade," Anna said, pulling Tula into a quick hug before heading for the door.

Taylor winked. "We'll make it a tradition. Girls' nights in sweatpants. None of that Hollywood glitter you're used to."

Jo smiled faintly as she left, her presence quiet but steady.

And just like that, the cabin was still again.

Tula cleaned up the last crumbs, then changed into the soft pajamas Anna had given her on that first night. She slid into bed, pulling the quilt up to her chin. The silence pressed in, but this time it didn't feel hostile. It felt ... safe.

It was nice to spend an evening with women who weren't trying to cut her down or edge her out. No competition. No cameras. Just honesty.

Gratitude tugged at her, surprising in its strength. She hadn't expected to find comfort here, of all places. Not in Hart's Ridge. But as she lay there in the dark, her mind drifted west. To Los Angeles. To what she'd left behind.

Her chest tightened. That mess was still waiting for her, stalking her mind and adding worry to everything already haunting her.

And beneath it all, the darker truth she hadn't told a soul here—that leaving L.A. hadn't been just about failure. It had been about fear.

She turned onto her side, pressing her face into the pillow, willing her thoughts to quiet.

But the questions followed her into sleep, relentless as ever.

Chapter Twenty-Two

Taylor pulled into the cracked driveway of the Gallagher home, killing the engine with a heavy sigh. A kid's scooter lay tipped over near the porch, its wheels caked with dirt. The potted flowers dotted along the edge bent over their rims, as if they'd given up.

The porch creaked under her boots as she climbed the steps. A faded wind chime tinkled weakly in the breeze, tangled around itself. The door opened before she could knock.

"Taylor."

Quig's mother, Beverly, stood there in jeans and a stained hoodie, her face drawn with the weight of grief and years of hard living.

"Hey, Beverly. Mind if I come in for a few?"

She nodded and stepped aside, waving toward the kitchen table and speaking weakly. "Coffee's cold, but help yourself."

Taylor didn't drink coffee, and she declined politely as she took a seat at the table. "I've heard that Quig may have had a second job. Do you know anything about that?"

Beverly looked confused. "No, I don't know of any other job besides what she was doing out at your place. Who said it?"

"Just someone from where Quig went to her meetings. Have you seen any paperwork she might've left here that can tell us more? Pay stubs, bank stuff, receipts ... anything that might help me understand where she was working? Who she was dealing with?"

Beverly shook her head as she slumped into a chair and pointed to the corner of the living room. "You're welcome to look, but the little bit I found is in that plastic tote over there. She didn't get much mail here."

Taylor knelt beside the bin and lifted the lid. A few old framed photos, some kids' art, a dried-out mascara tube. Nothing of use.

"I already went through every scrap of paper in her cabin. Twice," Taylor said. "Bank statements, jury notices, even junk mail. Not a single mention of Shuffle Lounge. No pay stubs, no deposits, nothing."

"Oh, I do have her on my phone bill, and I had them pull the records." Beverly went to the China hutch and opened a drawer, then pulled out a fat envelope. "There were no strange numbers, or out of the ordinary text messages."

"That means she probably had a burner phone," Taylor said. She snapped the lid shut and sat back on her heels. "She was hiding it. That means she was scared, or ashamed, or both. But why?"

"Yes, but tell me why? I just don't understand what went wrong. I thought she was doing so well." Beverly rubbed her temples. "The boys ... they're not doing good. And Addie keeps asking when Mama's coming home. She knows Quig has passed, so I don't know what to tell her anymore."

Taylor's heart cracked. "I'm so sorry. Sounds like she's in denial." She reached across the table. "I'll see what I can do about getting them some pro bono counseling. There's a group out of Athens that sends therapists out here once a month. It's not much, but it's something."

Beverly blinked fast, nodding. "Thank you."

As Taylor stood to leave, she glanced back at the bin one last time. It looked like a coffin for the life Quig had been trying to build.

———

The Den was half-full when she walked in—midday crowd sipping coffee and taking advantage of the bakery case while the town's Wi-Fi glitched in and out.

Shane was already at the back table with two mugs set out and a manila folder spread open. "You look beat," he said as she slid into the seat across from him. "I ordered you green tea."

"Thanks." She took a sip, letting the warmth of the liquid settle in her chest. "Quig's mom had nothing. Said she cleaned out everything. The only bin left was filled with old memories. I'm telling you, Quig scrubbed her trail clean before she died— or someone else did it after."

"Same on my end," Shane said. "I drove back out near the Shuffle Lounge. Walked the tree line again. No cameras. No evidence they've ever had any."

He pulled out a few photos. "But I did catch this guy again —same black Benz from the stakeout. Different day, different time. He never goes inside. Just talks to whoever's manning the door, then drives off."

"We need to set up surveillance and follow him," Taylor said. "If you can do that, I'll go up and talk to Lana again. I can tell she knows something, she's just afraid. One more meeting might do the trick. She is scared of something that's connected to that place, and I want her to tell me why."

Before he could respond, a voice drawled from behind.

"Well, if this ain't the dream team."

Sheriff Dawkins.

He slid in next to Taylor without asking, slapping a hand on the back of Shane's back before settling in like he owned the place.

"Didn't know I had an auxiliary task force running point on an open case. Appreciate the enthusiasm." His voice was dry, but the warning was there.

Taylor opened her mouth to object, but Dawkins raised a hand. "Save it. I'm not here to chew you out—just a gentle reminder. Weaver works for me, and, last I checked, the murder of a former addict wasn't top priority."

Taylor stiffened. "She wasn't just a former addict. Quig was sober, working, and trying to get her life back."

Dawkins exhaled like a man tolerating a tantrum. "I know you well enough to know by now that you aren't going to listen to me when I say to let it go, so I'm not saying don't look into it. I'm saying keep it in perspective. That assault and robbery case up near Lanier Heights? That's priority one. Shane, you're still point on that."

Shane gave a tight nod. "Understood. I've been on it."

"But," Dawkins added, his tone easing slightly, "I am curious what you've turned up in regard to the Gallagher case."

Taylor relayed her visit to the NA meeting, how Quig had dropped hints about a second job, and the name Lana—now linked to the Shuffle Lounge.

He nodded.

"You know the place?" she asked.

"Shuffle Lounge? Huh." He glanced down at the table. "Can't say I've been out that way. But I'll have a look into it. If there's something shady going on, I'll sniff it out."

Taylor wasn't sure what she'd hoped for, but his blasé attitude wasn't it.

Dawkins stood. "Weaver, keep me in the loop. And for God's sake, Taylor—don't you have enough to do with that new PI company you started? Whatcha going to do, let your man handle all that? I thought you wanted to be the lead detective? Isn't that why you left us?"

He obviously didn't expect an answer to all these questions. He clapped Shane on the shoulder and walked off, whistling as he left.

Taylor watched him go, then turned to Shane. "Why doesn't he care?"

Shane gave her a look. "He cares. Just not about Quig. She was a nobody, Taylor. To most, her death is just a blip on their radar, until the next big story of the town."

Taylor swallowed hard and looked down at her tea, the bitterness spreading through her like wildfire.

"She wasn't a nobody to me."

Chapter Twenty-Three

Taylor parked near the edge of the Eastside Marina and stepped out with a flat of lettuce starts in one hand and a tomato plant tucked in the crook of her other arm. The sun was high and already warming the deck boards as she made her way along the dock. Boats rocked gently beside her, their ropes groaning softly with each shift of water.

It was oddly peaceful, removed from the chaos, from investigations and the quiet grief of children left behind. For a fleeting second, she let herself imagine what it might be like to live on a boat. To wake with the sun filtering through portholes, her tea steaming in hand, surrounded by water and quiet.

Her sister Lucy had done it for a while, back before Jorge Vanzo and the whirlwind life they'd built together.

Taylor reached Lana's boat and scanned the deck. No movement. No Lana.

She set the plant tray down and looked around.

"Hey," she called toward the next slip, where an older man sat on a folding chair, squinting at a crossword puzzle.

He looked up. "Help you?"

"I was looking for Lana. She around?"

He scratched the back of his head. "Haven't seen her the last couple days, now that you mention it. That's not like her. Maybe she went to see her people."

Taylor frowned. "Mind if I just drop these off inside? I brought her some garden starts. Don't want them to cook in the sun."

The man waved her off. "Go ahead. She never locks up anyway."

That raised Taylor's concern even higher.

She stepped onto the boat, her boots thudding softly against the deck. The sliding hatch to the living cabin creaked open with a tug, and cool air drifted out, thick with the faint scent of fried eggs and fabric softener.

Inside, the space was tight but tidy. Mismatched curtains framed two small portholes, and a half-eaten piece of toast sat on a plate beside a coffee mug. The eggs were barely touched. Hard and congealed. A line of ants carried away crumbs, forming a line from the plate, across the table, to underneath and beyond.

How did ants get on a boat?

Taylor's pulse quickened. She set the tomato plant on the counter and carefully moved forward.

"Lana?" she called, voice low but firm.

No answer.

The living area was narrow, with a tiny galley kitchen and a foldout bench for sitting or sleeping. A small TV hung crookedly from a wall bracket, its screen dark. On the counter, a thin stack of library books sat beside a pink Bic lighter and a jar of coins.

Everything looked like it had been frozen mid-morning.

She passed through the galley and toward the sleeping berth.

The bed was unmade. A blanket hung halfway off. An open

magazine rested on the pillow. It didn't scream alarm, but something in Taylor's gut clenched tighter. She let out a soft breath of relief that Lana wasn't lying there.

Then she turned to keep walking—and saw it.

A foot.

Bare. Pale with chipped polish on the toes. Motionless.

It stuck out from under the cot tucked along the wall.

Time slowed.

Taylor's hand moved to her sidearm, unclipping the holster. She turned, scanned her surroundings. No one. Just the quiet lap of water outside.

She crouched down slowly, heart thudding, her breath caught halfway in her throat.

Lana's face was turned away, but Taylor could see a trail of vomit. A hand curled near her face. One fingernail broken. Eyes closed.

Taylor swallowed hard.

A needle hanging from just beneath an elbow.

She backed up a step and grabbed her phone, thumb shaking as she dialed 911.

"This is Taylor Gray of Hart County. I'm at the Eastside Marina in Monroe. I've found a body—female, probable overdose. Name's Lana ... unknown last name."

The dispatcher asked a flurry of questions, but Taylor's voice remained flat and calm. She'd done this part before.

"Yeah, I'll wait. Just get your people here fast."

She ended the call and leaned back against the doorframe, her head spinning.

While she waited, she moved carefully, taking in every detail. She wouldn't touch anything, but she could still observe. A broken drawer knob. The location of the mug. The indentation of the mattress. The faint scuff marks near the entrance like someone had dragged something—or someone.

Lana might be an addict, but this wasn't an overdose. It wasn't an accident.

It was a message.

Taylor was sure of it.

She stepped back into the sunlight just as sirens began wailing in the distance. Two patrol cars skidded into the marina parking lot, followed by a black SUV with county plates.

———

She paced the narrow dock, phone clutched in one hand, eyes darting between the flashing cruiser lights pulling into the marina and the gently rocking boat she'd just stepped off. Her pulse still hadn't returned to normal. Every time she closed her eyes, she saw Lana's lifeless form again—limp and pale under the cot.

A young deputy from Monroe approached, already jotting notes. "You're the one who called it in?"

Taylor nodded, offering her identification. "Yes. Graystone Investigations from Hart County, but I just recently left the sheriff's department after more than a decade."

He didn't look impressed. "You shouldn't have touched anything."

"I didn't. I walked in to drop off some plants for her—she was helping us with an open case—and I found her. I stepped out and called it in immediately."

The deputy muttered something under his breath and motioned toward a female officer arriving with gloves and an evidence kit. "You'll need to give a full statement."

Taylor already knew the drill. She backed away as the officer passed, her gaze instinctively tracing the path from the dock, across the deck, and into the small cabin where Lana's body still waited. She fought the urge to go back in. To see if she missed anything.

She wanted to question everyone on every boat in the marina. And those at the restaurant. But that would only get her into trouble.

"Ma'am?" The deputy was watching her. "Need you to hang tight here. A detective will want to talk to you."

She nodded again and pulled out her phone to text.

> Lana won't be any help.
>
> She's dead. Monroe PD is here.
>
> They're treating me like I'm just another nosy local.
>
> Please come.
>
> Marina on Eastside Monroe.

She hit send and dropped onto a bench at the edge of the dock, knees still shaky.

This didn't feel right. Not even close. Lana had been scared last time Taylor visited—jumpy, eyes darting, hesitant to say too much. And now she was gone.

Another loose thread tied off. Another witness silenced.

Her thoughts raced. The Shuffle Lounge. DFC. Quig. Now Lana.

Taylor had assumed she was chasing a single story. But now it was becoming clear—this wasn't just about one girl's murder. This was bigger. Someone was scrubbing the narrative clean. And they were moving fast.

She had to warn Tula that her brother might be in danger.

A short, stocky man in a blazer walked up—Detective Harlan, according to his badge.

"Deputy Gray, is it?"

"Not anymore. I am a private investigator now."

He raised his eyebrows, then looked back at his phone.

"You found the body?"

Taylor explained everything again. From the plants to the open cabin to the awful moment she saw Lana's foot.

"She'd been cooperating with you?" he asked, scribbling.

"Somewhat. She knew the victim of a crime I've been investigating over in Hart County. She'd hinted she might know something more. I was working on building trust."

He looked unimpressed. "Why'd you go in the cabin?"

"I got permission from the marina tender. It was unlocked. I didn't touch anything inside."

He gave her a long look, then finally nodded.

"We'll need to keep you here for a bit. Standard procedure. Then you're free to go, but stay available for follow-up."

Taylor stood. "Can I at least call in a partner from my department to help coordinate in case this is connected to our case?" She didn't mention she'd already done so.

"I won't stop you from making a call. But this is Monroe County now. Our crime scene, our jurisdiction."

She held his gaze. "Fine. But let me tell you something, Detective. This isn't just some junkie OD. Two women who had ties to the same establishment are now dead in a matter of weeks. That's not a coincidence."

"We'll look into that," he said evenly. "But until we find evidence, that's all speculation."

Taylor bit back a sharp retort. Instead, she stepped away to call Shane.

He answered on the second ring. "I'm already halfway there."

"She had a needle in her arm," Taylor said.

Silence. Then, "Hell."

"And her breakfast was interrupted. Maybe two days old. I

don't believe she put that needle there, Shane. Someone did this."

"Let's hypothesize. If it wasn't accidental, you think she knew her killer?"

"Well, she let them in. Didn't put up a fight. It was someone she didn't see coming." She rubbed her eyes, her voice cracking. "Shane, I feel like this is my fault. I pushed her. She was scared, and I kept coming back. I might've led them straight to her."

"No," he said firmly. "Don't do that to yourself. The person who killed her did this. Not you."

She blinked hard against the sting in her eyes.

"Sit tight," he said. "Is Harlan the detective on scene?"

"Yes," she replied.

"Good, I'll deal with Detective Harlan and get the scene report."

She ended the call and stood still, staring out at the water.

Another name added to a list that should've never started.

Who was next?

And how much time did she have to figure it out before the answers disappeared for good?

Chapter Twenty-Four

The next few days blurred together in an exhausting rhythm. Tula ferried paperwork back and forth for her mother, called insurance reps, and sat through visits from home health aides. Two had already quit after just arriving and meeting the family and seeing the environment and Dixie's attitude. Fingers crossed the third one would at least last a month.

Tula cooked simple meals her mama mostly picked at, scrubbed the kitchen until her knuckles ached, and made sure the oxygen tubing was never tangled.

Whenever she had an hour to herself, she drove. Past the high school where her face had once grinned down from banners and between the yearbook pages. Past the football stadium where she'd been the captain of the cheer squad, adored and envied in equal measure.

For a second she could almost hear the band, feel the anticipation of the team playing their rivals, the fall chill of Friday nights. The moment her name was called, and she walked out on the field, the feel of the crown put on her head.

For a moment, she was someone else. Not Tula Rose Skaggs.

That was probably when she'd gotten the idea to leave town and change her name. To really embrace a new identity, far from the dysfunction she called her family.

A few miles past the campus, she slowed near a familiar park, pulling into the cracked lot. The picnic tables were still there, warped with age. She'd met boys there, and remembered one in particular—how he'd lifted her up onto a table, all hands and lips, clumsy and eager.

Her first kiss, messy and unforgettable. A boy named Anders. He was an exchange student from Norway and, with his blond hair and icy blue eyes, all the girls had fawned over him. He'd chosen her.

What had happened to him? she wondered, a pang of nostalgia hitting her hard. He'd loved being in America, he'd said. Claimed he never wanted to leave and, if he had to, that he'd come back once he graduated. Said he'd marry her when he did.

Her phone rang, shattering the memory. Waylon.

She answered on the first ring. "Hey—what's up?"

His voice was strange, tight. "Come get me. Now."

"Where are you?"

"The old church. On 17. Don't ... don't tell anyone."

"Waylon, what—"

But the line went dead. The abandoned church sagged against the sky, its white paint peeled to gray, its steeple leaning like a weary man. The graveyard behind it was quiet, stones half-swallowed by moss and time. Tula parked, scanning for him.

"Waylon?" she called, stepping out. The silence felt too heavy.

She wandered into the graveyard, brushing moss from one headstone: **Mary Sue Lawson, 1842–1901. Beloved**

midwife. Another bore a lamb etched at the top, the name of a child who hadn't lived past three. **Lenora Louise**.

What a sweet name.

So many lives, so many endings, she thought, a chill running over her. Graveyards always reminded her that one day she'd be nothing but a memory. Or maybe not even that.

Movement flickered at the edge of her vision. She turned.

Waylon staggered from behind the church. Her breath left her in a gasp.

"Waylon!" She ran toward him. His face was swollen, one eye nearly shut, dried blood crusting along his lip. He clutched his ribs, each step pained.

"What happened?"

"Don't ask," he rasped. "Just ... take me somewhere I can rest."

"No. You need a hospital."

"I said no." His voice broke, fear raw in it as his eyes widened. "If you try, I'm not going in with you. I'll run. I swear it, Tula Rose."

Her throat closed. She had never seen him like this. She slid an arm under his shoulder, half-dragged him to the car.

"Where's the truck?" she asked.

"Curtis took it about ten miles back."

"Tell me what's going on." Anger flooded through her. She'd annihilate whoever did this to her little brother.

"Not right now. Let me rest." On the drive to the farm, he leaned against the window, silent tears slipping down his face. Tula's own vision blurred. She hadn't seen him cry since he was a little boy.

"You have to confide in me," she whispered, her anger turning to despair. "I can't help you if you don't."

He didn't answer for a minute, then he whispered.

"Do you ever wonder what our lives would be like if we'd have had different parents?"

"I used to," she answered honestly. "But then I decided I could be something more than they had planned for their kids. I took my own life into control and got the hell out of here. You can do that, too, Waylon."

"Nah," he said, drawing the word out slowly. "Too late for me, big sister."

"Nonsense. Tell me why you think that?"

Before he turned his head the other way, the sadness in his eyes just about did her in.

"Fine," she said shakily. "Let's just get you to my place and see what we have going on here."

The rest of the ride was in silence.

As they turned in through the farm gates, Waylon straightened despite the pain, eyes darting around the tidy pastures and barns. "How'd you slide into this?" he asked bitterly. "I work my ass off, and I still live in a dump. And you just ... end up here?"

Tula swallowed hard. "I didn't end up here. This is temporary until I get back home. Anna is just being kind."

He didn't answer, just let her help him out of the car and guide him into the cabin.

She settled him on the couch and grabbed a rag, dampening it with warm water. He winced as she dabbed gently at his split lip, his bruised temple.

"Hold still," she murmured. "I know it hurts."

It looked worse than she'd first thought. When he closed his eyes, she pulled out her phone and texted Anna:

Need you at my cabin stat. Bring a first aid kit.

Anna arrived within the hour, hair still damp from her

shower, tote bag slung over her shoulder. The moment she saw Waylon, her jaw tightened. "Lord, Tula. Who is this?"

Waylon tried to wave her off. "I'm her brother, and I'm just fine."

"No, you're not." Anna crouched, her hands gentle but firm as she examined his ribs. "These are at least bruised. Maybe cracked. You need imaging, but, for now—ice, rest, careful breathing. And you need to file a police report."

"No." His voice was sharp, panicked.

Tula stared at him, heart aching. "Who did this, Way?"

"Doesn't matter." He turned away, his shoulders curling inward.

Anna stood, pulling her phone from her pocket. Tula caught the quick movement of her thumbs, the text sent off fast.

Minutes later, a knock sounded on the door.

Taylor stepped in, her eyes sweeping the scene. She set her jaw and crouched in front of Waylon. "Listen. You've been assaulted. I've got contacts at the sheriff's department. Whoever did this doesn't get to walk free."

Waylon's good eye flickered with something—fear, shame, defiance.

He shook his head hard.

"No cops," he said. "I mean it."

Tula's stomach sank. Whatever he was caught in, it was darker than she wanted to admit.

And she had no idea how to pull him out.

Taylor sighed loudly. "I don't like to talk about my investigations, but there's something strange about the place you are working at, Waylon. Are you sure there's nothing you can tell us about what's happening there?"

He stood, stumbling to the couch and laying down. He turned his back to them.

Tula met Taylor's eyes and held her hands out helplessly. They didn't speak.

By the time the clock on Tula's phone clicked past eleven, he was asleep. He shifted now and then, a pained groan slipping out, but exhaustion had dragged him under.

Tula stood at the small kitchenette, rinsing out the rag she'd used on his face. Anna sat at the table, jotting notes for follow-up care, while Taylor leaned against the counter, arms crossed.

Tula lowered her voice. "You two know something you're not telling me."

Anna glanced at Taylor, then back at Tula. "What makes you say that?"

"Because when I said Waylon was working at Shuffle Lounge the other night, Taylor looked at me like I'd just set off a bomb. And then today, she's suddenly here the second you text. Don't play me. I'm not stupid. What is my brother tangled up in?"

Taylor's eyes softened. "You're not stupid. And you're right. I do have suspicions about Shuffle Lounge. About what's going on there. People connected to it are dying."

Tula's pulse ticked up. "People? What people?"

Taylor hesitated, then nodded toward Waylon. "I can't say. I also don't know, but, whatever happened to him tonight, my gut says it's tied to that place. And it's the same gut that's telling me it's all connected to Quig."

"Quig?" Tula echoed.

"Yes. She lived here, in this cabin, before you," Taylor said quietly. "Her real name was Margaret, but we called her Quig. She was a friend. She'd been working so hard to turn her life around—got clean, started trying to earn back trust from her kids. I was rooting for her." Taylor's throat worked. "Then she was found dead in a burned-out car. Someone said she was moonlighting at the Shuffle Lounge."

Anna's pen stilled, her gaze dropping.

Tula's chest clenched. "God." She sank into the chair across from Anna, her voice soft. "I'm so sorry. She sounds like ... a broken soul. Like someone who deserved better."

"She did," Taylor said, her jaw tight. "And I think the Lounge had something to do with her not ever finding it."

Silence pressed in, heavy and thick.

"Who else is dead?" Anna asked. "Can you tell us, please?"

"You don't know her, but she was a friend of Quig's and had also worked out at the Shuffle Lounge for a short time."

Tula looked from Taylor to Anna, terror fueling her thoughts into chaos. Waylon was never going back there. She couldn't lose him. Not the one family member she had who truly cared about her.

Finally, she whispered, "So what do you want me to do? How can I help?"

Taylor looked at her, something flaring in her eyes—determination, maybe even hope. "I have an idea. We'll talk to your brother tomorrow."

And in that quiet moment, with Waylon asleep in the next room and shadows stretching long across the cabin floor, Tula felt the stress of it all settle on her shoulders and, suddenly, her return to her own life seemed like it would be eons away. Whatever this was going on in her hometown, she was being pulled in deeper, like it or not.

Chapter Twenty-Five

Waylon was up, but barely. He sat hunched on the edge of the old plaid sofa, cradling a chipped mug of coffee in both hands like it was a lifeline. The right side of his face was a war zone—both eyes swollen and purple, lip split, a bruise curling down the side of his neck like a vine.

Tula had tried to offer eggs, toast, even some instant grits she found buried in the pantry, but he'd refused it all with a shake of his head. She didn't push.

She was trying. God, she was trying. But seeing him like this —broken, silent—was ripping something loose inside her.

"Anything you wanna talk about?" she tried gently, crouching down in front of him.

He shook his head again. "Ain't ready."

She blew out a breath, nodding. "Okay. But you will. And when you do, I'll be right here."

Then it happened.

The sharp blare of a truck horn, long and angry, shattered the morning stillness. Waylon flinched so hard he spilled coffee on his jeans.

Tula shot to the window.

"Oh, hell no," she breathed. "Shit. It's Curtis."

She spun back around, fire already building in her chest. "Did you tell him you were here?"

Waylon's eyes were wide, terrified. "No. I swear, Tula, I didn't."

Another honk. Louder this time. Followed by a familiar voice outside, bellowing, "WAYLON! Get your ass out here!"

Tula's fists clenched. Who did he think he was?

Memories flooded her, mornings that he thundered around the house after her daddy had left, trying to prove he was some kind of big man. Ordering her and her siblings around and, if they didn't jump when he said jump, they'd be in for it.

He always was a bully.

Damn if he was going to do it now. She wasn't scared little Tula Rose any longer.

She stormed to the door and flung it open so hard it banged against the side of the porch. The morning sun was blinding, but there he was, leaning against the rusted hood of his flatbed truck, a cigarette dangling from his lip, arms crossed like he owned the world.

"Shoulda known you'd be the one hidin' him," he drawled when he saw her. "You always did think you were better than the rest of us."

Tula stepped down the porch stairs like a woman on a mission. "What the hell do you think you're doing here, Curtis?"

He grinned, eyes cold. "Come to get my worker. I got a call that he didn't show up for work. Was supposed to be there an hour ago."

"Worker?" she snapped. "You mean your little punching bag? No. You're not getting him. He's not going anywhere with you."

159

Curtis straightened, tossing the cigarette to the ground. "You don't tell me what to do, girl. This ain't your town anymore. Hell, it never was."

Tula's voice shook with fury. "Why don't you admit you beat him up?"

Curtis smirked. "You really wanna go down that road? What're you gonna do, torture me 'til I talk? Don't worry. Waylon knows how to take a punch and keep his mouth shut. If he doesn't, I'll squeeze his head off and shit down his throat."

And that was it. Tula snapped.

She charged at him, fists swinging, catching him off guard. Her fists landed against his chest—wild, desperate, enraged.

"You bastard! He's your brother!"

He laughed, then shoved her backward.

She stumbled hard and fell into the dirt, skidding on her palms.

"Tula Rose!" Waylon's voice from behind her. She whipped her head back—he was at the door, halfway down the porch, eyes wide with panic.

"Stay inside!" she barked.

But before she could rise to her feet, a slow voice rolled in like thunder from the side of the barn.

"Don't know who the hell you are, son ..." Cecil, dressed in his usual stained overalls and boots, stepped out into the yard. In his hands, steady as a stone, was a shotgun, aimed directly at Curtis. His eyes were so dark with anger, they looked black. "But on this farm, we don't push women around."

Curtis froze.

Hands went up slowly.

"Now, let's not get crazy," he said. "It was just a misunderstanding. She's my sister, and I didn't even push her hard."

Cecil didn't blink. "I didn't ask how hard, and it don't make a lick of difference if she's your sister, you don't put hands on a woman."

Then, another vehicle pulled into the drive—Taylor's truck, gravel spraying behind her tires. She jumped out before it even stopped rolling.

"What the hell is going on?" she demanded, eyes locking on Curtis, then the gun, then Tula, who was still brushing herself off. "Okay, let's all calm down."

Tula pointed at her brother. "That's Curtis. He's the one who beat the hell out of Waylon. And now he won't leave."

Taylor's eyes went to the porch, where Waylon stood looking like a shadow of himself. Her jaw tightened and her hand hovered on her side piece.

Cecil's voice cut in again, cool and level. "Oh, he'll leave alright. Question is whether it'll be on his own ... or in the back of the county coroner's van."

"Jesus, okay!" Curtis snapped, still holding his hands up. "I just came for Waylon. That's it. Y'all people are crazy."

"Before you go," Taylor said, stepping closer, her gun now visible. "Just know that, if you lay another hand on either of them, I'll make damn sure you're wearing orange and eating bologna sandwiches for the rest of the year."

Just then, Ellis stepped out from the barn, quietly assessing the scene as he walked up. He carried no weapon, just that still, calming presence of his voice.

"Morning," he said, nodding to each of them. Then to Curtis: "Whatever business you have with your siblings, it'll have to be somewhere else. This land is protected. And these people? They're under our protection now."

Curtis looked between them—Cecil still holding the shotgun, Taylor with her hand hovering over her hip, Ellis calm but firm. His options were dwindling fast.

Waylon still looked terrified.

Curtis sneered at Tula one more time. "You should've never come back to this town."

Tula lifted her chin. "Yeah, well, I did. Live with it." She took a shaky step forward. "Now get in your truck—and go!"

Curtis hesitated, then spat to the side and climbed into his cab. The engine coughed and rumbled, tires spinning as he peeled out of the drive and disappeared down the road.

The silence that followed was heavy. No one moved.

Then Tula turned to Waylon. "You okay?"

He nodded faintly, but she could see the shame in his eyes.

Taylor touched her arm. "You handled that better than I would've."

Tula gave a brittle laugh. "I don't feel like I handled anything. I feel like I want to set the whole damn world on fire."

Cecil finally lowered the shotgun and walked back toward the barn without a word.

Ellis offered Tula a soft smile. "We'll be close if you need us to come back."

Tula didn't answer.

She looked back at the porch where Waylon stood, then at the horizon beyond the trees.

If she was going to protect him—and herself—she'd need more than strength.

She'd need answers.

Chapter Twenty-Six

The door to Tula's cabin creaked as Taylor stepped in behind her, gently guiding Waylon past the threshold. He moved slowly, favoring one side of his body, his face still mottled with bruises, both eyes puffed and rimmed in black. The tension inside him buzzed like static. He hadn't said a word since Curtis sped away in a cloud of gravel dust and exhaust.

Tula hovered nearby, arms crossed tight over her chest, radiating protective fury.

Taylor pulled out a chair from the tiny dining table. "Sit," she said softly to Waylon.

He did, wincing.

Tula retrieved a cold pack from the fridge, wrapped it in a towel, and handed it to him. "You keep this on your face for a while. Swelling's worse today."

"Thanks," he mumbled.

Taylor took the seat across from him and leaned forward. "Waylon, I need you to be honest with me. I'm not here as law enforcement, okay? I'm here because Quig mattered to me. And

I think you know something about what might've happened to her."

He kept his gaze on the tabletop.

Tula's voice was sharper. "She's trying to help you, bud. You're not gonna last long if you keep letting Curtis treat you like that."

Waylon winced again—this time from shame. He ran a hand over his buzzed head and exhaled through his nose.

"I don't know much," he finally said. "I didn't see anything. But I know the Shuffle has more goin' on than poker machines and cheap beer."

Taylor sat up straighter. "Tell me what you do know."

Waylon hesitated, glancing toward the door as if he half-expected Curtis to crash through it again.

Tula noticed. "You're safe here. I won't let him touch you again."

Waylon nodded once, then looked back at Taylor. "I was makin' deliveries. Envelopes, mostly. Sometimes stuff in small boxes. They'd give me a list of addresses, cash up front, and that was it. No receipts. No names."

Taylor's stomach knotted. "Were these local deliveries?"

"Some are. Others up toward Athens. Once I had to go all the way to Macon." He shifted, the cold pack sliding slightly. "Quig ... I did know her a little. I swear, though, I don't know what happened to her or why."

"Was Quig slipping? Do you know if she was using again?" Taylor asked.

He bit his lip, then winced. "I don't think so. I really don't. She seemed clear-headed. Focused. But she was scared. We were out back together one night, and she was acting all paranoid. I asked her what was going on, and she said she saw something she wasn't supposed to."

Taylor's breath caught. "Did she say what?"

He shook his head. "Only that it wasn't what she signed up for. She thought about quitting, but said they wouldn't let her. That she'd 'already seen too much.'"

Tula gasped. "God, Waylon. Why didn't you tell someone?"

"I was scared," he said. "Still am."

Taylor leaned forward. "Do you remember any names? Anyone she mentioned? Or anyone you saw her talking to?"

Waylon hesitated, then slowly nodded. "A girl named Lana. She and Quig started around the same time. Lana told me to keep my head down, don't ask questions."

Taylor's chest turned to lead. "Lana's dead."

Waylon looked up sharply. "What?"

"They're calling it a drug overdose, but I'm not buying it."

He slumped back against the couch. "Jesus."

Taylor leaned forward, voice calm. "Look, I need you to be honest with me, Waylon. We're not trying to trap you. But if someone hurt you—and if it's tied to Quig—I need the truth."

Waylon didn't answer. He stared into the mug like it held the secret to disappearing.

Tula broke the silence. "You know we're not giving up until we get answers, baby brother. So go ahead. Start talking."

He exhaled sharply through his nose, shoulders sagging. "It wasn't supposed to be a big deal. Curtis said they needed someone reliable to do some deliveries. Said I'd make good money."

Taylor's pen paused. "Deliveries of what?"

He rubbed his palm against the leg of his jeans. "Just packages. In big manila envelopes. Sometimes small bags. Always sealed."

Taylor exchanged a quick glance with Tula. "Tell us more about those deliveries. What kind of places did you deliver them?"

"Some bars. A vape shop out by the bypass. Once to a

garage over in Lavonia. One time to a lady's house. She had a little white dog that barked the whole time." He blinked slowly. "Sometimes they'd say leave it in the mailbox. Other times, knock and hand it off."

"Did you ever see what was inside?"

"No. I didn't ask, and they didn't tell. Curtis said, if I kept my mouth shut, I'd stay in the clear."

Taylor's jaw tightened. "Waylon, did Quig make deliveries, too?"

He hesitated. "A few months ago, when I had to rest up after that stomach bug. Quig said she'd take the route for me— just that one day. I gave her the list and the packages. I didn't think nothin' of it. But afterward ... she acted weird."

"Weird how?"

He shrugged. "Tense. Like she was mad. Didn't say much, just told me it was done and walked off. Next few days, she didn't hang around the Lounge much."

Taylor's mind raced. "Did you tell Curtis she filled in for you?"

His lips pressed together. "No. He'd told me not to let anyone else do the job."

Tula's voice sharpened. "So, she took the route for you? And now she's—" She couldn't finish it.

"I didn't know," he whispered. "I didn't know they'd do anything."

Taylor sat back slowly. "Waylon, I need you to make a list. Everywhere you've delivered. Every name you can remember. Even descriptions."

He nodded faintly. "Okay."

She tapped her pen against her notebook. "And this whole time—you don't have a driver's license?"

Waylon grimaced. "It's suspended. I figured if I was just

driving local, it wasn't a big deal. Cops never stopped me. Not until that last time."

Tula stood, hands on her hips, voice rising. "Curtis knew he didn't have a license. And he used him anyway. That's not just shady—it's criminal. Can't he be arrested for that?"

Taylor stood, too. "No. Waylon's an adult and responsible for his own choices. I'm more worried that if Quig saw something she wasn't supposed to ... and now she's gone ..." Her throat tightened. "We might have a chance to get to the bottom of this. But only if we're smart."

Waylon's voice was quiet. "What if they come after me next?"

Taylor's reply came without hesitation. "Then we make sure they don't get the chance."

She pulled out her phone and fired off a text to Shane:

> I've got a lead. Come to the farm. I need backup.

Chapter Twenty-Seven

Taylor waited for Shane near the porch, arms folded, eyes shadowed. Her smile was tight, her voice steady —but, just beneath it all, something was burning. She didn't wave. Just nodded once and turned toward the cabin. He followed without a word.

Inside, Tula sat stiffly at the small kitchen table, her lips tight. Waylon slouched nearby, a frozen bag of peas pressed against one cheek, eyes puffy and dark like he hadn't slept in days. Probably because he hadn't.

"Rough week, huh?" Shane said lightly, trying to gauge the kid's state.

Waylon gave him nothing.

Taylor filled him in quickly—the beatdown from Curtis, the "delivery job" at Shuffle Lounge, the list of drop-off locations, and the vague, shady details Waylon could remember.

"And inside are a dozen or so poker machines, and a secret back room."

When she finished, Shane let out a slow breath. "Okay, first of all—Waylon, I'm not here to bust you. You're not under arrest. But I need you to be honest with me. No dodging. What were you delivering?"

"I am being honest," Waylon muttered. "I never looked inside the packages. Curtis told me not to."

"He's already said, he doesn't know," Tula said, crossing her arms defiantly.

Taylor sat on the edge of the counter and took a friendly tone. "You never even peeked?"

Waylon shook his head. "Swear to God. Just dropped them off and left. Sometimes it was envelopes. Sometimes small, padded bags. I figured it was something illegal, but the less I know, the better."

"You figured," Shane echoed, eyeing him. "But you don't know."

Waylon looked away.

Shane sighed. "I can't call it distribution. Not yet. Hell, I don't even know what I'd be accusing them of distributing. But that kind of operation? Off-the-books deliveries? Remote drop points and cash payments? It walks and talks like something dirty."

He pulled a chair out and sat, looking between them. "I'll say this, though. The sheriff's on my ass. Called me in this morning, asked what the hell I thought I was doing getting involved in the Monroe business. Said Lana's death isn't our jurisdiction. Not our problem."

Taylor's jaw clenched. "She was our witness."

Shane nodded. "Exactly, but he says I'm using scarce resources where they don't matter. We're going to have to proceed carefully."

"It's all connected," Taylor said, voice low. "Why can't he see that?"

Shane turned to Waylon. "We need to know more. Anything. People you saw. What kind of places you dropped off to. Who opened the doors. Did anyone ever say something that felt ... off?"

Waylon hesitated. "There was one time ... I was supposed to leave the bag inside this old ice chest. Behind a fireworks shack on 106. No one there. Just a note saying to drop and go."

"A note?" Shane asked. "You still have it?"

Waylon shook his head. "Curtis took it after."

"Damn," Taylor muttered.

"Start writing down everything you remember," Shane said. "Every location. Time. Cars that were there. What Curtis said. Even the music on the radio—anything that could jar a memory."

At the mention of his brother, Waylon put his head in his hands. "Curtis will kill me if he finds this out."

Tula stepped behind him, placing a firm hand on his shoulder. Protective. Fierce. "Waylon's not doing another job. Not for Curtis. Not for anyone. Not after this."

"No argument there," Shane said. "But anything you might think of could help get justice for Quig. And Lana."

Waylon glanced up. "You think that's what happened? That what I did ... got them killed?"

He looked crestfallen.

"No," Taylor said quickly. "You didn't kill anyone, Waylon. But you were used by people who might've."

Shane stood. "If we can get eyes on another delivery, or find someone else in the operation to talk to, we'll have more to go on."

"I still don't understand why Quig kept this a secret," Taylor murmured. "Why she didn't just tell me. Why she didn't ask for help."

"Probably because she thought she could handle it," Tula said. "Or because someone made sure she knew what would happen if she talked."

The silence that followed hung heavy.

Finally, Shane said, "I'll start digging on the LLC, see if any new business permits or liquor licenses are connected. Also check addresses that Waylon is going to give us."

"If I can remember them," Waylon warned.

"I still haven't talked to a girl named Rae," Taylor said. "I'll see if I can round her up. If Lana was killed for what she knew, someone else might be next."

Shane reached for the door but paused. "Oh—and Taylor?"

She looked up.

"If you're going to keep running point on this, you better be careful. Sheriff's looking for a reason to reel you back in and slap that badge back on your chest. Without it, he doesn't want you in the picture."

Taylor gave a humorless smile. She'd loved her job, but not enough to go back to a good ol' boys' club that she would never advance in. "Not happening."

Chapter Twenty-Eight

I f motherhood, marriage, and murder investigations were a circus act, Taylor was the tired clown duct-taping the tent. The sound of Lennon squealing with happiness at Jo in the next room was in Taylor's ears when she turned back to the whiteboard, her marker poised mid-air. Sam was at the shop, going over month-end numbers with his dad, for a report due to the accountant by Friday.

Thankfully, Jo had agreed to come watch Lennon for a few hours while Taylor worked her case. The house was full now, with the four of them, so, instead of a dedicated room as an office, Sam had removed their dresser and created a space in the corner of their bedroom where she'd put a desk and surrounded it with her investigative tools. It wasn't a conference room with all the newest gadgets, and it didn't afford her a lot of room to work, but at least she was at home more than she wasn't.

She'd added Lana's name to the bottom corner and drew a thin arrow back to Quig, and another to a box that said SHUFFLE LOUNGE.

Lana had mentioned Quig was working for the Lounge. Lana had at one time, too.

Two women with a connection to a business. Both now dead.

A part of Taylor wanted to scream. The other part, the rational side, knew she had to move methodically. Keep her emotions locked away where they couldn't make a mess of her logic.

She stared at the board, eyes jumping from box to box. From Quig's last few days to the night she died. From the NA meetings to the side job she'd never spoken of, to the shell company—DFC—that had somehow escaped even a whisper of law enforcement attention for two years.

Taylor felt it in her gut. They were connected.

She needed to get back to a meeting and see if she could talk to the girl who was supposedly Quig's friend, Rae.

She snapped the cap on the marker and grabbed her keys.

Fifteen minutes later, she was heading toward a back road that she and Shane often used in order to talk without being seen. The windows were down, and the scent of pine and distant rain filled the air.

He was already there, and she pulled up behind him, got out and met him at the hood of his truck.

"Did Waylon hand over the list yet?" Shane asked, stepping up into the cab.

"No. Tula said she'd have him work on it today, once he was up and feeling better. He finally said why Curtis whupped him. He'd delivered something to a wrong address, said it was a learning moment. Tula's like a mother hen over him right now."

"I still don't like how much he's holding back," Shane said, tapping his fingers on the wheel. "If he knows more, he's going to have to talk."

"He's scared," Taylor said. "You saw what he looks like. That was a hell of a beating. And whatever this is, he's been threatened enough to believe they'd follow through."

"Then maybe we need to move faster. Before someone else ends up dead."

Taylor nodded slowly. "Okay, recapping. He told us he was delivering sealed envelopes. Cash probably—is my guess. No packages, no drugs—at least none that he saw. Just in and out."

"But to where?" Shane asked. "If he's making drop-offs, then someone's making pick-ups."

Taylor frowned. "He mentioned a bar outside of Lavonia once. Said it was always dark, and the owner never spoke more than five words to him."

"Didn't give an address?"

"No, but I can find it. I remember passing a dive out there that looked like it hadn't seen a paintbrush since the '80s. It had a neon palm tree out front even though it was five hours from the coast."

"That sounds about right." Shane exhaled. "We should check it out. Or, you should. I don't want to get Dawkins stirred up again, so you're going to have to do more of the footwork here."

"We've got two dead girls, an assaulted young man, and a shady business, yet the only people who seem to care are sitting in this damn truck."

Shane shrugged. "We've done as much with only the two of us before. Let's just focus," he said, flipping a page in his notebook. "Okay, so I ran by the place again last night. More of the same. Loud music, mix of rough and flashy cars, same crew hovering around the side door. I caught a glimpse of the machines Waylon mentioned."

"The poker machines?"

He nodded. "Straight up Class B Coin-Operated Amusement Machines. COAMs. Legal ... technically."

Taylor's brows lifted. "So, we're back to square one. Having machines don't make it criminal."

"Right. Technically, they're approved under the new state law," Shane said, flipping to another note. "As long as they're skill based. Players have to make a decision before they win anything—keeps it from being classified as gambling."

"I read about that," Taylor said, frowning. "House Bill 353, right? The one that passed last year. Now they can give out prepaid gift cards instead of just prizes from the store where the machine's located."

"Exactly. That shift in law turned every sketchy gas station or small pop's store into a little Vegas. And the Shuffle is tucked out just far enough to avoid attention."

Taylor sipped from the coffee Shane pushed toward her, appreciating the sustenance, but wishing it was tea. "So, let's say they're gaming the system—literally. I'd bet half those machines are being used for more than just winning free sandwiches."

Shane's expression darkened. "We don't know that for sure but, yes, that's a scenario to look into. Machines take in hundreds in cash every night. You inflate the winnings, fudge the books, skim the rest."

Taylor nodded slowly. "So, on paper, it's 'Oh wow, we had a lucky night, lots of winners.' But, in reality, you're feeding money into the machine from illegal activity and pulling it back out as legit earnings. Classic money laundering."

They lapsed into silence for a moment, the tension stretching between them.

Finally, Shane said, "I also ran background on her brothers—Curtis and Earl Skaggs."

Taylor turned toward him. "And?"

"Curtis has a rap sheet as long as my arm. Assault, petty theft, resisting arrest, you name it. Earl's not much better. Half the charges are shared between them—same dates, same locations. Looks like they've been getting in trouble together for years."

Taylor gave a low whistle. "No wonder Tula tried to escape her roots. God. That family's a mess."

"Yup. And now Waylon's caught in the middle of it all."

Taylor's gaze hardened. "Then we've got to get him out. Before they pull him under completely."

Shane nodded slowly. "One wrong step, and it's going to get worse. We need to move. Smart, but soon."

Taylor looked out at the trees. "Let's find the cracks and start prying."

"Which brings us back to Waylon," Taylor said. "If he was doing deliveries—cash or otherwise—he could be the key. But he doesn't want to talk much."

"He's scared. I don't blame him. And we still don't know what exactly he was delivering. We could be totally off about the machines. All he's said is it was 'just errands.' If we can get him to trust us, maybe he can wear a wire. Something small. Just to get a feel for what's happening inside."

Taylor hesitated. "Shane, he's barely an adult. Tula doesn't want him to go back there, either."

"But he's already caught up in it somehow. Don't you think, if he just stops going to work, it will be more suspicious?" Shane sat back, blowing out a long breath. "I think he can do this. We'll have to be careful. Discreet. We aren't going to get much insider info about what happened in Monroe, either. Dawkins is still set that it's not our problem."

Taylor's jaw clenched. "It is our problem. Lana's death is related to Quig's, I just know it. You know how much I care about the sheriff, Shane, but this feels discriminatory. Just because Lana and Quig didn't have money or clout doesn't mean they don't matter. Sometimes I think he might be too focused on reelection. He's busy doing whatever his biggest supporters want him to do."

"I agree." Shane's voice dropped. "But he's watching me now. Closely. You, too, if I had to guess."

Taylor's gaze hardened. "Then we stay sharp. Quiet. Build the case without tipping anyone off."

They sat in silence for a beat before Shane added, "And what if the Shuffle's got more protection than we thought?"

Taylor stirred her coffee slowly, her voice low. "Like I said, we have to be careful."

Chapter Twenty-Nine

Taylor parked her truck at the far edge of the church lot, just outside the line of neatly painted white spaces. Inside, the Tuesday night NA meeting had already begun to thin. A few stragglers stood chatting on the front steps while others made quiet exits toward their cars.

She spotted the woman in charge—Helene, if she remembered correctly—stacking chairs near the side entrance. She approached slowly, hands in her jacket pockets.

"Helene?"

The woman turned, her expression guarded. "Taylor. Back again, huh?"

Taylor gave a small nod. "I was hoping to speak with Rae. You mentioned her last time; said she might know something."

Helene sighed and folded her arms. "Yeah, I did. And I also told her you might want to talk to her. Funny thing is, she hasn't been back since."

Taylor frowned. "You think that's more than coincidence?"

"You tell me," Helene said sharply. "We work hard to make this a safe place. People come here to stay clean, not get interrogated. I think you scared her off."

Taylor bit back the urge to defend herself. "That's not what I'm trying to do. I'm just trying to find out what happened to Quig."

Helene shook her head. "Then maybe find another way. We all miss Quig and are sad about what happened, but you showing up here is doing more harm than good. These people walk a delicate line every day. More stress can make that line impossible to follow."

Just then, a man brushed past them, heading toward a beat-up sedan near the curb. He glanced over his shoulder at Taylor before unlocking the driver's door.

Taylor watched him for a moment, then turned back to Helene. "If Rae comes back—"

"Don't count on it," Helene cut in. She walked away without another word.

Taylor started back to her truck, frustration buzzing in her chest. She was just climbing in when the sedan pulled up beside her. The man rolled down his window.

"Hey."

She turned, surprised. "Yeah?"

He leaned across his seat. "I overheard you asking about Rae. I know where she's staying."

Taylor squinted at him. "Why are you telling me?"

He scratched his jaw. "Because I'm not dumb. I know something went down with Quig. Then Rae stopped coming. She's scared, and I don't want anything bad to happen to her."

"You know her well?"

"Well enough. Delivered a fridge to her place a couple weeks ago. She's with her parents—up in Ledgewater Way. Big place that overlooks the lake."

Taylor blinked. That was one of the more upscale neighborhoods in Hart's Ridge. Not where she'd expected Rae to be holed up.

"Thanks," she said. "You got a number or address?"

He gave her the info, and Taylor jotted it down. As he pulled away, she stared after him for a long moment, then turned on the ignition.

The houses in Ledgewater Way were set back from the road, with long winding driveways, stone facades, and lake views that could make you forget all your problems. Taylor pulled up to a sprawling ranch with white columns, a manicured lawn, and two golden-doodles barking happily at the front window.

She rang the bell. The dogs—one apricot, the other cream—pressed their noses against the glass, tails wagging. A moment later, the door opened.

A girl stood there, barefoot in leggings and an oversized sweater, her hair damp and twisted up in a messy knot.

"Can I help you?"

"Rae?"

"Who's asking?"

That answered the question. Taylor handed her a business card. "Hi, Rae. I'm Taylor Gray, and I'm just here to ask you some questions about your friendship with Quig Gallagher."

Her eyes widened. "Oh."

Taylor held up a hand. "I'm not here to start trouble. I just want to talk. Off the record, I swear."

Rae hesitated, then looked over her shoulder. "My parents are home."

"I won't stay long. Give me ten minutes, and you'll never see me again."

Rae stepped aside. "Come on. Out back."

The back terrace overlooked a glassy stretch of lake, a dock with a pontoon tied to it, and a pair of kayaks leaning against the railing. The dogs—Churro and Maisie, as Rae introduced them

—bounded down the steps to chase something invisible in the yard.

They sat on a stone bench beneath a pergola.

"You've got a beautiful place," Taylor said.

Rae shrugged. "It's my parents'. Not mine."

A woman stepped outside then, her face pinched with worry. "Rae, you okay?"

"I'm fine, Mom. This is ... Taylor. She's looking into the death of my friend from my meetings; remember I told you about that?"

The mother's face paled. "Yes, but what do you have to do with it?"

"Nothing, ma'am, but she was friends with Quig. I'm just following up on the case," Taylor said.

The mother hovered another moment, eyes darting to her daughter, before going back inside. She stood just inside the door, her profile evident in the shadows.

Rae stared out at the lake. "Sorry about that. She's been through it with me. Rehab. Relapse. Hospital. Rinse and repeat. This time, I think she's holding her breath, waiting for me to mess up again. I can't blame her. I wouldn't trust me, either."

"How long have you been sober?"

Rae gave a small smile. "Six months. The longest I've gone yet. I got my chip the day before Quig ..." Her voice cracked. She swallowed. "She brought me a gift to celebrate. A journal with a gold pen. She said, 'You're writing your new story now.'"

Taylor's chest tightened. "You were close."

"Not really. We didn't hang out. But there was something about her. She wanted to be better—for her kids. For herself."

Taylor nodded. "How'd you get into using?"

Rae didn't flinch. "I broke my ankle on the track my junior year of high school. They gave me Oxy. The rest is a cliché. Ten years of making mistakes. I've stolen from my parents. Lied. Been arrested. Put them through hell. Humiliated them. So has my brother. He's now lost in the streets after leaving a rehab that cost my parents most of their retirement fund. He's hiding out, only God knows where."

"I'm really sorry to hear that," Taylor said. "I grew up with an alcoholic father, so I know a little about it, but only from an outsider's view. I've been afraid to touch alcohol all my life, because of what he put us through."

"Yeah, but, in my case, it's turned upside down. My parents are as straight as an arrow, but I've heard about some uncles and such. I guess you can say that addiction runs deep in my family tree. We have a ton of skeletons in the closet that my parents try to keep secret."

Taylor glanced toward the lake, then back at Rae. She was being more transparent now. Now was the time to ask. "Did Quig ever talk to you about her job at the Shuffle Lounge?"

Rae shook her head. "I never even heard of that place until after Quig—well, was gone. All I know is that some girl—someone she wouldn't name—got her the job. She was excited at first. Said she was finally saving enough to get a real place. But a few weeks later, she looked rough. Tired. Said she was struggling not to use again."

"Do you think she did?"

Rae hesitated then swiped a few tears from her eyes. "I want to say no, that she stayed strong. But I don't know. Maybe. And if she did ... maybe that's what killed her."

That wasn't what killed her.

Taylor stood, her heart heavy. "Thanks for talking to me. I know it wasn't easy."

Rae nodded. "If you find out what happened to her, will you let me know?"

"I will."

As Taylor walked back to her truck, she looked over the homes lining the lake, perfect lawns and perfect porches. But inside, she knew no one was immune. Not from pain. Not from the disease of addiction that left no class untouched.

And still, she had no new answers. Just more grief.

Chapter Thirty

Waylon was on his feet again, pacing the small cabin like a caged animal, his ribs still tender but his temper sharper than ever. Tula tried to stay patient, but what she really wanted to do was lock him inside until she could be sure he wouldn't go back to their mother's house.

"I'm not sitting around hiding like some scared kid," he snapped, hands clenching at his sides.

"You can barely walk straight," Tula shot back. "You need to rest, not plot revenge. If you came back with me to L.A., we could start over. Both of us. No Curtis, no Earl, no Mama dragging you down. Just a clean slate."

Waylon's head whipped toward her, eyes blazing. "And pretend it never happened like I always do? I've had enough, Tula Rose. I'm not running anymore."

Her heart lurched. "Revenge won't fix you, Waylon."

His jaw tightened. "Maybe not. But it'll fix the way he looks at me. Like I'm nothing."

They were still at a standoff when a knock came at the door.

Tula swallowed her fury, brushed her hair back, and opened

it. Taylor stood there, calm as ever, notebook tucked under her arm.

"Sorry to interrupt," Taylor said. "Thought I'd check in."

Tula stepped aside. "Come in."

Waylon flopped into the chair by the table, glaring at the floor.

Taylor pulled a chair close, her voice even. "I want to talk about what's next. About how we can—"

"I'm going home and back to work," Waylon blurted, cutting her off.

Tula's chest seized. "No, you are not."

"Yes, I am." He leaned forward, fire sparking in his eyes. "I'm not a baby anymore, Tula Rose. I'm not innocent in this, and I wish I could take it back, so if there's anything I can do to help your investigation"—he looked squarely at Taylor—"I want to do it. I don't want to be a loser like Curtis and Earl. I want to do something good. I want to matter."

Tula's breath hitched. For a moment, all she could see was the little boy he used to be—dragging a scuffed teddy bear by one arm, his too-big hand clutching it tight like it was armor. Curtis and Earl had tormented him for it, sneering that he was soft, shoving him down until the bear's stitched smile was ground into the dirt.

Tula had pulled him up a dozen times, wiped his tears, told him to ignore them. But the words had never stuck, not when the mockery came day after day. And now, here he was, bloodied and bruised, still fighting to prove he wasn't the weak one.

It was so damn unfair. That he'd grown up with fists instead of guidance, ridicule instead of respect. Her anger rose like bile —at her mother, for coddling Curtis and Earl while ignoring Waylon's potential. At their father, for vanishing when they'd needed him most. And most of all at her brothers for grinding Waylon down every chance they got.

She wanted to hug him. But that wasn't the Skaggs way. Her eyes burned. "You're not worthless," she whispered. "You never were."

He looked at her, a flicker of doubt on his battered face.

Taylor had stayed out of it, but now she said gently, "If you really want to help, here's what we can do. Let's take a ride. Go by some of the places you delivered to for Shuffle. You tell me what you know, I'll take notes. And while we're at it, we can talk about other ways you can help."

Tula straightened and grabbed her purse from the kitchen counter. "Then I'm coming, too."

Waylon shook his head, stubborn as stone. "No. You aren't coming. This time, I stand on my own two feet. You can't always save me, Tula. If I'm going to change my trajectory, I've got to do it myself."

Her throat closed, but she saw it—the steel in his spine, the thing she'd been waiting for a long time. Slowly, she nodded. "All right. But you come back to me. You hear me? You come back safe, and then we'll talk about you going home tonight."

She had to find a way to convince him not to.

Waylon managed the barest of smiles. It lit up his face and showed just how handsome he really was, so unlike their deadbeat brothers. "Deal."

Chapter Thirty-One

The world constantly asked Taylor to be strong. Home let her be soft. Their house was finally settling in for the evening. She was comfortable in a pair of Sam's joggers, and an old sweatshirt, her hair up and her face shiny clean. Lennon was asleep in her crib, a warm bundle of lavender lotion and soft snores. Alice was in the living room, headset on, her laughter rising and falling as she clicked furiously through a video game that she'd talked Sam into letting her download.

Dishes were still piled in the sink, the living room could use a vacuum, and the trash needed taken out, but those could wait. Taylor sat at the desk in their bedroom, her notes spread in neat rows, addresses circled and annotated in red ink.

Sam was stretched across the bed, laptop balanced on his thighs, scrolling with a practiced frown.

"All right," Sam said, tapping a key. "This first one—East Side Bowling. Been dead for years. Every time we drive by it, the parking lot's empty except for a couple cars."

Taylor leaned back, chewing her pen cap. "Then why is it still open?"

"Good question." He clicked again, then glanced at her. "Guess who owns it?"

She arched a brow. "Don't tell me."

"Same LLC as Shuffle Lounge."

Taylor's pulse quickened. "That can't be coincidence."

Sam's mouth tightened. "Nope."

She scribbled the connection on her pad: Bowling alley. Shuffle Lounge. Same shell company.

Sam scrolled down the list. "Next three are residential. Rental houses. I pulled the property tax info—different owners, all local, but no tenant names listed. We'd need boots on the ground for that."

"Could be stash houses. Safe spots."

"Could be," he echoed grimly.

"And this one—" Taylor pointed to the final address. "Small laundromat. Open odd hours, barely any foot traffic. I drove by with Waylon. Place gave me a bad feeling."

Sam snapped his laptop shut and set it aside, rubbing his jaw. "So, what's the angle? They running gambling through laundromats and bowling alleys now?"

"Or laundering money." She tapped her pen against the desk. "Pun not intended."

He chuckled, but it faded quickly. His gaze lingered on her. "I need to talk to you about something. You've been spending a lot of time with Shane lately."

Taylor blinked. "Shane? Hardly. We meet now and then to compare notes, make plans. That's it."

Sam's jaw worked. "I still don't trust him."

The fact that he was jealous might be a little endearing to Taylor, but she didn't want him to worry needlessly. She pushed back from the desk and came to sit beside him on the bed, resting a hand on his knee. "You don't have to. You can trust me, Sam. And I promise—Shane and I aren't together on this as much as you think. You're the one I tag-team with, every night. Not him."

Some of the tension in his shoulders eased, though his eyes still held a flicker of doubt.

From the living room, a small crash rang out. Both bolted upright.

"Everything okay?" Taylor called.

"I'm fine!" Alice's voice floated back, tinged with laughter. "Just knocked over my soda."

Taylor sat back, heart thudding, then let out a shaky laugh. "She's getting louder by the day. It's kind of unnerving considering she usually barely makes a peep."

Sam's smile was softer this time. "She is. She's coming out of her shell. Not just buried in books anymore—games, friends. Teachers say she's raising her hand more at school."

"I've noticed," Taylor admitted. "She seems lighter."

Sam reached for his phone, scrolling. "Yep. Oh, she's got that field trip coming up next week, too. To the Atlanta Aquarium. They're asking for a parent chaperone."

Taylor's heart twisted. "Oh, Sam, I'd love to. But until we get closer to figuring out what happened to Quig ..." Her voice trailed off.

He gave a slow nod, disappointment flickering across his face. "I figured you'd say that. I'll go instead. And I'll ask Cate if she can watch Lennon."

Taylor touched his hand. "I'm sorry. I hate missing these things."

His fingers laced with hers. "I know."

"Tomorrow I'm planning on going to check out that place in Lavonia that Waylon mentioned."

"Mmm," he murmured.

The silence between them was thick but tender, the pressures of family and duty pressing in from both sides. Taylor squeezed his hand once more, then picked up her pen. "All right. Back to work. Let's crack this thing wide open so I can get back to minding our own business."

Sam nodded, his eyes steady on her. "Ditto to that. Graystone Investigations and just the two of us."

Chapter Thirty-Two

The Lavonia place looked exactly as Waylon had described—maybe worse. Taylor pulled onto the gravel shoulder and let her truck idle for a moment. The bar looked like it had been patched together from the scraps of other buildings—a low-slung rectangle of warped siding and sun-faded shingles tucked between two weedy stretches of woods. Over the door, a flickering neon palm tree buzzed against the dark like a broken promise.

Two old trucks sat out front, one missing a side mirror and the other sagging to one side like a tired dog. Red clay painted their undercarriages. No security cameras. No marked parking spaces. A place meant to be forgotten.

Taylor climbed out and let the door thud shut behind her. Heat wrapped around her shoulders, sticky and unrelenting.

She passed a rickety table near the entrance, half-covered by a battered beach umbrella. A wiry old man in a sweat-stained ball cap manned the setup, selling small brown paper bags of boiled peanuts, fried pork skins, and plastic-wrapped honey buns stacked in a cracked cooler.

"Need a snack for the road?" he asked.

"Maybe on the way out," she murmured, already pulling open the door.

Inside, the shift was immediate—dim, smoky, and stale. Years of cigarette smoke clung to every wooden surface. The only light came from a string of dusty Christmas bulbs along the back wall and the glow of the video poker machines near the bathrooms. A fan turned overhead like it was spinning through molasses.

Country music rasped from a jukebox in the corner, barely competing with the clack of pool balls and the buzz of conversation.

She headed to the bar.

The bartender, a thick guy with a ZZ Top beard and mirrored sunglasses—indoors—watched her approach like she might bite.

"You lost?" he asked.

Taylor smiled. "Heard y'all might be looking for help. Part-time. I waitressed before."

He gave her a long, slow look. "You don't look local."

"Just moved to Lavonia. My sister's sick. Figured I'd be around for a while. Need some cash to hold me over."

He nodded toward a warped cork board near the register. "Leave your number."

Taylor jotted down a burner name and number on the corner of a gas receipt. She added a star, like she meant business. "Y'all do food?"

"We fry stuff," he said. "Wings. Nachos. Mozzarella sticks if the truck came in."

She gave a nod, then casually turned her back to him and scanned the room.

Three men hunched over a pool table. A woman at the far end of the bar scribbled in a notebook, sipping a beer with chipped nails and a faded tank top. But it was the poker machines that caught Taylor's eye.

Two sat nestled in the back, dim but still glowing. One man was camped out on a stool, hunched over, methodically feeding bills into the slot. He had a sweating cup of soda in one hand and a look in his eyes like he hadn't blinked in ten minutes.

Then she saw it—the navy baseball cap on his head. DFC.

Her heart thudded once, heavy.

DFC. The same shell company tied to the Shuffle Lounge. The same name that had cropped up on paperwork that no one seemed to own.

For such a small town, Lavonia sure knew how to keep its secrets buried deep.

Taylor eased toward the back, just close enough to glimpse a doorframe behind the machines. Something was back there. Another room maybe. A side office. It was impossible to tell.

She turned slightly to get a better angle when a voice rang out behind her.

"Hey! Ain't you that deputy from Hart County? Gray?"

Her stomach dropped.

The woman at the bar was now standing, pointing straight at her. Pool balls stopped mid-play. The bartender straightened. Chairs creaked as heads turned.

"I saw you on TV last year," the woman added. "Press conference. That missing girl. You were in uniform."

Taylor forced a light laugh. "You must be thinking of someone else."

"Nope. You're Taylor Gray. I'd swear on my mama's grave."

The bartender frowned. "You lied. Said you were looking for work."

"I was," Taylor said. "Still am."

"You came in under false pretenses," he said. "We don't like that here. Time to go."

Taylor didn't argue. She'd stayed long enough. Long enough

to see the DFC connection. Long enough to feel the rot under the floorboards.

She walked slowly toward the door, imprinting every detail she could—faces, tables, license plates through the smoky window, and especially the man on the poker stool who never once looked up. As if the machine were whispering something only he could hear.

Outside, the sun had already dipped behind the trees. The man at the peanut table gave her a curious look as she passed.

"Didn't like the smell of the wings?" he joked.

"Didn't like the smell of something," she muttered, brushing past him.

She climbed into the truck, her pulse still drumming in her ears. One hand gripped the wheel as she stared through the windshield.

She'd been recognized.

And if she'd been recognized here—in a podunk bar in Lavonia—then someone from the top would hear about it. DFC, Shuffle, whoever was still pulling strings behind the scenes. Her cover was blown, and that meant she'd have to be even more vigilant from here on out. One wrong step, and she wouldn't just be outed—she'd be targeted.

She drove off without turning the headlights on for the first half mile, the peanut vendor shrinking in her rearview mirror.

She didn't get much.

But she got enough.

Chapter Thirty-Three

The minute Tula pulled into the yard with Waylon, her stomach knotted. The place looked the same as ever. Half-lit, half-broken, half-lived-in. But there was a hum in the air, like the house itself knew a storm was brewing.

Inside, Earl was already in the kitchen. He had the refrigerator door wide open, leaning on it like it might hold him up. He didn't acknowledge them, just reached in, pulled out a jar of pickled pig's feet, and fished one out with his fingers before shoving it into his mouth.

A saucepan of spaghetti sauce simmered on the stove, turned up too high and making plopping noises as it escaped the pan.

Waylon went to the couch, leaning back and picking up the remote. The sudden sounds of old *The Dukes of Hazard* sitcom chaos filled the room, mixing with the smell of stale beer, smoke, and grease.

Earl continued to dig in the open jar with his dirty fingers, then make loud sucking noises as he ate the goods.

It was all enough to turn Tula's stomach.

"Nice to see you puttin' Mama's food to good use," she said dryly. "And someone's been smoking in here again."

Earl chewed slow, eyes flat, then turned his back without a word. Silent treatment. Typical from a brother who had always been passive-aggressive.

From the hallway came the shuffle-thump of her mother's walker. She appeared in her nightgown, oxygen tubing snaking along the floor, tangled around one wheel. Her hair stuck out in wiry clumps, her skin gray, and she smelled like she hadn't touched soap in days.

"Well, there she is," her mother said, squinting at Tula. "Our very own superstar, Tula Rose Skaggs. You finally decide to bring my boy home, I see ..." She waved her hand, the other gripping the walker. "And, Lord, do I need a bath. Ain't nobody in this house cares if I stink. I haven't had dinner yet, either."

Tula pressed her lips together, fighting the words that wanted to leap out. *You've been sick as a dog, and they let you shuffle around hungry, with your tubing dragging the floor?* Instead, she said, "We'll get you cleaned up in a minute, Mama. Let me fix you something to eat, first."

Tula went to the kitchen and waited for Earl to move away from the fridge.

The door slammed so hard behind them that the thin windowpanes rattled. Curtis stomped in, his boots heavy, his scowl darker than a thunderhead.

"Well, look who finally crawled home," he barked, eyes locking on Waylon. "Two days gone. You think you can just disappear from work and not answer for it?"

Waylon froze. His bruises stood out even under the weak light, and Tula could feel him shrink in on himself.

Before he could speak, Tula surged forward, planting herself between them. Her blood boiled hot.

"You lay one more hand on him," she spat, "and I swear to

God, Curtis, you'll regret it. He's not your punching bag. Not anymore."

Curtis leaned down, so close she caught the sour stink of beer and sweat. His smile was mean, jagged. "Or what? You think you scare me, Hollywood? You're just passing through. Don't forget whose house this is."

Tula's fists itched to swing, but, before she could, another voice cut through.

"Y'all shut up a minute!"

Lorene stood in the doorway, her hands on her hips, eyes glittering. For once, she looked almost triumphant.

"I got news," she announced.

Nobody moved. Curtis cocked a brow. Dixie paused mid-wheeze. Even Earl turned around, pickle jar still in hand.

Lorene smirked, slapped a hand against her belly. "I'm pregnant."

The room fell into stunned silence before Dixie burst into tears. "Another grand baby! Oh, Lord, ain't I blessed?" She shuffled forward, hugging Lorene awkwardly around the walker.

Curtis let out a sharp laugh. "Well, hell. Guess we'll have another little shithead running around soon."

Earl muttered and shot Lorene a dirty look, "Like this place ain't already bustin' at the seams. Don't you know how to prevent that shit?"

She narrowed her eyes at him, and he looked away.

There was no mention of who the father was, and Tula was afraid to ask. Her stomach churned. The last thing this house needed was another child dragged into the mess, another life starting out under the shadow of the Skaggs name. She wanted to scream, to shake Lorene until she understood she was only burying herself deeper into dysfunction. But Dixie was beaming, and Lorene's smirk only widened at the attention.

In the middle of it all, Waylon's jaw tightened. He stepped

forward, ignoring Tula's warning glance. "I'll be ready for work in the morning," he said flatly, his eyes fixed on Curtis. "Count on it."

Curtis gave him a long, hard look, then nodded once, satisfied, before stomping into the kitchen to rummage with Earl.

The noise rose again—Dixie cooing over Lorene, Earl slamming the fridge door, Curtis cracking open another beer. The TV blared from the corner, some game show nobody was watching. Outside, the dogs started a chorus of howling and barking.

Tula's head pounded.

She caught Waylon's eye, but he was already pulling into himself, jaw set, bracing for tomorrow. He headed for his room.

At the stove, she turned down the sauce and wiped up the splatters before starting a pot of water, for the pasta. She wasn't sure who was in charge of the meal, and there was no meat in sight. Not even a loaf of Italian bread or makings for a salad.

"I'm not eating that unless someone goes to the store for hamburger meat," Dixie called out from the living room.

Tula's throat burned. She couldn't breathe in here—the stench, the noise, the suffocating madness of it all. She turned the stovetop off, grabbed her bag from the chair, muttered something about needing air, and walked out before she did something she couldn't take back.

The night air wrapped her in blessed silence. She gulped it in, heart hammering, staring up at the stars. Relief washed through her, but worry clung stubborn, heavy as a chain.

She could leave the house. She could walk away from the chaos.

But she couldn't walk away from Waylon. Not when he was still inside, standing on the edge of something that could swallow him whole.

Chapter Thirty-Four

"I t's cash," Waylon said. "At least a few thousand, if not more. I'm afraid to touch it too much, so I'm not counting."

His voice trembled slightly through the Bluetooth earpiece Taylor had insisted he wear. From where she sat—two cars behind him in her truck, windows cracked to listen for sounds beyond the mic feed—she could hear his nerves louder than the rustle of the envelope.

Taylor kept her voice low and steady, the calm anchor he needed right now. "Good job. At least now we know what you're delivering. Next, we'll see who's getting it. You ready?"

They were running what Shane had called a "controlled delivery"—not quite sanctioned, but discreetly observed. It was a chance to see what Waylon had been pulled into, and who might be waiting on the other end.

Waylon hesitated. "You really think this'll help?"

He was gripping the wheel too hard. She could hear the vinyl creak under his fingers. Taylor glanced down at the mini-tablet in her lap, where a GPS ping traced his slow progress toward the edge of town. "Yes. We need more than hunches, Waylon. This helps."

He exhaled a breath that sounded more like a whimper. "Even if I'm being watched?"

"If you are," she said firmly, "they won't see me. I know what I'm doing."

There was silence on the line. Then, in a small voice, he added, "I—I'm beginning not to like this."

Taylor's jaw tensed. "I don't like that Quig's dead. Or that your brother has you tangled in something this dangerous. You said you wanted to help. So let's go."

Another beat of silence, then his turn signal clicked on.

Message received.

Waylon pulled the old truck—their uncle's battered Ford Curtis had finally returned to him—onto a cracked side road. North of Hart's Ridge, past the derelict mill, where cell service dropped to one bar as the trees grew thicker.

Taylor followed at a distance, headlights off until she hit a bend. The gravel crunched under her tires like bones as the forest closed in.

When Waylon's truck veered onto a gravel drive, she parked behind a screen of pine saplings and cut the engine. A wide clearing opened in front of her. At its center sat an old auto shop with a sagging roof and a yard littered with rusted cars, as if time had forgotten them. A bent chain-link fence bordered one side, more symbolic than functional.

Taylor adjusted her binoculars.

Waylon parked beside a dented Mustang with no hood. He climbed out, the manila envelope tucked under one arm. His steps were hesitant, but steady. He knocked on the side garage door.

It slid halfway up.

A man inside stepped into view—broad frame, face shadowed under a hoodie, hands gloved despite the warmth in the air. He didn't say anything, just held out his palm. Waylon handed over the envelope and nodded once. No words exchanged.

Then the garage door dropped again with a hollow bang.

Waylon didn't linger. He got back in the truck, glanced toward the trees, and gave the smallest nod as he passed Taylor's hiding spot.

Mission done.

Taylor didn't move right away. Her pulse had picked up, but she forced herself to stay still, eyes sweeping the yard, noting every car, every path out.

She was just reaching for her ignition when the sound of tires on gravel turned her blood to ice. A black SUV nosed out from behind the shop, slow and deliberate. Tinted windows. No tags.

Recognition slammed into her chest.

That SUV had been parked outside the Shuffle Lounge. Twice. Same make, same dark chrome wheels. Too specific to be coincidence.

She ducked down slightly and watched it ease past the tree line, then turn onto the same gravel road she'd just come from.

Her breath caught.

This wasn't just some under-the-table gig with gaming machines and side cash. It was organized. Watched. Protected.

She thought again about Quig. About the poker room. The second job. The way Quig had been afraid.

This wasn't a girl who relapsed and died in her car.

This was something darker.

Taylor sat in the stillness, heart pounding against her ribs, fingers tight around the wheel. Waylon was lucky he hadn't been followed. And now that she'd seen the SUV again, there was no doubt in her mind—DFC wasn't just a shell company.

It was a front.

And someone, somewhere, had their eye on the small town of Hart's Ridge with bigger ambitions.

She started the truck, backed out carefully, and drove with her lights off for another mile before flicking them on.

Her thoughts swirled as she passed back by the little roadside boiled peanut stand she'd passed earlier. The table now sat empty, bags fluttering in the light breeze under the tattered umbrella. Next to it, a cracked cooler held sodas and bright-orange cheese crackers.

She'd grown up thinking Hart's Ridge was a place where you could leave your door unlocked. Where a crooked smile was more dangerous than a gun. But now?

Now she saw the truth.

Beneath the friendly shopkeepers and country diners and Saturday flea markets, the rot was spreading.

And tonight had just proven—it had roots.

Chapter Thirty-Five

T ula gripped the steering wheel tighter than she needed to, knuckles pale in the glow of the dashboard lights. Beside her, Lorene sniffled into a wad of tissues, her pale hands trembling against her lap. The sight should've softened Tula, but all it did was stoke the irritation already buzzing under her skin.

Why was it always her?

Why did she have to be the one to drop everything and play savior?

She'd barely had time to breathe in the last few weeks without some family crisis falling into her lap. Now here she was, hauling her sister to the ER because Lorene hadn't managed to get herself to a doctor yet. Tula's stomach clenched with a mix of resentment and worry. What had they all done when she was gone all those years? Just let everything rot, and wait for her to come back and clean it up?

When she glanced over, though, she saw Lorene's face—the blotchy cheeks, the red-rimmed eyes, the way she held her stomach as though sheer will could hold the baby in—and the anger gave way to something heavier. Fear.

She slammed the gearshift into park and shoved her door open. "Come on," she muttered, marching around to help Lorene out.

Inside the hospital, the smell of disinfectant wrapped around her, sharp and metallic. Lorene leaned against her as they shuffled to the desk, answering the intake questions in a voice no louder than a whisper. "Spotting blood and cramping," Tula explained briskly when Lorene faltered. "She's pregnant. Needs to be seen right away."

When the triage nurse tried to usher Lorene back, Lorene clutched Tula's arm and said, "Will you ask for Nurse Anna Gray? Please? She's ... she's nice."

Tula exhaled hard, nodding. If it made this easier, fine.

"I don't know if she's working, but we'll try."

Anna was contacted by the other nurse and arrived a few minutes later, ushering them into a curtained room with the easy calm of someone who'd seen every kind of crisis. She asked her questions gently, clipboard balanced against her hip.

"How far along are you, Lorene?"

"Maybe ten weeks."

"Any other health concerns? Medications? Substance use?"

Lorene shook her head quickly. "Not anymore. I quit. I promise, I want to do good by this one." Her voice cracked on the last word.

Tula crossed her arms and stared at the floor, because hope was dangerous when it came to her family. Lorene had terminated past pregnancies. Why was this one any different? Suddenly her selfish little sister wanted to be a mother?

It would not go well.

She asked quietly, "You're sure, Lorene? No more using? They have to know."

"I said no, Tula Rose," Lorene whispered angrily.

Anna scribbled something on her form, then asked softly,

"Do you know who the father is? Sometimes that helps us understand medical risks."

Lorene's whole face crumpled. She buried her face in her hands, shoulders shaking. For a long moment she said nothing, just let out jagged sobs that filled the small room.

Tula frowned. "Lorene?"

Finally, Lorene lifted her tear-streaked face. The words tumbled out, raw and broken. "It's Earl. The baby's daddy is Earl."

The air went thin. Tula's ears roared like she was under water. "A different Earl, right?"

"No. Earl, our brother," Lorene wailed. "Oh God, Tula Rose. What if the baby comes out looking wrong? What if it's ... messed up?"

Tula was speechless. Every fiber of her being froze, pleading with her that she hadn't heard what she thought she'd heard.

Anna crouched down beside Lorene, speaking in the kind of steady tone meant to anchor someone in a storm. Not a smidgen of judgment. "Not every baby born to related parents has problems. But, yes, there can be higher risks. That's why it's good that you told me, so we can take care of you and your baby the right way. We'll find you an obstetric doctor, and they will talk to you about genetic counseling and tests that can be done if you choose to proceed with the pregnancy."

Lorene nodded. She looked more like a small child than her thirty years.

Tula couldn't breathe. Her chest seized, bile rising in her throat. She backed out of the room before Lorene could reach for her again, before Anna could say anything else. Down the hall, she stumbled into the first bathroom she found, then gripped the sink until her reflection steadied.

Her family was rotten clear to the roots. Sick. Broken. Twisted. How could she have ever thought she could patch them back together? The thought of the whole town knowing about this made her vision blur. Everything in her was ready to bolt.

This wasn't just shame. It was humiliation that could strangle every one of them.

She wished she could kill Earl.

An innocent baby was going to be born into a house of shame. A child who would probably face a lifetime of trauma and humiliation. Maybe medical problems. Development issues. Possibly even deformities.

Would the child know his father was also his uncle?

Moving quickly inside a stall, she retched, emptying her stomach into the toilet, then back to the sink rinsed her mouth and pressed her forehead against the cool mirror. If she could blink her eyes and disappear from Georgia that instant, she'd choose anywhere.

Hell would even be better.

When she returned to the hallway, Anna was scribbling on a chart outside Lorene's room. Tula grabbed her wrist, desperation burning in her voice.

"You can't tell anyone," she begged. "Please, Anna. I can't take this getting out. I can't—this town will eat us alive. You've got to promise me you won't breathe a word. Not even to your family. It's so—so disturbing."

Anna looked down at Tula's hand, then back up with steady eyes. She didn't say yes. She didn't say no. But the silence stretched heavy, full of things Tula wasn't sure she wanted the answers to.

Anna's expression softened, but she gently pried her wrist free from Tula's grip. "Listen," she said quietly, keeping her voice low so it didn't carry beyond the curtain. "I can't lie in my notes. I must document what Lorene told me for her medical record. That's the only way we can make sure she and the baby get the right screenings."

Tula's heart slammed against her ribs. "So, you are going to report it?"

Anna shook her head slowly. "I didn't say that. They're both adults. It's not my role to call the police or child services unless there's abuse or a minor involved. That's the law. But the information can't just vanish either. If another doctor takes over her care, they'll see it."

Tula's breath came sharp and shallow, panic clawing at her throat. "So, anyone could read it. Anyone could talk."

"I'll chart it in the right way," Anna said, steady and calm, "clinical, not sensational. My responsibility is to your sister and her baby's health—not to spread gossip. But I can't promise no one will ever see it. You need to prepare for that possibility."

Tula swallowed hard, her stomach rolling again. She pressed the heel of her hand against her forehead, fighting to hold herself together. "If this gets out, Anna, it'll destroy my family for good. You don't understand what this town does with rumors. I'm begging you."

Anna placed a hand lightly on Tula's arm, a gesture of compassion rather than promise. "What I can tell you is this: I'll treat Lorene with dignity, and I won't share a word outside of the people who absolutely need to know. For her prenatal care. For the genetic counseling that she needs to do. That's the best I can give you."

Tula nodded, though the motion felt brittle. Her family's filth was now ink on paper, tucked into hospital files that could surface at any time. She felt the walls of Hart's Ridge closing in on her, squeezing out every damn ounce of self-respect she'd built since she'd left so long ago.

Chapter Thirty-Six

Tula had barely slept. She'd sat up most of the night with the light of her laptop glaring back at her, scrolling article after article until the words blurred. Search term after search term. "Pregnancy between siblings." "Risks of inbreeding." "Termination options."

By 3 a.m., she'd stopped clicking the links and just stared at the headlines, numb.

She'd learned too much. That children born to sibling parents have a significantly increased risk of serious genetic disorders, birth defects, and developmental problems ... increased homozygosity ... harmful recessive genes ... higher infant mortality rates ... congenital malformations ... metabolic disorders ... intellectual disabilities.

She rubbed her temples now, her stomach still sick.

Lorene. Her baby sister. Pregnant by their brother.

Tula had always known the family was broken, but this? This was something dark enough to make the old shame flare like a sunburn. She couldn't let Lorene go through with this. She had to talk her into terminating the pregnancy—if not for Lorene's sake, then for the child's.

Lorene had always been a little lost. She'd tailed around after Earl for her whole life, putting him on a pedestal. Her big brother that, more times than anyone can count, had used his fists to defend his sisters. But Lorene had had boyfriends. Many of them, as Tula could recall. Why would she do something so heinous? Allow herself to be used by Earl, who obviously had no compass of right and wrong.

Sick.

So damn sick.

She shoved the laptop into her bag and grabbed her keys. The sooner she got Lorene set up with a doctor who would hopefully talk her into terminating the pregnancy, the sooner she could get out of this hellhole town again.

But when she turned into her mother's rutted driveway, she slammed on the brakes.

Curtis and Earl were out front.

Two grown men, shirts off in the sticky morning heat, wearing what looked like homemade bulletproof vests—duct-taped nylon with hunks of metal shoved under the fabric. They were laughing like kids in a schoolyard, guns in hand. Curtis' toddler was sitting on the steps of their trailer, a red Popsicle dripping from his hands as he watched.

Earl fired first, the blast echoing off the tin roof of the carport. Curtis swaggered forward, chest puffed. The bullet hit the vest with a dull clank, and he threw his arms wide like a gladiator. "See? Told you it'd hold!"

Tula threw her door open. "Are you two out of your minds?" she shouted. "You're gonna kill each other!"

Curtis just grinned, swinging his pistol like a toy. "Lighten up, Homecoming Queen. We're stress-testing our gear."

"What gear?!" she snapped, stomping toward them. "That's not a vest, that's a death wish! And you've got a kid out here right under your nose."

Curtis fired, but this time the sound was sharper. Earl staggered back, eyes wide. His hands flew to his chest. Blood seeped between his fingers.

"Shit," Curtis muttered, the color draining from his face.

Tula froze. The bullet must've ricocheted off the corner of the plate, slipping past the duct tape. Earl dropped to his knees, gasping for air.

"Oh God," she whispered, fumbling for her phone. "I'm calling 911!"

In the frantic minutes that followed—sirens in the distance, Curtis pacing, hands in his hair—Tula found herself caught between two warring instincts.

She hated Earl. Hated what he had done to Lorene. Hated what they all represented. Part of her wanted him gone and thought this might be divine intervention. But another part—some stubborn, vestigial sibling loyalty—wanted him to live.

By the time the ambulance pulled up, she was shaking.

They loaded Earl in, still conscious but pale, his breathing wet and shallow. Curtis tried to climb in after him, but a paramedic shoved him back. "You can follow in your own vehicle," the man barked.

At the hospital, Tula stood in the hallway outside the trauma bay, arms crossed, while chaos unfolded around her. Over an hour later, the doctor emerged, stripping off his gloves.

"The bullet collapsed a lung," he said. "We've repaired it, but the slug's lodged in his back. It's safer to leave it for now. He'll need a few days' observation. Unfortunately, even though this was an accident, we must file a report. Someone from the sheriff's office will be here soon."

Tula just nodded. She would love to see Curtis in handcuffs.

Down the hall, Waylon had appeared, pale and tight-lipped. Lorene stood beside him, her arms crossed. Their mother, too, who was in full meltdown mode, clutching a balled-up tissue, sobbing about her "baby boy" in a voice so shrill it made Tula's teeth ache.

Lorene, on the other hand, looked bored. Almost vacant.

Tula watched her sister for a long moment. Lorene didn't look fazed by what had just happened. Maybe she was numb. Or maybe she'd already detached from all of it—the same way Tula had tried to do. Or maybe she was mentally ill.

Tula turned on her heel and walked out.

She couldn't do this anymore. Couldn't stay in Hart's Ridge, where her family's dysfunction spilled out onto the dirt like oil.

But first, she was going to finish what she'd started.

Get her mother situated. Take care of Lorene's problem. Talk Waylon into leaving. And then the two of them were getting the hell out of this town.

Chapter Thirty-Seven

Taylor pulled into the gravel turnout off Old Lakeview Road. It was their usual spot now—off the beaten path, out of sight, where they could talk without ears in the walls.

Shane was already there, sitting on the tailgate of his truck, phone pressed to his ear, tension carved into his face. When he saw her, he ended the call and hopped down to meet her. "Everything okay?"

She gave a half-shrug, ending her own phone conversation. "That was Anna. She's at the hospital. Said Earl Skaggs came in with a gunshot wound to the chest."

Shane blinked. "What?"

"Curtis shot him. They were playing with guns out in front of the house like idiots—wearing homemade bulletproof vests. One of the bullets caught Earl just off the edge of the plate and collapsed a lung."

"Jesus. Is he alive?"

"Yep. He'll be fine, but he's staying a few days. Anna says Mama Skaggs is losing her mind, Waylon was afraid, and Lorene looked like she couldn't care less."

Shane muttered something under his breath. "That family's like a bad horror film. Just when you think it's over ..."

"Yeah," Taylor said, rubbing her forehead. "Tula was there, too. Anna said she left right after the doctor reassured her that Earl would be fine, and that law enforcement was going to be up there."

"Well, hell. That's an easy aggravated assault felony arrest. Surprised I haven't heard anything about it on the radio. Sheriff know about this yet?"

Taylor shook her head.

"If he goes in on a felony arrest, maybe we can get a search warrant for his truck and his home." Shane said, opening the door of his truck.

He pulled out a thermos, offering her some.

She declined, then leaned against her vehicle. "That might be just what we need to get ahead of this thing before it swallows anyone else. Waylon's in deeper than we thought, and Quig and Lana—they didn't just die in the same few weeks by coincidence."

"I've been thinking about that," Shane said, flipping through his notepad. "Everything Waylon gave us—small cash deliveries, weird drop locations, no names, no receipts. It all feels like smoke."

"And smoke means fire," Taylor followed up, matter-of-factly. "The question is where."

He nodded. "You still tailing him?"

"I will, just as soon as he takes another shift. Tula said he might be willing to do one more drop. I'll stay back. No contact, just eyes. If he walks into something risky, I'm pulling him out."

"Good." Shane paused. "But if this operation's tied into something bigger—and I'm starting to believe it might be— Waylon could be the thread that unravels the whole thing. Or gets cut first."

"I know," Taylor said quietly. "That's why we're careful. We use him once, then get him the hell out. He's not like the rest of them, Shane. He and Tula are different. They don't deserve to be in this mess."

"I have something else to tell you."

The way he said it made her instantly on alert.

"What?"

"I decided to drive by the Lounge again late last night. I recognized a truck in the parking lot."

She waited for the axe to fall.

"It was your dad's," he said. "Think you can talk to him? Get some intel?"

Just when she thought things couldn't get worse, now her dad might be involved? That was not what Taylor was expecting at all.

"He might be innocent in it," she said finally. "Just stopping by."

Shane shrugged. "Maybe. I'll leave it up to you if you want to pretend like I never saw it. But he also might know something helpful."

They stood in silence for a few beats. The trees whispered in the breeze around them, like they were keeping secrets of their own.

Shane's voice dropped low. "I'd better get to the department, see what's going on with Curtis. I'll talk to you soon as I find out."

She pushed off the truck, the tension in her shoulders pulling tighter. If she were still at the department, she wouldn't have to wait on news. She'd have been the one doing the arrest. It was times like this that she missed the badge. Patience was never a virtue she'd been known to uphold.

"I'm headed to go on a video footage hunt again," she said, avoiding talking about her dad any further. "Someone near the crime scene had to have caught a clip of Quig's car going by. Maybe that gas station up the road. If that leads to nothing, I'll knock on some doors. See if anyone's doorbell cam caught anything. Surely I'll be able to find something. Jeez, these days you can't do anything without it being filmed somewhere or somehow."

Shane was already getting into his cab.

"Sounds like a plan. Talk at you later." He waved a goodbye and started the engine, then pulled out and onto the highway, where he gunned the motor, squealing the tires.

Why are men such little boys? Taylor thought, shaking her head at the plume of smoke he left behind, then thinking, *Why not?*, as she gunned her engine.

Chapter Thirty-Eight

There's no clean line between family and duty—only the blur of what you're willing to lose for each. Taylor pulled off the cracked asphalt road and onto the dirt path that led to her father's trailer. The weeds had grown high along the fence line again, and the mailbox leaned like it had finally given up standing watch. Diesel let out a low whine from the passenger seat, tail starting to thump at the familiar turn.

"Yeah, I know. You love him," Taylor muttered, cutting the engine. "You just don't know him like I do."

She stared through the windshield, taking in the sagging mobile home tucked beneath a canopy of pines. From a distance, it didn't look half-bad—not since Ellis and Cecil helped put on a new roof last spring, and built him a porch to replace the crumbling steps. The porch had even held flower boxes for a while. They'd tried. They all had.

Taylor grabbed Diesel's leash and stepped out, gravel crunching beneath her boots. She climbed the porch, knocked twice.

No answer.

She waited a full minute before using the key he always left hidden outside. Diesel trotted in ahead of her, nose twitching, tail still wagging.

The smell hit her first—stale grease and something sour underneath. The kitchen sink overflowed with dishes crusted in gravy and bits of food. The garbage can had a greasy sheen, surrounded by balled-up paper towels and crushed fast-food bags. Her eyes landed on an empty liquor bottle poking out from the top of the trash.

Her stomach dropped.

He was supposed to be sober.

Taylor stood frozen, hand still on the doorknob, Diesel hovering near her hip like he sensed the shift in energy.

She moved quietly toward the back room, pushing the door open with her foot. Her father was passed out on the bed, one arm flung over his eyes, the TV flickering static in the corner. He hadn't even heard her come in.

She turned back to the kitchen, yanked open the cabinet under the sink, and started cleaning. Dishes stacked in the drying rack. Spoiled leftovers tossed. The counter scrubbed with mechanical precision. Anything to keep from yelling.

She'd done this before. Too many times. And she just didn't have the bandwidth anymore.

When she finally slammed the trash lid closed, her father's voice rasped from the hall.

"Who's there?"

She didn't answer.

A moment later, he shuffled into the kitchen in wrinkled sweatpants and a VFW tee. His hair stuck out sideways. Diesel padded up to him, tail wagging harder now.

"Well, hey there, buddy," he murmured, crouching to scratch behind Diesel's ears. The dog leaned into it, thumping the floor.

Taylor crossed her arms. "You been drinking again?"

He froze, then slowly straightened. "It was just a little something for sleep. I've been having a rough week."

"You're always having a rough week. At least now I know why you've skipped the last few Sunday dinners."

"Tay—"

"No. Don't 'Tay' me." Her voice cracked despite her effort to keep it even. "You told me you were done. You swore on Johnny's grave."

He looked away, rubbing the back of his neck. At least he had the dignity to look ashamed. She knew from experience it would do no good to talk to him about his drinking. She would, however, let Cecil know and send him over later.

She exhaled and grabbed a chair. "I didn't come here to argue about the bottle. I came to ask about the Shuffle Lounge."

That caught his attention. "What about it?"

"You been going there?"

He shrugged. "Maybe once or twice."

She narrowed her eyes. "Don't lie. Shane saw your truck there last night."

He leaned back against the counter, face hardening. "What, now you got that scumbag spying on me?"

Taylor ignored that. "Are you gambling, Dad?"

"Just playing the machines a bit. Nothing serious. Jeez. Get out of my business, Taylor. I'm a grown man."

"You know they're supposed to follow the new regs, right? No cash payouts. Points only. Legal limits."

"Hell, I don't pay attention to that crap. I just play."

"Are they paying out?"

He scratched his beard. "Some places get around it. You know how it is."

She stared. "So it's shady."

He gave a long sigh. "You always think I'm part of something bad."

"I think you're not telling me everything. You working?"

He shook his head. "Ain't much out there for a busted-up knee and no references."

"Then how are you feeding the machines?"

He didn't answer.

She stood. "You know what? I can't do this. I've got my own family now. I've got my daughter and Alice and Sam—and a young woman died, Daddy. Quig is dead. And this thing—this 'small-town poker room' crap—it's bigger than you want to believe. Bigger than any of us thought."

He turned toward the dog, resting a hand on Diesel's head. "This world's changed, girl. You don't always get a clean fight anymore."

"No. But you can still pick a side."

She walked to the door. "Fine. I won't be cleaning up your messes anymore. Not literal or otherwise. I hope you figure it out, 'cause I'm done trying to save you."

Diesel followed her, pausing just long enough to look back, then trotted down the steps.

As Taylor got behind the wheel, she felt like her chest might cave in. Another thread fraying. Another loss she didn't have time to mourn.

And deep down, she knew—seeing Cate so happy with Ellis? It ate at him. He could act like it didn't, but it did. He'd never stopped loving her. Never stopped losing her. And now, in a town full of secrets, even her own father might be part of what she was unraveling.

Chapter Thirty-Nine

T he worst part wasn't the silence—it was knowing the truth was out there, just one door, one lie, one dead end away. The warm breeze stirred the edge of Taylor's notepad as she sat across from Shane at a secluded picnic table at the edge of Hardin Park. Kids' laughter echoed from the swings in the distance, but she barely heard it. Her mind was on Waylon. On Quig. On Lana. Three people connected to something much darker than anyone in Hart's Ridge wanted to admit.

She'd come up empty on finding any video footage from neighbors or businesses. Knocking on doors in the country was always dangerous, and this round had netted her a dressing down from one old farmer, and a small bite on her ankle from a Chihuahua who identified as a Rottweiler at another home.

Shane tapped at his laptop, the screen tilted to avoid the glare.

"I got something," he said, sliding it toward her.

Taylor leaned in.

"This came through the department's anonymous tip line this morning," Shane added. "I don't know who sent it, but it came with a return IP from a public library system in Gainesville. Someone's being careful."

The video loaded slowly. Grainy black-and-white footage taken from what appeared to be the back lot of Shuffle Lounge. The timestamp blinked: 10:42 p.m. – two nights before Quig's body was found. Someone had gotten nosey and taken a video.

Taylor's breath caught as the frame came into focus.

There she was—Quig—wearing a light hoodie, as she spoke to someone in the shadows. Seeing her looking lively made Taylor's heart lurch. It still seemed impossible that she was gone forever.

The man in the video stepped forward, and the camera caught his face full-on.

Curtis Skaggs.

"Son-of-a ... I knew it," Taylor murmured.

"He's agitated," Shane said. "Look at his hands. That's not just a disagreement. He's losing it."

The final few seconds showed Curtis lunging forward, finger stabbing the air as Quig backed away. Then she turned and stormed off toward the line of parked cars.

Shane closed the laptop and met her gaze. "We've got motive now. Maybe not proof of murder, but this puts him square in her orbit right before she died. Shows he's angry about something."

Taylor's jaw tightened. "Then it's time we paid Curtis another visit."

"I'll meet you there."

They headed for their separate vehicles.

Once there, Taylor waited outside the interview room while Shane got Curtis brought down. When they finally opened the door, he swaggered in like he owned the place, smirking under a fading bruise on his cheekbone.

"Look who it is," he drawled, slumping into the chair across from her. "The nosiest Gray sister of them all."

Taylor remained standing, arms crossed.

"I hear your charge was downgraded to reckless conduct, Curtis," she said, voice flat. "Not aggravated assault. Not attempted manslaughter. Just a misdemeanor. That right?"

Curtis grinned. "I didn't mean to hurt him. Hell, ain't my fault Earl's lungs are made of tissue paper."

Shane, leaning against the wall, cut in. "Actually, it is. You acted with gross negligence. Playing with guns like it's a game. You got lucky he didn't die."

Curtis shrugged. "Not dead. Not a problem."

Shane added, "You endangered everyone around you by consciously disregarding a substantial risk. You know—like firing live rounds into a homemade vest."

Curtis snorted, but his jaw clenched.

Taylor leaned in. "Funny, how someone with that same poor lack of judgment just happened to be in the parking lot with Quig the night she died."

Curtis' smile faltered. His fingers drummed on the metal table.

"We know you were there," she said quietly. "And we know you were angry. She was going to blow up your little side hustle, wasn't she?"

"No idea what you're talking about," he muttered, but there was a flicker in his eyes. Just for a second before he shuttered them again.

"You see someone named Lana lately?" Taylor asked next. "She was trying to help us, too, but that was curiously put to a stop."

His eyes narrowed, lips twitching.

"Don't know anyone by that name," he lied.

"What about Marcus Jenks?"

"Nope. Him either."

"Yeah, I think you do," Taylor said.

Shane opened his mouth, but Taylor gave him a small shake of her head.

They heard keys jangling and a knock at the door. Penner poked his head inside.

"He's been sprung," he said, sounding apologetic.

Curtis looked from one to the other, then pushed his chair back with a smile. "I guess that means we're done here. It's been good to chat, but I have other appointments to take care of."

Shane glared at him, and Taylor could see the tick in his jaw pulsating.

"That's fine, Curtis" she said, diffusing the situation. "The way you treat Waylon, he's going to talk eventually, you know. And when he does ... I hope you've got more than a smart mouth to protect yourself."

The bailiff escorted Curtis out of the room. Taylor and Shane followed and, when they neared the bond counter, they heard stomping footsteps and raised voices.

There, at the end of the hall, stood Dixie Skaggs, decked out in leopard-print leggings, a stained shirt, and fury in her eyes as she held onto her walker. Earl, pale and hunched, stood behind her with gauze still visible under his shirt.

"If y'all think you can keep one of mine," Dixie hissed when she saw Taylor, "think again."

Taylor ignored her, but her eyes flicked to the stack of cash being handed to the bail clerk. Small bills. Crumpled. Someone had been scraping together what they had.

She glanced at Shane. "Where are they getting this kind of money?"

He shook his head.

Dixie leaned in, jabbing a nicotine-stained finger toward

Taylor. "Don't worry about it. You best stop pokin' your nose in our business. We handle our own."

Taylor smiled tightly. "Yeah. I can tell. Real family values."

Curtis sneered, but Taylor caught the tremble in his hand as he took the receipt from the clerk. Then he stepped through the double doors, a free man—for now—and flashed them both a smug smile.

Taylor's stomach churned.

This wasn't over.

Not even close.

Chapter Forty

Taylor turned off the main road and onto the long gravel drive leading up to the Dawkins' place.

The old oaks still framed the lane, but the house at the end looked newer, cleaner. The paint on the siding gleamed, the porch had fresh latticework, and flower boxes hung beneath the windows. Someone had been spending both money and time.

She parked beside the mailbox and sat for a moment, watching a gust of wind lift the edge of the sheriff's American flag. A motorhome sat in the side drive—sleek, silver, and brand-new, with a small SUV hitched behind it. Both still had temporary dealer tags.

A prickle of unease stirred low in her stomach. Shane would be furious that she'd come out here, especially without his approval. But he'd never understand the relationship that she had with the sheriff.

It was time to figure out why he wouldn't be more helpful.

When she stepped out, the air smelled like cut grass and gasoline. The front door opened before she reached the porch.

"Well, look who it is." Patty Dawkins smiled, surprise flickering across her face. "Taylor Gray, in person. I was just saying the other day, we never see you anymore."

"Hey, Patty," Taylor said. "Sorry to drop by unannounced."

"Oh, you're fine. Matt's out in his shop. He practically lives in there these days—got himself a little museum, I swear. Go on through the side gate."

"Appreciate it," Taylor said, then hesitated. "You've done a lot with the place."

Patty's smile brightened, proud and nervous at once. "We finally decided it was time to enjoy life a little, you know? He's talking about retirement now, but don't let him fool you. I predict that he'll work until he falls over."

"Retirement?" Taylor repeated, but Patty waved her off.

"Oh, I probably shouldn't have said anything."

From inside, a voice called, "Patty! You see who's out there?"

She jumped slightly. "Go on back, honey. He'll be glad to see you."

Taylor followed the gravel path toward the shop.

It wasn't the same old tin shed she remembered. This one was neat, freshly painted, with a metal sign over the door that read MAD DOG'S GARAGE in bold block letters. She pushed the door open and stepped into cool, filtered air.

The shop was immaculate—everything in its place. A wall of neatly arranged tools, polished work surfaces, even a recliner in one corner with a small TV and mini fridge. The walls were lined with framed photos: Dawkins in his glory days as the Hart's Ridge High quarterback, "Mad Dog Matt Leads Team to State!" headlines, his old jersey framed in a shadow box.

It looked less like a workspace and more like a shrine to better years.

"Well, I'll be," Dawkins said, turning from his workbench

with a grin that reached his eyes but not quite his tone. "If it ain't Taylor Gray herself. You slumming it, or just missing the smell of motor oil?"

She flashed back to the many times he'd fixed her cars for her when she was younger. Brakes. A water pump, once.

Repairs that she couldn't afford, so he'd stepped in and done them, helping her the way her father should've been sober enough to do.

"Just came to talk," she said. She was going to try to skirt around Quig's case as much as possible, unless otherwise forced to bring it up.

"Talk, huh?" He wiped his hands on a rag and nodded toward a stool. "Then talk."

"I wanted to ask about Curtis Skaggs."

His expression didn't change, but his shoulders shifted slightly. "That situation's handled."

"Handled how? I heard the charge got dropped down to a misdemeanor."

"Reckless conduct," he said, matter of fact. "That's all it ever was. Two dumb boys showing off. Earl's gonna make a full recovery, thank God."

"Lucky for Curtis," Taylor said, her tone even. "Shooting your brother in the chest usually earns a little more than a slap on the wrist."

He chuckled softly, shaking his head. "Oh, hell. You know how those boys are. None of 'em ever learned what good judgment looks like. And Earl—well, he'd never testify. He's too proud for that. In their world, testifying against your own is worse than the crime itself."

"Convenient," Taylor murmured.

Dawkins gave her a sideways glance, one brow lifting. "You saying something?"

"I'm saying it seems like the Skaggs family keeps walking

away clean while everyone around them winds up hurt or dead. Have you ever heard of a Marcus Jenks?"

He leaned against the workbench, casual, almost amused as he dodged the question. "You've always had that fire. Don't lose it. But sometimes a thing's not corruption, Taylor—it's just life being messy."

"Life didn't shoot Earl," she said quietly. "Curtis did. And he was the last person seen arguing with Quig the night she died."

"Ah," Dawkins said, rubbing his jaw. "We're back to that again."

"I never let it go," she said.

"I can tell." His smile didn't waver, but something in his eyes cooled. "Listen, I know how hard that one hit you. She was your friend. But you can't chase ghosts forever. We've got no evidence, no witnesses, and whatever was left burned in that car."

Taylor swallowed her frustration. "There are always other paths to investigations."

That made him laugh, quiet but sharp. "You always did think everything had a conspiracy behind it."

She didn't take the bait. "You used to tell me not to back off when something didn't add up. Remember that? Follow my gut. Rely on instinct."

He smiled faintly. "Yeah, well, I used to tell you a lot of things. Didn't mean I expected you to go tearing through every locked door in the county."

She started to reply, but he lifted a hand gently.

"I mean that kindly," he said. "You've always been driven, Taylor. That's why you went as far as you did. Hell, you wouldn't even have made it into investigations if I hadn't put you there with Weaver. You could've been doing school traffic or pencil-pushing your whole career, like Penner. I gave you that chance, in case you've forgotten."

The words were soft, friendly on the surface—but underneath, there was a warning, and it landed heavy.

"I remember," Taylor said.

"Good," Dawkins said with a small nod. "Because we all look out for our own here. That's what keeps Hart's Ridge steady. Loyalty. Respect. Knowing when to hold your cards and when to fold 'em."

He smiled as if they were talking about poker, but the message was clear enough: don't push too far.

Taylor glanced around again, taking in the high-end coffee machine on the counter, the spotless Harley, the neat rows of chrome tools. Then, through the window, the reflection of that brand-new motorhome gleamed like a warning beacon.

"Looks like life's treating you well," she said.

He shrugged, reaching for his tea. "Thirty-five years in the job. Figured I'd finally make the place look like I've done something with it."

"Patty mentioned you might be retiring soon."

That earned a flicker of something across his face. Not surprise exactly—just calculation. "Did she now?"

"She did. How come I haven't heard about it?"

He set the tea down carefully. "No one has. Not official yet. Got a few loose ends to tie up. Don't want talk of that out there, either."

"Must feel strange," Taylor said softly. "Letting go after all these years."

He gave a slow nod. "A little. But a man knows when it's time. This town's changing. Too many young faces with big ideas." He looked at her then, holding her gaze a beat too long. "Not all of 'em bad, mind you."

She smiled thinly. "That almost sounded like a compliment."

"It was," he said. "You've come a long way, Taylor. You should be proud. Some of us older dogs like to think we helped shape that."

Her pulse ticked up. There it was again—gentle, polished, and perfectly placed.

"Yes, you helped shape my life," she said, realizing he wanted verbal confirmation.

He nodded, satisfied. "Then you know I've always had your back. Still do."

She wanted to believe that. But the warmth in his voice now felt too smooth—like honey masking something sour.

"Well," she said finally, pushing off the stool, "I won't keep you."

He smiled. "You never do. But it's good seeing you, Taylor. Just try not to chase every dark corner. Sometimes they're just shadows."

"Sometimes," she said. "And sometimes shadows mean there's something standing in the light."

Dawkins chuckled. "Still poetic. Always liked that about you."

As she walked toward the door, his voice followed her, calm and measured. "Don't lose sleep over the Skaggs mess. It'll sort itself out."

She turned slightly. "That's the problem, Sheriff. It already has—just not the way it should."

He didn't answer, only smiled, that same practiced grin that had once made her feel safe.

Outside, the afternoon light glinted off the motorhome. She paused beside it, running her fingers along the shiny chrome. The air smelled faintly of diesel and something artificial—new leather, maybe.

When she looked back, Dawkins was standing in the doorway of his shop, hand lifted in an easy wave, the perfect image of a good man winding down a good career.

But as she drove away, her chest felt hollow. The relationship she'd always had with the sheriff was slowly swirling the drain, and it didn't feel good.

Chapter Forty-One

Tula lay the phone on the counter, putting it on speaker as she rinsed out a coffee mug in the sink. After nearly an hour on hold, the conversation was even more frustrating than the wait.

"I understand, but she's not gonna fill out a form," she told the woman from Meals on Wheels. "She's not even gonna open the door unless the delivery person's someone she knows or who brings her a damn cigarette."

A pause.

"No, I'm not trying to be difficult. I'm trying to be honest. Look, just start her off with two days a week. I'll work on getting her used to the idea."

She shut off the faucet and dried her hands on a towel just as the front screen door creaked open. Waylon stepped in, his hoodie pulled low despite the warm breeze outside. His left eye was still tinged yellow around the edge, the remains of a black eye fading, but the deeper bruises were in his posture—stiff, withdrawn, like he'd folded in on himself.

Tula turned and picked up the phone. "Okay, thank you. I'll talk to her and get the paperwork back."

She clicked off and raised an eyebrow. "Well, look who's alive."

Waylon gave a half-smile, but it didn't reach his eyes. "You really tryin' to get her signed up for that old people food delivery thing?"

"Trying, is the key word."

"She don't even need it," he muttered. "Mama's got money. Always has."

Tula paused, towel in hand. "What do you mean, she's got money?"

He shifted his weight. "Just ... she's not broke, is all. Don't mean she's spendin' it smart, but it ain't like she's starving."

Tula stared at him for a beat, then tossed the towel on the counter. "Come on. Let's get out of here and go for a drive."

The botanical garden sat on the edge of Hart's Ridge, nestled beside a stream and shaded by a canopy of ancient oaks. It wasn't big or flashy like the ones in bigger cities, but it had its own kind of magic. They wandered through winding gravel paths bordered by day lilies and camellias. Wooden sculptures stood nestled in beds of greenery—owls carved into tree stumps, a raccoon peeking out of a hollowed log. One old barn had been converted into a "bug hotel" with handmade signs painted by local kids.

They walked quietly for a while, past a gazebo overgrown with wisteria and a small koi pond where fat orange fish floated lazily beneath lily pads.

When they reached the old bench near the edge of the garden, Tula gestured for him to sit.

He did.

She waited, letting the silence stretch. Birds chirped overhead. Somewhere a wind chime clinked softly.

Waylon let out a lengthy sigh. "Tula, why are we here? You going to lecture me? We could've done this in the truck."

"I didn't ask you to come so I could nag," she said finally. "I just ... I want to understand. You're not a bad kid, Waylon."

"I didn't say I was," he mumbled.

She looked at him. "You're scared. And that's fair. But I need you to know something. You're safe with me. Always. You're my brother. I'd lay my life down for you. You hear me?"

He didn't answer.

"I know you think staying quiet is the smart move," she went on, "but an innocent girl is dead. Quig didn't deserve what happened to her. What if it had been me, Waylon? What if someone killed me and burned me in a car, and the only person who knew anything about it decided to stay quiet?"

His eyes flicked to hers, the hint of moisture gathering.

"You wouldn't, right?" she pushed. "You'd want someone to fight for me. To find the truth. You know more. I can feel it."

He swallowed hard.

"Quig's babies lost their mama," Tula said softly. "They're left with nothing but a broken system and two sorry excuses for fathers."

Waylon stared at the ground. "I didn't kill her."

"I know," she said. "But I think you know who did."

He was quiet a long moment. Then he whispered, "Curtis was pissed. Said she was poking around. Asking too many questions."

Tula's chest clenched.

"She told him she was done," Waylon added. "Said she didn't want to risk anything that could screw up her custody. She was working hard to get her kids back."

"What did Curtis say?"

"Called her a traitor. Said she was weak and stupid if she thought she could just walk away."

"Did you see them arguing?"

He nodded. "In the parking lot. The night she died. He

grabbed her arm. She pulled away. Told him he didn't scare her."

"And?"

He went still. "She left. I thought that was the end of it. That's all I know."

Tula placed a hand on his. "Thank you for telling me."

She stood up and pulled out her phone.

"Who you calling?" He looked concerned.

"Taylor Gray. She needs to hear this."

Waylon looked down at the ground, face pale. "She gonna arrest him?"

Tula hesitated. "I don't know. But we're gonna make damn sure he never hurts anyone else again."

Chapter Forty-Two

Taylor and Shane turned off the main road and bounced down the dirt lane that led to the Skaggs property. The air hung thick and humid, the smell of hot dogs and motor oil drifting on the wind. They parked a few yards from the crooked trailer that had seen better decades. It appeared there were two new pit bulls, chained to a tree, their heavy collars rattling as they barked.

Cate would be really irritated.

Curtis Skaggs sat shirtless on the front steps, beer in hand, a smirk on his face. A little boy darted around the yard in a pair of sagging shorts, his face sticky with red Popsicle juice. He ran dangerously close to one of the pit bulls, who lunged against its chain, growling.

Taylor's heart clenched. "That chain's gonna snap one day," she muttered under her breath. "And the dog."

"Wouldn't surprise me," Shane said grimly as they climbed out of the car.

The screen door creaked open behind Curtis, and the rest of the Skaggs clan spilled into view—Mama Skaggs on her walker, Lorene slumped against the rail, chewing gum, Earl half in shadow, looking like he hadn't slept since his gunshot wound. His dirty wife-beater tank top didn't hide the crusty-looking bandage on his chest, and he was paler than usual.

Waylon stood a little apart, on the far end of the porch, eyes startled and face pale. Tula wasn't there. Taylor had advised her not to come, so that she didn't get the blame for their visit.

Taylor and Shane approached slowly.

Curtis grinned, leaning back on one elbow. "Well, if it ain't my two biggest fans. Come to congratulate me on being reunited with my family so quickly?"

"Not exactly," Shane said evenly. "We've got some more questions about the night Quig Gallagher died."

The laughter drained from Curtis' face, replaced by that familiar smirk that never quite reached his eyes. "Told y'all before, I don't know nothin' about that. Never even knew the girl."

"Funny," Taylor said, "because someone saw you and Quig arguing in the parking lot behind the Shuffle Lounge."

Curtis' eyes flickered. "People say all kinds of things after a few drinks."

"Yeah, but this one had proof," Shane said, pulling his phone from his jacket pocket. He tapped the screen, and grainy footage filled it. "This came in from the anonymous tip line this morning."

Curtis' smirk froze as the black-and-white video played— Quig, animated, angry, pointing at him. Then Curtis lunging forward, finger in her face as he raged. The rest of the porch had gone quiet, all eyes on the little screen. Even the kid had stopped running, watching from behind the railing, the Popsicle melting down his hand.

"Don't you need permission to come bothering my kids?" Dixie said, glaring at them from her perch. "A warrant or something?"

"Why? Have they done something else illegal?" Shane retorted.

"That's you, isn't it, Curtis?" Taylor asked softly, ignoring the matriarch.

Curtis laughed, but it came out hollow. "That could be anybody."

"Could be," Shane said. "Except it isn't."

The screen door slammed. The child's mother—a tired-looking young woman in cutoff shorts and a tank top—stepped out and walked down the porch steps. "Curtis, get your son inside," she said sharply. The boy giggled and ran the opposite direction, straight toward the pit bull.

Taylor's heart lurched. "Hey!" she shouted, but the girlfriend scooped the boy up just as the dog snapped at the air. The child screamed, the pit bull barked louder. The chaos spilled over like a match hitting oil.

Earl stepped down from the porch, his chest puffed out. "You don't come out here accusing my family of nothin'. Get the hell off our property!"

Shane lifted a calming hand. "We're not here to cause trouble, Earl. Just asking questions."

Earl shoved him—hard enough that it wasn't a misunderstanding. Harder than he should've been able to do, considering his recent injury.

Shane reacted faster than Taylor could blink. He caught Earl's wrist, pivoted, and in one fluid motion brought him down to the dirt with a heavy thud. Earl let out a grunt of pain, face pressed into the ground.

That was all it took.

Curtis roared, launching himself off the steps toward Shane. Waylon lunged after him, grabbing Curtis around the shoulders. "Stop it! Stop!"

The dogs went wild, straining against their chains. Dixie

screamed. The little boy started crying, wailing so loud it split the humid air. Lorene chortled with laughter.

Taylor's instincts kicked in. She drew her pistol, fired one shot straight into the air.

The crack echoed through the yard. Everything froze.

"Enough!" she shouted. "Everybody stand down!"

The chaos stilled—except for the child's sobs. Shane had Earl pinned, handcuffs snapping around his wrists. Curtis stood breathing hard, his chest rising and falling, eyes wild as Waylon stood between him and everyone else.

Shane hauled Earl up by the arm. "You're under arrest for assaulting an officer. You, too, Curtis. Taylor, cuff him."

She didn't get a chance before Curtis moved quickly out of reach.

"Bullshit!" Dixie shouted, slapping the porch rail. "You can't take them!"

Taylor's gaze stayed locked on the woman as she considered the best way to go after Curtis. "You want to add resisting arrest to your sons' charges? You'd better tell them to go peacefully."

Curtis spat into the dirt. "I ain't going nowhere. This is crap. Y'all don't know what you're talkin' about. Quig was a damn liar, anyway."

Shane's voice was calm but sharp. "Maybe so, but she's not the one who got caught on video threatening her the night she died."

Curtis' jaw flexed. "I told her to just do her job and keep her mouth shut, but, no, she couldn't even handle that. She was gonna blow up everything—she—"

He stopped, realization flashing across his face.

Taylor's voice was steady. "Go ahead, Curtis. She was gonna blow up what?"

He stared at her, eyes narrowing. "Nothing. I didn't say anything."

"Sounded like the beginning of a confession to me," Shane said quietly.

Curtis barked out a short laugh. "Nah. You don't know nothin'."

But Waylon did. He was shaking now, fists clenched. "You should've left her alone," he said suddenly, voice cracking. "She had three kids, Curtis. Three! Now they ain't got nobody—no mama, no daddy—they'll be as screwed up as we are!"

"Shut up," Earl growled from where Shane held him.

But Waylon wasn't stopping. Tears streaked his dirty face. "You think I wanted any of this? I just wanted to make some money, man! Deliver packages, stay out of trouble—but you dragged me in! You dragged all of us in!"

Curtis turned on him, voice low and deadly. "You keep your damn mouth shut, boy. You talk, and you go down with me."

Earl nodded toward him, sneering. "You'd better listen, little bro. Snitches get stitches."

Lorene leaned against the rail, smirking. "He ain't lyin', Waylon. Keep it zipped."

Waylon's whole body shook, but he didn't speak again.

Taylor's stomach turned. She holstered her gun slowly, watching the broken family tableau before her—the crying child, the snarling dogs, the grown men acting like little boys, the old matriarch glaring daggers.

Curtis stomped past her, into the trailer, slamming the door and locking it behind him.

It was the epitome of a certified shit show.

"Let's go," Shane said, pulling Earl toward the car. "We'll be back with a warrant for Curtis. That video evidence is exactly what we needed. Tell him don't go anywhere."

A window opened above them, and Curtis peeked out. He spread his arms, mocking. "I won't' be going anywhere, my friend. Mark my words."

Taylor didn't answer. She just turned away, her boots crunching through the dirt.

Behind her, she heard the pit bulls start barking again—loud, angry, relentless.

And somewhere in that noise, she could've sworn she heard Waylon crying quietly, his voice breaking through the chaos as he staggered back into the house.

Chapter Forty-Three

Taylor had learned to live with frustration—it was practically part of the job. But patience? That was harder. Especially when the truth was close enough to taste but still out of reach. With Sam already gone to work at the garage for the day, the house was quiet except for the low hum of the refrigerator and the steady rhythm of rain against the back porch.

She sat at the kitchen table, looking at her laptop, Shane in the chair opposite her. The confrontation at the Skaggs place kept replaying in her head like a loop she couldn't pause. Waylon's face. His tears. The way Curtis had shouted that Quig was "gonna blow up everything."

She reached for her tea, cold now, and took a sip anyway.

The bitterness helped her think.

Judge Crawford had denied an arrest warrant for Curtis, stating not enough evidence. It hadn't surprised her. He was right. They needed more.

At least Earl was in jail, until the next morning, anyway, when his bond would be set.

Shane hunched over his own laptop, elbows propped on his

knees. The two of them looked like detectives out of time, two ghosts still chasing the truth long after everyone else had given up.

"I pulled the DFC Hospitality Group, LLC, and found a few more businesses under their umbrella."

Taylor frowned. "What else?"

Shane scrolled, the light flickering across his face. "Four properties across the county. Shuffle Lounge, a dive bar in Lavonia, a short-term rental company, and a local vending business. All cash-heavy."

Her brain clicked into motion. "That's the same place Waylon told me about. They ran me out of there. Let's focus on what could've gotten her into trouble at the Shuffle." She stood, pacing the small room. The floor creaked under her feet. "She was trying to save money for a custody attorney. Lana said they paid in cash and didn't track hours. Maybe Quig stumbled onto the books—or off-the-record deposits."

Shane's fingers flew over the keyboard. "Hold on ... here we go. DFC Hospitality is registered out of a P.O. box in Hart's Ridge."

He read off the number. Taylor froze mid-step.

"Repeat that," she said.

"P.O. box seventy-two."

She leaned forward, pulse hammering. "That's Dawkins' box. He's used it for years—for campaign mail, fundraisers, even county correspondence before the new address system. I checked it for him a lot, years ago."

Shane turned the laptop toward her. "Registered agent name is Marcus Jenks."

Taylor blinked. "Weird."

"Can't find much about him online, either. No social media, no driver's license renewal since 2014. He's a ghost."

Taylor grabbed a notepad and scribbled. "What about tax records?"

Shane clicked through a few screens, muttering. "Filed on time every year. Perfect quarterly payments. No payroll, no debts, no assets listed other than the properties."

"Too clean," she said. "Whoever this Marcus Jenks is, he's not real."

Her mind went back to Dawkins' shop—the perfectly aligned tools, the framed newspaper clippings, the expensive coffee machine.

"Wait." She moved to her filing cabinet and yanked open the bottom drawer, fingers rifling through old folders until she found what she was looking for: a copy of an old budget approval form from her days as deputy. Dawkins' signature was scrawled at the bottom.

She slid it across to Shane. "Pull up Jenks' electronic filing for DFC. Check the signature block."

He did. Then he looked at her, eyes widening. "Holy shit."

The handwriting was identical. Same swooping M, same narrow D.

Taylor's throat went dry. "Marcus Jenks ... is Matt Dawkins."

For a long moment, neither of them spoke. The only sound was the steady patter of rain against the window.

Shane leaned back in his chair, running a hand through his hair. "That old bastard built an empire right under everyone's nose."

She sank into her seat, numb. It was nearly unbelievable. The sheriff, her unofficial hero. Stand-in father figure. The man she trusted more than her real dad.

"We don't know that for sure, yet." She had to defend him.

How could he be a criminal? More importantly, how could she have misjudged so badly?

Shane continued. "This is what I think. Dawkins set up the LLC. Laundered cash from the poker machines through fake business accounts. Probably used guys like Curtis and Waylon to move the money so it never touched his hands."

"And Quig found out," Shane said.

Taylor nodded slowly. "She saw his name somewhere. Overheard it. Maybe she didn't even realize what it meant until too late." Her chest tightened. She could almost hear Quig's voice again—nervous, hopeful, promising she was finally getting her life back together.

"I'll just bet she was going to tell me," Taylor whispered. "She was going to blow the whistle. I know it."

"And Dawkins made sure she didn't," Shane said quietly.

The truth settled between them like a weight.

She thought of something that had been niggling at her. "If we're right about money laundering, we still don't know where it's coming from. Whose money is it?"

"That's going to take longer to figure out," Shane said. "And more resources than just you and I."

Taylor turned toward the window, watching the rain streak down the glass. "We can't take this to the department. Dawkins still has people loyal to him there. If this gets out before we're ready, Waylon's as good as dead."

Shane exhaled. "So, what do we do?"

"We hold it," she said, voice low and steady. "We build around it. Quig's video, Waylon's testimony, the LLC, the P.O. box—every thread that points to Dawkins. When we've got enough, we take it straight to the state bureau. But not yet."

Shane studied her face. "You realize what you're saying, right? You're going up against the man who trained half this department."

"No, he trained *most* of the department," she said. "This town loves that man. He also taught me everything I know about covering tracks. He's good, and that's how he's made this thing work. As much as he's done for me, and as much affection as I carry for him, it's more important that justice is done."

She stood and crossed to the table, gathering the printouts and shoving them into a folder marked DFC.

On the cover, she wrote four words in bold ink: DO NOT TRUST ANYONE.

Then she looked at Shane, her voice barely above a whisper.

"He thinks he's going to get away with it. But we're not done."

The thunder rolled outside, slow and distant, like a warning. Then Taylor's phone buzzed with a text message. She looked to see Tula's name on the screen.

Come to the cabin. Waylon wants to talk.

Chapter Forty-Four

The rain hadn't let up by the time Taylor and Shane reached Tula's cabin. The dirt road had turned to sludge, their headlights catching sheets of water that slashed sideways through the night.

Shane killed the engine and sat for a moment, watching the soft glow of light coming from Tula's living room window. The silhouette of two figures moved behind the curtain—Tula and Waylon.

"Ready?" Shane asked, though his voice said he wasn't sure he was.

Taylor nodded, gripping the folder in her lap. "Let's get this done before he changes his mind."

They stepped out into the rain, hurrying up the short path to the porch. Tula opened the door before Taylor could knock. Her face was pale, her hair pulled back in a messy knot.

"He's not doing great," she whispered. "Hasn't eaten all day. Just sits there staring at the fire."

Taylor gave a small nod. "We'll be gentle."

Inside, the air was warm but heavy. A fire crackled in the stone hearth, throwing gold light across the cabin's wooden walls. Waylon sat on the couch, arms folded tight, staring at the flames like they might answer him if he waited long enough.

When he saw them, he blinked fast, rubbing at his eyes with the heel of his hand.

"Hey, buddy," Shane said carefully, taking the chair opposite. "Mind if we sit a minute?"

Waylon gave a small nod but didn't look up.

Taylor set her folder on the coffee table. "Thank you for calling us," she said. "We just need to understand what really happened with Quig."

His throat worked, but no sound came out.

Tula perched on the arm of the couch beside him, a hand resting lightly on his shoulder. "Tell her, Way. You don't have to carry this by yourself anymore."

He looked at her, his eyes raw. "It won't change nothin'."

"It might," Taylor said softly. "It might change everything."

He took a long breath, shaking. "She ... Quig ... she was just tryin' to do right. Said she found somethin'—something big—when she was working over at that diner. The one off Highway 17. She was cleaning after hours. In the back room, she found a file in the trash with a name on it—DFC Hospitality Group. She didn't know what it was, but she thought it was connected to the poker machines at Shuffle."

Taylor's pulse quickened. "Did she mention any names?"

Waylon nodded weakly. "She said there was a man's name on the paperwork. Marcus Jenks. But she laughed when she said it—said she knew that name from somewhere. She was gonna come see you, Taylor. She said she finally had proof."

Taylor's heart twisted. She knew it. "What happened next?"

"I told Curtis about it," Waylon said, voice cracking. "I didn't mean to. I just ... he was gettin' suspicious. Asked why Quig was actin' strange. I said she'd found something. Thought maybe, if I told him, he'd calm down. But he freaked out."

He stared into the fire, his face hollow. "Said she'd ruin everything. That the whole group—and I didn't know who he was talking about—would lose everything if this got out. I didn't know what he meant then. But now I do."

Tula's hand tightened on his shoulder. "What did he do, Waylon?"

His breath came out in shudders. "He went after her. That night. Said he just wanted to scare her. But she must've argued with him and—I think he snapped."

The sound of rain on the roof filled the long silence that followed.

Shane spoke first, his voice low. "Then what?"

Waylon swallowed hard. "The next morning, he showed up at Shuffle. I was supposed to make a drop that night—just envelopes, like always—but, when I got there, the back door was open. Curtis was pacing, freaked out, when Sheriff Dawkins pulled up. They told me to go inside, but I heard them talking. Dawkins told him to shut up and no one would figure it out."

Taylor leaned forward. "You heard him say that?"

"Yes, ma'am. He said, 'No evidence, no arrest. It's done.' I didn't see what they did after that. I left. But I know Curtis did it. I just know it." He dropped his head into his hands. "I can't sleep without hearin' her voice. I keep seeing her there, burned in that car, and keep thinkin' about her kids. They're never gonna know why their mama didn't come home."

Tula slid down beside him, wrapping an arm around his shoulders. He sobbed against her, raw and unfiltered.

Taylor looked away, blinking hard.

Across the firelight, Shane sat rigid, jaw tight.

When the sobs finally quieted, Taylor stood and crouched in front of Waylon. "Listen to me. You didn't kill her. But you can help make it right. We're going to get this information to the state, to people outside Hart's Ridge. Curtis won't touch you again. Not if I can help it."

He looked up at her, eyes red and shining. "You can't stop him. He's got the law behind him. I really think that the sheriff's in his pocket."

Taylor shook her head slowly. "Not for long. You just need to keep your mouth shut a little longer. Then you'll need to be a witness. You'll be asked to testify, Waylon. Can you do that?"

He didn't look convinced, but he nodded, defeated.

Shane rose, glancing at Taylor. "We should let him rest."

"I'll call Cecil, see if he can come stay with y'all tonight. Keep vigil with his shotgun," Taylor said.

Tula nodded in agreement.

Outside, the rain had softened to a steady drizzle. When they reached the porch, Taylor stopped, gripping the railing.

"I keep hearing that line," she said quietly. "'No evidence, no arrest.'"

Shane zipped his jacket. "Sheriff Dawkins told Curtis how to clean it up. The fire, fingerprints—he made it all go away."

"And now he plans to ride off into the sunset with a new name and a pocket full of laundered money. I can't let him do that. What if he's responsible for Quig's death?"

Shane turned toward her. "I really don't think he'll do that, but, just in case, we'll take what we got to state police tomorrow. Involve them so we can get this buttoned down. You have to consider that Curtis did the murder on his own, too. We'll give Dawkins the benefit of the doubt until Skaggs starts talking."

"*If* he starts talking," Taylor added.

The rain eased, leaving only the quiet drip from the eaves and the distant sound of frogs starting their nightly chorus. Taylor looked out across the dark tree line, her reflection faint in the wet glass of her truck window. She recalled the way that the sheriff had talked to her at his shop. As though he thought no one would ever come after him. He'd treated her like the same snot-nosed kid he'd introduced himself to when she was in high school.

She'd show him. When she was ready, she'd make him understand that loyalty was important, but never before the pursuit of justice.

"Next time," she murmured, "we don't come knocking at the sheriff's house. We kick the damn door in." On those words, the sky opened again, and rain poured down, droplets mixing with the tears of betrayal on her face, and the pain of feeling disillusioned and let down. Sheriff Dawkins had just proved to her that there was no such thing as heroes in this world.

Chapter Forty-Five

The worst kind of heartbreak isn't sudden—it's the kind that creeps in when someone you trust makes you doubt what you saw in them all along. The morning after, the storm broke clear and sharp, the kind of day that looked clean but wasn't. The air still smelled like wet pine and diesel, and the puddles along the edge of Dawkins' drive reflected the sky like broken mirrors.

Taylor had woken feeling drained, and uncertain. Early enough to get the worm, she rolled out of bed, got Lennon organized, and headed over. Shane didn't know she was going, and he'd be angry, but, before they went to the state police, she had to be sure. And to be sure, she had to face the sheriff.

The motorhome sat in the open, sunlight flashing off the chrome. A small SUV hitched to the back, packed to the roof. The engine idled low and steady.

She parked behind it and stepped out. Her chest felt tight, her mind still replaying Waylon's voice:

He said, no body, no story. We clean it up now, and it's done.

She and the sheriff had such a long history. He'd been good to her. Changed her life, actually. She'd decided that she owed him at least a chance to explain. To prove to her that what they'd discovered wasn't true, that he was still the honorable man that everyone in Hart County believed him to be.

Quickly, before anyone could see, she took a quick photo of the license plate on the car being towed, and the motorhome, then slipped her phone back into her pocket.

Patty Dawkins came out to the porch. "Taylor," she said weakly. "Glad you stopped by so early. We're headed out in just a few minutes."

"Where?"

"I'm not supposed to tell anyone," She looked over Taylor's shoulder toward the motorhome, as if worried he might hear her. "But I'm sure he won't mind if it's just you. Matt has surprised me with a whole voyage planned. We'll end up in California to see the Redwoods. First stop is Asheville, then westward bound. I can't understand why he wants to go now— before his official retirement—but he said it was time. That this town doesn't deserve him anymore."

Taylor nodded, jaw clenched. "Mind if I talk to him before y'all leave?"

Patty hesitated, then stepped aside. "Go right ahead. I'm glad you came to say goodbye."

Taylor walked toward the open shop door. The scent of motor oil, coffee, and sawdust met her at the threshold.

Dawkins was inside, sleeves rolled up, polishing one of his trophies from his football days—"Mad Dog Matt" forever frozen in time, grinning from a framed newspaper cover.

He didn't turn when she entered. "Figured you'd show up," he said.

"Figured you'd be gone by now."

"Soon." He set the trophy down carefully, almost tender. "Can't leave without saying goodbye. Got some loose ends to tie up."

Taylor's voice was even. "Goodbye implies you're coming back."

He smiled faintly. "Who knows. Might wander back through someday. You never can tell."

"You planning to turn yourself in before you do?"

That earned a chuckle. "I'd have to be guilty of something first."

She took a step forward. "Please, Sheriff. Don't keep up this charade. We've got enough to prove who you are and what you're doing. LLC records, signatures, cash transfers—all under an alias. I just don't understand why. You had everything you need. And you jeopardize your good name, your pension, and Patty's future. For what, Mr. Marcus Jenks?"

That made him look at her, really look at her. "Took you long enough."

Taylor's pulse drummed in her ears. "Maybe, but I eventually got there, didn't I? Even without a badge. I cracked what you thought was solid. Figured out that you built DFC Hospitality to move gambling money and launder cash through the county. Curtis helped. Quig found out, and you made sure she never got the chance to tell me. What I don't know is whose money you've been laundering. Who got to you, Sheriff?"

He gave a slow sigh, like a man who'd carried too much for too long. "You ever stop to think, maybe what I've been doing has kept the town afloat? That money paved half our roads, funded the department you used to wear the badge for."

"Even if I believed that, that's not yours to decide," she said, voice sharp.

He smirked. "That's where you're wrong. In a place like Hart's Ridge, someone has to decide. Somebody always does. Small town budgets, small town politics, it's not done like it is in the big cities, Taylor. It can't all be above board. Surely you aren't naïve enough to think that."

The two of them stared across the workshop—the space suddenly too small for the history between them.

"Just tell me, Sheriff. Did you order Curtis to kill Quig?"

His head jerked around to her, eyes startled.

"I absolutely did not. That being said, you're going to ruin everything."

"No, what I'm going to do is stop you, and either you or Curtis are going down for Quig's death. I told you, she meant something to me. To my family. And to her kids. Someone will pay for what happened to her. I swore justice to her memory."

He let out a long sigh, shaking his head.

"No one ever really gets justice. I taught you better than this, too," he said finally. "I taught you to survive. To play the long game. There's always going to be collateral damage, Taylor. Even between the good deeds."

Taylor's reply was quiet but lethal. "And you taught me how to spot a liar, too."

Outside, the motorhome engine rumbled louder. Dawkins grabbed his bag from the counter, slung it over his shoulder, and started for the door. Taylor followed, her hand on her holster, unsure for a minute whether to try to take him in or just let him go.

Outside, he called for Patty to join him. She carried a large duffle bag with her as she left the porch, her eyes shining with excitement. She looked so happy.

And then he was gone—walking through the mist toward the motorhome.

The tears that ran down Taylor's face surprised her.

Or maybe they didn't.

Patty followed him aboard without a word, and, within seconds, the rig eased forward, turning down the long gravel drive.

Taylor stood there, crying and listening to the crunch of tires fade into silence.

When she turned, Shane's truck was rolling in.

She rubbed at her face quickly.

He climbed out fast, a folder clutched in one hand. "I had a feeling you'd be here," he said, watching the motorhome disappear around the bend. "He's really leaving, isn't he? That buttons up my last hope he was innocently involved."

"Yeah, he's running," Taylor said flatly. "But not for long. I got his license plate number, and I know where they're headed first."

Shane handed her the folder. "Good job. I pulled bank records from DFC Hospitality. Wire transfers match the cash amounts from the Shuffle Lounge drops. There's no doubt—it's him."

Taylor flipped through the pages. It was all there: the missing deposits, the shell business filings, the proof of everything Quig had died for.

Her throat tightened. "Then we're done waiting."

Shane nodded. "State bureau office opens at eight. I'm sure they'll do a quick transfer to the FBI, but I think we should start with them anyway."

Taylor looked down the empty road one last time. The dust from Dawkins' motorhome still hung in the air, golden in the rising light.

She took a slow breath. "Let's go."

They drove in silence, the miles rolling past in quiet rhythm.

Shane glanced over. "You sure about this? Once we hand it over, it's out of our hands."

Taylor stared ahead, eyes fixed on the horizon. "Good," she said. "Because some things are too big for Hart's Ridge to carry."

The sun broke through the trees as they reached the highway. Taylor reached for the folder between them, thumb running along the edge.

Inside was Dawkins' signature, the proof of his empire—and Curtis' connection to Quig's murder. One of them had blood on their hands. She prayed it wasn't the sheriff, but, for the first time in weeks, she let herself breathe.

They were almost there.

They rode in silence. Just under two hours later, as the state police headquarters came into view, its glass windows gleaming against the sky, Shane pulled into the lot and shut off the engine.

Before they climbed out, Taylor put her hand on Shane's arm.

"This is for Quig," she said quietly.

Shane nodded. "And for everyone Dawkins thought he owned."

Together, they left the truck, the folder in Taylor's hand heavy with the truth.

They walked through the doors side by side, ready to turn it all in.

The real fight wasn't over. But it had finally begun.

Chapter Forty-Six

The smell of fried food and cinnamon pretzels hung in the air, the kind of scent that stuck to your clothes and hair no matter how long you stayed. Tula walked beside Waylon through the mall, her hand hooked around a paper shopping bag filled with steel-toe boots and a few pairs of jeans sturdy enough for welding school. It had taken some convincing, but he'd finally agreed to enroll, and the proud smile he wore made every penny worth it.

She'd much rather he left town with her, but he couldn't be swayed. Instead, she'd spent the last three weeks tying up loose ends.

"You sure these are the right ones?" she asked, nodding toward the boots.

"Yeah," he said, checking the box. "They've got the steel in the toes and the ankle support. Instructor said that's all that matters. Guess I'll be breaking 'em in the hard way."

She smiled. "That's how you'll know they're yours."

He grinned a little. "Ain't had new shoes since Curtis outgrew his last ones. Feels weird."

"You deserve more than hand-me-downs," she said.

They walked in silence for a moment, passing storefronts plastered with fall sales and bright window mannequins. Tula caught their reflections in the glass—her in her cardigan and boots, Waylon tall and lanky beside her, trying hard to look like a man, but still with that little-boy worry around his eyes.

She planned to surprise him with a visit later to the craft store. Pick him up some art supplies. Canvases. Pens. Whatever he wanted. Something to encourage his talent and keep him focused on doing well and keeping out of trouble.

"Hungry?" she asked.

He nodded, and they found a spot in the food court—a small corner booth near the window. The place was half empty, just the hum of chatter and the occasional squeak of shoes on tile.

Tula ordered them both burgers and fries. When the food came, Waylon doused his fries in ketchup and took a long bite before leaning back in the booth with a satisfied sigh.

"Man, this is good," he said.

"You've been living on crap food for years," she teased. "Anything cooked fresh would taste good."

He grinned but didn't argue.

They ate in easy silence for a while. It had been a long time since either of them had a normal day—no drama, no chaos. Just a small stretch of peace.

When they finished, Tula sipped her sweet tea and leaned forward. "I've got us set up to look at that apartment over on Maple this afternoon."

Waylon raised an eyebrow. "You mean for me?"

"Yep," she said. "If it works out, I can help you get settled, then figure out what's next. It's close enough that you can walk to class and still check on Mama, like you said."

She didn't state that her mother didn't deserve someone like

Waylon looking after her wellbeing. It made her proud that he wasn't like their siblings. That he cared about something other than himself.

That gave her hope that he could really be something one day.

He stared at his empty wrapper for a moment. "I know you aren't thrilled about me staying here, Tula, but I feel like I'm just not ready to give up yet. I'll also have to testify against the sheriff, so I should stay and get it over with. You think I'm crazy, don't you?"

No, he wasn't crazy. Like her, he wanted to do the right thing. Her chest flooded with love for him.

"I think this is your home," she said gently. "The only one you've ever known, and, believe me, I know it's frightening to just up and leave everything you know and start over. You're also trying to do right. I agree, too, that Mama still needs somebody steady. Just ... not someone who'll let her pull him back in."

Waylon nodded slowly. "Yeah. I ain't goin' back to the house unless it's an emergency, though. Curtis bein' gone makes it easier, but that place still feels heavy. I can check on her from elsewhere. And drop things off and stuff. Maybe pick her up for doctor's appointments, but I'm not going in."

Tula hesitated. "And what about Earl? You can handle him?"

He shrugged, taking a sip of his drink. "Without Curtis, Earl ain't no trouble. Just talks big. You know him."

She smiled faintly. "Yeah, I do."

But her chest tightened. She didn't tell him about what she'd overheard at the hospital—about Lorene, about the baby, and the big, bad, horrific thing. The meeting with the genetic counselor was later this week.

Maybe Lorene would make the right choice on her own, and that would go away.

After that, Tula could finally leave.

Maybe she'd go back to Los Angeles. Maybe not. Part of her still ached for that old version of herself—the one who wore lipstick every morning and believed fame could fill the hollow parts inside her. But the thought of L.A. now felt like a stage she'd outgrown. If she could only get Eden out of her head, she might just move on to somewhere totally new where rumors and innuendo didn't follow.

Her eyes moved to Waylon, studying the soft lines of his face as he wiped his hands with a napkin. Maybe Hart's Ridge wasn't her home anymore, but it had a way of grounding her, even when she didn't want it to.

She stared off into the distance, daydreaming about a little beach cottage somewhere, or maybe a mountain cabin high up and away from everyone. A respite from the world and all the troubles it brought.

"You're awfully quiet," he said.

"Just thinking," she said. "Trying to figure out what comes next."

He smiled. "You'll figure it out. You always do."

She laughed softly. "That's what they say."

For a moment, they just sat there—two people who'd crawled through the same fire, trying to believe in fresh starts.

Waylon cleared his throat. "You think Quig's kids are doin' okay?"

The question pulled her back. "Yeah, I think so. Taylor checks on them every week. Says they're settling in with their grandma. The boys joined band and football. Addie's doing ballet."

He nodded, staring out the window at the parking lot. "That's good."

Something about his tone made her watch him closer.

"They're good kids," she said. "They'll make it."

Waylon's voice dropped low. "Wish I could do somethin' for them. Maybe talk to the boys. Keep 'em outta trouble."

"That might be possible," she said softly. "You'd be good at that."

He smiled faintly, but it didn't reach his eyes. "The least they should know is that their mama didn't suffer."

Tula's heart stopped mid-beat.

Her hand tightened around her drink. "What did you just say?"

He blinked, startled. "What?"

"You said she didn't suffer." Her voice was quiet, but the air around them shifted. "How do you know that, Waylon?"

The color drained from his face. His fingers twitched against the table, his throat working like he couldn't swallow.

"Tula—"

"Don't," she whispered, her pulse roaring in her ears. "Don't lie to me. Not this time."

He was trembling, and that terrified her. Something that looked too damn close to guilt flooded his face, making him turn red from the collar up.

She leaned forward, her voice shaky but steady enough to cut. "Tell me, Waylon. Tell me all of it this time."

He looked down at his hands, and, for a long, breathless moment, the world outside their booth fell away—no clatter, no music, just the sound of two people caught between truth and fear. Tula held her breath, terrified for what his next words would bring, her mind already scrambling for a backup plan, for ways to protect the only sibling that she had worth saving.

When Waylon finally looked up and locked eyes with her, his sudden fear had dissolved into a state of hopelessness, and she knew what came next would be the catalyst for where fate would lead them next.

"Fine," he began, sighing long and loudly, "but you'd better cancel the appointment to look at the apartment tomorrow. I don't want you to lose a deposit and first month's rent."

"Why would I?" She dreaded his answer, but she had to know.

"Because what I have to tell you ... changes everything."

Chapter Forty-Seven

Loyalty had taught Taylor who to protect. Justice taught her who she had to stop protecting. And life—well, it taught her that neither was ever simple. She sat in her old wooden chair near the edge of the grass, Diesel lying beside her, chin on his paws. A small breeze stirred his fur and brushed her bare ankles. The air smelled like honeysuckle and bait.

On the dock, Sam sat cross-legged beside Alice, both holding fishing poles, their lines trembling across the water. Every so often, Sam pointed something out—how to tell when the bobber dipped, how to stay still enough to let the fish come to them.

Lennon slept in her stroller behind them, one small hand curled around her blanket.

Watching the three of them soothed her soul.

It had been a peaceful week. No work, other than at the farm. No chasing leads, or dead ends. No drama, and no Shane.

The state police had picked the sheriff up at a small camp-ground just outside of Asheville. Shane was a part of it, but Taylor hadn't wanted to be there. She couldn't stomach the thought of seeing the sheriff in handcuffs, being led to a car, disgraced.

It hurt her heart to even think about it.

The state police were now investigating just who DFC Hospitality Group consisted of, and Dawkins wasn't talking. They'd figure it out soon enough. The Attorney General had already formally suspended Dawkins until his trial and the Chief Judge was considering who would serve as interim sheriff until things were decided. So far, Dawkins' charges were racketeering and conspiracy to commit racketeering.

After he was taken into custody, she'd gone to her dad again. Gave him the news and squeezed just a bit out of him. He confessed that he and a few others were given cash every week and told to put it through the machines, and lose more often than not.

Money laundering at its finest.

They were allowed to keep the small wins. According to him, it hadn't added up to much more than pocket change. What hurt the most was that he knew how she felt about crime, and knew what he was doing was wrong. His respect for her was put aside just so he could buy a bottle or two and still be able to pay his bills.

Not that he'd ever treated her as something valuable. One of these days she was going to stop wanting his love and respect. Stop chasing it altogether.

Her eyes drifted to the little memorial stone by the rocks— smooth granite with Quig's name carved into it. She reached out and touched the top of the stone, her thumb brushing away a bit of pollen. "Hey, Quig," she murmured. "It's been a while."

Diesel lifted his head and pressed against her leg, as if he knew who she was talking to.

"They took the case," Taylor said softly. "State's got everything now. It's not over, but it's moving. Curtis is sitting in jail, and this time won't be bailed out. We're getting there."

The sound of the lake filled the space between her words—the rhythmic hush of water against the dock, the soft creak of Alice's line pulling taut before settling again.

"Your kids are doing okay," she continued. "They've all got new shoes, the kind that don't fall apart when it rains. Your oldest made the school band—plays trumpet. The middle one's trying out for football next week, and little Addie's taking ballet. First recital's in June. I promise, I'll be there."

She paused, watching the sunlight shimmer across the lake. She didn't say the rest—that the Gray family had quietly covered the costs of lessons and uniforms. That she and Sam had made sure those kids could stay busy, could stay kids with good, clean hobbies.

"You'd be proud of them, Quig," she whispered. "They're strong, just like you."

Diesel sighed and laid his paw across her foot.

Taylor looked up toward the dock, where Sam helped Alice unhook a small bluegill, both laughing quietly. The moment was so simple, so alive it ached.

Her phone buzzed on the arm of the chair. Shane.

> On the second go-thru, they were able to pull up a partial print from the car. Enough for an ID.

Taylor's stomach clenched. Her thumb hovered above the screen. Please, God, don't let it be the sheriff.

Her first reply set off a series of back-and-forth.

> Curtis?

> Nope—but same family.

Earl.

Try again.

Her mind jumped to Lorene. Surely not ...
Shane's next text made her stomach drop to her knees.

Waylon.

Taylor stared at the screen, the sound of the water suddenly too loud in her ears.

Diesel shifted beside her, resting his head on her knee.

On the dock, Alice held up her catch for Sam to admire, her laughter carrying softly across the lake.

Taylor forced a smile, lifted a hand to wave, but her thoughts were already drifting—back to Waylon, to Quig, to how every truth in this town seemed to bleed into another. She looked out across the lake, the last light flickering on the water like shards of glass.

This wasn't over. Not by a long shot.

The water was calm, but Taylor knew better than anyone—calm never lasted long in Hart's Ridge.

The End

Next in the Hart's Ridge Series is TICKET TO RIDE. When a teenage girl disappears after leaving rehab, the small town of Hart's Ridge is thrown into turmoil.

As the search widens, whispers emerge of other girls who vanished under eerily similar circumstances. Families who once trusted the system now fear it. Every answer uncovers a darker question, and every lead pushes the case closer to secrets powerful people would do anything to keep buried.

Then tragedy strikes closer to home—Someone near and dear to Taylor and Sam is missing. With her family fractured and time running out, Taylor is forced to confront dangers on two fronts: the predators luring vulnerable girls and the shadowy forces determined to silence anyone who gets too close.

Gripping and emotional, *Ticket to Ride* is a story of betrayal, resilience, and the unbreakable bond of family when innocence itself is under attack.

A NOTE FROM THE AUTHOR

Hello, readers! I hope you enjoyed **Tell Me Why**, the fourteenth book in the Hart's Ridge series. The true crime wrapped into the fictional town of Hart's Ridge and its fictional characters was loosely inspired by a sheriff in central Florida who was arrested and charged in connection with an alleged massive gambling operation and public corruption scheme that generated more than $21 million in profits. Wrapping Quig's death into the story was purely fictional. If you've enjoyed the so far fourteen books of Hart's Ridge, you'll be happy to know that I've decided to continue the series. Next up is TICKET TO RIDE.

If you'd like to be notified when there is a new title and pre-order button, you can sign up for my monthly newsletter at the following link: JOIN KAY'S NEWSLETTER HERE

While you're waiting on the next in this series, I have many more books for you to read! I'd love for you to check out my *By the Sea* trilogy, starting with True to Me, a mystery with lots of family drama that packs a heck of a twist! I'd also like to invite you to join my private Facebook group, Kay's Krew, where you can be part of my focus group, giving ideas for story details such as names, livelihoods, sneak peeks, etc. in this series. I'm also known to entertain with stories of my life with the Bratt Pack and all the kerfuffles I find myself getting into. Please join my author newsletter to hear of future Hart's Ridge books, as well as giveaways and discounts.

Until then, scatter kindness everywhere.

Kay Bratt

True To Me

*Learn More about **True to Me** at this link: My Book or keep scrolling to see the book description:

From the bestselling author of *Wish Me Home* comes a breathtaking novel about the secrets that families keep and one woman's illuminating search for the truth.

Quinn Maguire has a stable life, a fiancé and what she thinks is a clear vision for her future. All of that comes undone by her mother's deathbed confession—the absentee father Quinn spent thirty years resenting is not her real father at all. With that one revealing whisper, Quinn embarks on a journey to Maui, her mother's childhood home, a storied paradise that holds the truth about her mother's past and all its secrets Quinn is determined to uncover.

But settling on the island has its complications, and, with the fiancé she left behind questioning every choice she makes, Quinn's quest for her truth is even more difficult than she expected. As time passes and she digs deeper into her family history and her own identity, one thing becomes clear: Maui is as beautiful as she'd always imagined, and its magic is helping uncover the woman that Quinn was always meant to be.

Get ***True to Me*** in eBook, Paperback, and Audio here:
My Book

About the Author

Writer, Rescuer, Wanderer

Kay Bratt is the powerhouse author behind 40 internationally bestselling books that span genres from mystery and women's fiction to memoir and historical fiction. Her books are renowned for delivering an emotional wallop wrapped in gripping storylines. Her Hart's Ridge small-town mystery series earned her the coveted title of Amazon All Star Author and continues to be one of her most successful projects out of her more than two million books sold around the world.

Kay's literary works have sparked lively book club discussions wide-reaching, with her works translated into multiple languages, including German, Korean, Chinese, Hungarian, Czech, and Estonian.

Beyond her writing, Kay passionately dedicates herself to rescue missions, championing animal welfare as the former Director of Advocacy for Yorkie Rescue of the Carolinas. She considers herself a lifelong advocate for children, having volunteered extensively in a Chinese orphanage and supported nonprofit organizations like An Orphan's Wish (AOW), Pearl River Outreach, and Love Without Boundaries. In the USA, Kay served as a Court Appointed Special Advocate (CASA) for abused and neglected children in Georgia, as well as spearheaded numerous outreach programs for underprivileged kids in South Carolina. Most recently Kay spent a year volunteering as a hospice companion.

As a wanderlust-driven soul, Kay has called nearly three dozen different homes on two continents her own. Her globe-trotting adventures have taken her to captivating destinations across Mexico, Thailand, Malaysia, China, the Philippines, Central America, the Bahamas, and Australia. Today, she and her soulmate of more than 30 years find their sanctuary in St. Augustine, Florida.

Described as southern, spicy, and a touch sassy, Kay loves to share her life's antics with the Bratt Pack on social media. Follow her on Facebook, Twitter, and Instagram to join the fun and buckle up for the ride of a lifetime. Explore her popular catalog of published works at Kay Bratt Dot Com and never miss a new release (or her latest Bratt Pack drama) by signing up for her monthly email newsletter.

For more information, visit www.kaybratt.com.

Printed in Dunstable, United Kingdom